SECRETS AND SIN

BOW STREET WALLFLOWERS TRILOGY
BOOK TWO

CHERI CHAMPAGNE

Cover design and illustrations by Cheri Champagne, Image inspiration purchased from PeriodImages.com

Editing by Jen Graybeal and Amanda Bidnall

Logo design and creation by Rachel Champagne

Edition: 1

ISBN: 978-1-7386935-5-9

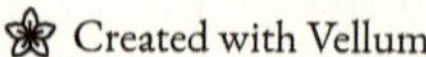 Created with Vellum

DEDICATION

For those who struggle to advocate for themselves, and for everyone willing to be vocal on behalf of those who need it.

CONTENT WARNINGS

Dear reader,
There are certain aspects of this novel that might be triggering to
some readers. (Spoilers ahead) They are as follows:
** Death (both accidental, and not-so accidental)*
** Poisoning*
** Swearing*
** Violence (particularly hand-to-hand combat and the use of*
daggers and pistols)
** Biting (not for pleasure)*
** Abusive family members*
** Death of an animal (death not on-page, but the remains are)*
** Threats*
** Discussions on death*
** Fire (arson)*
** Explicit sex*
** Sex without a condom (without pregnancy)*

Things to also keep in mind:
** One of the side characters has Tourette*
Syndrome. Tourette's was only first

*described/named in 1885. So, at the time
this book takes place, people displaying
signs/symptoms of Tourette's were either
hidden by the family or put in a place like
Bethlem Royal hospital. For that reason,
there is conflict between Maria and their
parents.
As a mom to three kids with Tourette's, I am a
staunch advocate for folks with this neuro-
logical disorder, and would advise you do
some reading on the subject.
* One of my protagonists is nonbinary. And
while countless nonbinary people existed in
the early 1800s, there weren't the more
modern descriptive words we have today
with which people might explain their feelings. I've done my best with Maria, and
hope I've done their character justice.
Maria's pronouns throughout are she/her,
but I imagine if they were around today,
they would prefer they/them, with frequent
uses of he/her, depending on what their
heart said that day.*

PROLOGUE

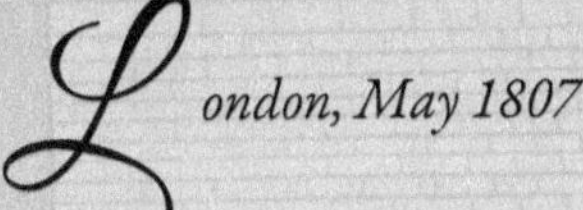

London, May 1807

GLITTERING CHANDELIERS HUNG HIGH OVERHEAD, casting light upon the swirls of colour below. Miss Maria Roberts flipped open her fan and waved it before her rhythmically as her stomach swooped in anticipation. Music filled the grand ballroom, and hope swelled in her chest.

The ballroom was large and full, the air fragrant with perfume and heavy with humidity. It was utterly delightful.

She scanned those in attendance, enjoying the bustling activity and high energy, and her gaze irrevocably slid sideways toward a group of young men. Despite her best efforts to the contrary, she frequently found herself watching the handsome profile of Jasper Sinclair, the future Duke of Derby.

The young man was the focus of all the society mamas, who were no doubt studiously directing their newly out daughters in the art of fan flirting in his direction—a practice which continued to mystify Maria. He was charming, affable, and knew precisely what to do to get a woman's heart fluttering.

Her stomach twisted in knots, and she suppressed a sigh. With every one of the man's breaths, he stole hers away. With every flash of his single dimple, tingles skittered over her skin. And, Lord help her, with every word he spoke, her belly trembled. His hair was black as pitch and appeared feathery to the touch—heavens, but she wanted to touch it—and his eyes...

"Have you any names on your dance cards?" her dear friend Lady Juliana Sinclair asked, jolting Maria out of her ill-timed musings about the woman's brother.

The third of their trio, Miss Heather Morgan, shook her head. "I do not expect to receive any. My aunt says that I ought instead to focus on—"

"Come now, dearest," Juliana murmured, a delicate frown puckering her brows. "You ought never to take what she says to heart. Your aunt's treatment of you is abysmal. You may set your heart on whomever or whatever you desire. And I daresay you should."

Heather nodded. "Yes. Of course you're right, Juliana."

"Indeed." Juliana turned her gaze to Maria. "And you, Maria? Have you any names on your dance card?"

"No." Her stomach gave a sad wobble. "We are only in our second season; not on the shelf *already*."

"I should say not," Heather mused, her expression rueful. "It would appear, however, that we *are* wallflowers."

"*Wallflowers*." Juliana scoffed. "Surely not! You two are lovely, and I'm... Well, you two are very pretty."

Hiding a perplexing flinch at being called *pretty*, Maria gently chided her friend. "Oh pish. While our intelligence might be intimidating for men—and therefore *must* be disguised—our beauty is undeniable."

Juliana mightn't believe it, but she *was* beautiful: tall and shapely with stunning hair. And, for pity's sake, she was the daughter of a duke! It seemed impossible that men would not line up for the opportunity to dance with her. But her friend had experienced several disheartening encounters with disingenuous men and fortune hunters—and was, Maria knew, understandably jaded.

Dancers whirled past, and Maria watched them with longing. How odd that she'd never been particularly fond of dancing, and yet she now found herself missing it.

"Besides, how handsome a woman is scarcely determines how marriageable she is. One must also consider their breeding," Heather mused, listing the items on her fingers, "the suitability of their relations, or whether madness runs in their blood—" Her eyes flashed wide. "Oh Maria, I'm sorry. I—"

Maria waved a gloved hand through the air, her empty dance card dangling limply from her wrist. "I know that you meant no harm by it, Heather."

"Your brother is a genuinely lovely person; not mad, at all," Juliana put in. "I fail to comprehend society's lack of acceptance."

Maria nodded. "Thank you."

"Nevertheless," Heather continued, "we are undeniably wallflowers."

"I daresay it matters naught..."

Her friends' discussion continued as they strode to the refreshment table, giving Maria an opportunity to gather herself. All the while, her thoughts turned inward. Her brother, Thomas, was indeed wonderful. And Juliana was correct: he was by no means mad. With the *haut ton's* skewed definition of madness, however, Thomas was forced to—

Maria discreetly cleared her throat in an attempt to dislodge the lump that had abruptly formed there. Thomas wasn't the only reason she was a social pariah. It was also because of her boisterous and overbearing mother, her too-familiar father, and her own...peculiarities.

A heavy sigh escaped her.

She looked downward at her attire. That evening, she wore white, like the other debutantes of the *ton*. Her bodice was modest, her sleeves capped, and her brown hair done fashionably high. Her gown wasn't threadbare or out of style, but for some reason she felt mundane, and wished she were permitted to wear a colour that brightened her grey eyes and detracted from her too-strong jaw.

No, her inner voice challenged. She didn't just feel *mundane*. Today, this dress felt...*wrong*. Mayhap it didn't perfectly suit her body—despite the modiste's assurances to the contrary—or perhaps the lack of colour made her look drawn. But whatever the reason, the wrongness itched along her spine and curdled high in her belly.

And yet... She still wanted to dance.

Raucous laughter erupted from several paces away, drawing Maria's attention to the group of handsome young men gathered around Jasper. The young pups gazed at him in admiration, clearly pleased that they'd been included among his circle.

Maria angled her slender neck, notching her chin higher in the hope of making her jaw appear less harsh should one of them deign to look her way. *Please let it be Jasper*. She shifted her stance near the wall, affecting nonchalance in an attempt to lure the men toward her. Would that they asked her to dance!

"It's unfortunate, really," one man said mockingly.

"Indeed not," another young man replied. "It's their own fault."

Maria stilled. Did men gossip? She trained her ear on them while she focused her gaze on the dancers.

"How so?" Jasper asked, sipping on his champagne.

"If," the man responded, "they truly intended to attract a husband, they would lower their necklines and fix their flaws.

And, of course, one cannot go wrong with allowing a man some liberties."

The men laughed again, and Maria pursed her lips.

"You just want to get under their skirts, Billingsly," the first man said with a superior sniff.

"Doesn't every man?" drawled another.

More laughter erupted, and Maria's stomach dipped unpleasantly.

"But one must have standards," Jasper interjected. "Unlike Billingsly, of course."

The man named Billingsly lightly shoved Jasper with his elbow. "Sod off, Sinclair. I wager that even you haven't the cods to seek a dance with a wallflower."

"And your sister doesn't count," another young man put in.

Sounds of discreet interest and boorish delight surrounded the men, and Maria set her jaw against a scowl. Outrage, affront and, she was ashamed to admit, *hurt* pulsed through her with every beat of her pounding heart. How could men speak thusly about women? They ought to know that she and the other wallflowers were not truly out of the range of hearing—though perhaps that was their wish, for they'd not attempted to lower their voices despite their proximity to the outskirts of the ballroom. She'd not imagined Jasper would be capable of something so...so *crass.*

Indeed, not the Jasper she knew.

"A wager?" Jasper asked.

"I do love a wager!" another man interjected, interest and devilment ripe in his voice. "What are your terms, Billingsly?"

There was a moment of silent interest while the swirling dancers and the overwhelming scent of candle wax, sweat, and perfume dizzied Maria.

"If we're wagering, I'll make this interesting," Billingsly

urged. "If you can encourage a wallflower to fall in love with you, then snub her, I'll give you ten quid."

Maria's eyebrows rose and her heart stuttered at both the large sum and the abhorrent terms.

"Because I'm charitable," Billingsly continued, "I'll give you ten shillings just for asking the ugly wench to dance, and another seven if she accepts."

Out of the corner of Maria's eye, the smug, challenging smile on Billingsly's face was almost menacing. Surely Jasper would not accept the wager. He was Juliana's brother, after all, and Juliana was among the wallflowers that the other man found so distasteful.

Maria refused to believe Jasper capable of something so hateful. He'd joined in their discussion, but he would refuse, of course. He would defend his sister's honour, and would unquestionably not ruin a woman merely for the sake of a wager.

Struggling to keep her breathing slow and even, the din around her was drowned out by the rush of blood in her ears. Out of the corner of her eye, she could see the men gesturing, but could no longer hear their conversation. *Jasper will refuse.*

Abruptly, he moved. Dragging his fingers through his hair and straightening his coat, Jasper sauntered toward the wall of women.

Sharp pain burst beneath her sternum as her heart broke. The ache spread over her chest and tingled down her arms. *No, Jasper. Don't do it.*

Then he stood before her, his two-toned blue-and-brown eyes glittering with false appreciation, his smile broad and gleaming. He appeared for all the world like a young man in earnest as he bowed. And it hurt her all the more.

"Good evening, Miss Roberts," he said charmingly.

Maria was very aware of the other wallflowers' awe at his presence. But all Maria felt was a mix of indignation, disappointment, and...anguish. The man had let himself down with this barbaric choice.

She nodded coolly and dipped into a shallow curtsey, deliberately leaving off his title as she replied. "Good evening."

His smile deepened, and she was struck by his ability to be so affable to a woman's face and yet so dismissive and cruel behind her back.

"Might I claim the next waltz?"

A waltz. The most intimate of dances. Her chest clenched. He'd accepted the larger wager, then—to make her fall in love with him. Another twist of the proverbial knife to her heart, to be sure.

Well, she would not give him the satisfaction.

"I thank you for the request, but I am otherwise engaged."

He blinked, his gaze sliding downward toward the empty dance card dangling from her wrist. Maria indiscreetly hid it among the folds of her skirts.

"Brother!" Juliana exclaimed delightedly, drawing nearer with Heather at her side.

The strains of another quadrille echoed through the ballroom from the orchestra's balcony, and a flurry of motion and swirls of hot air filled the space. Maria could not countenance another moment. Her heart ached and her stomach churned.

"Please excuse me," she muttered. Ignoring the surprised —and penetrating—glances of all those around them, including the dishonourable Jasper, Maria spun on her heel and strode determinedly toward the refreshment table.

If that *gentleman* and his friends were representative of her choices for a marriage, Maria wanted nothing to do with it. She would find a way to support herself in the future without relying on a man. Indeed, from that moment forward, she would gladly accept—nay, *welcome*—her role as a wallflower.

CHAPTER 1

London, Spring 1817

Bodies jostled against Jasper as he made his way out of the crowd on Newgate Street. Morbidly energetic cheers rose up around him. The elbow of a man pumping his fist into the air narrowly missed Jasper's temple as the dying struggled for breath.

Francis is coming for you, Jasper. Miles' chilling last words raced through Jasper's mind, and his pulse rushed dizzyingly through him.

Francis had not made it to the gallows. But why? *How?*

Dazed from the stench of unwashed bodies, urine, manure, and the dreadful reality that his cousin was loose, he made his way out of the crush and down the street to his awaiting carriage.

"Home," he called to the coachman as he entered.

He settled back just as the carriage jolted into motion. He

would have to warn Juliana and her new family. Sending them away would be the safest option, of course.

Christ. She'd want to help him again. She and her friends had become runners for Bow Street, of all things. Jasper had indulged their fantasy, but what could they truly accomplish facing off against Francis? The man was utterly mad. And while they'd been successful in capturing his cousins once before, he simply couldn't risk their lives on luck.

And Maria, his inner voice whispered. She would wish to help, would put herself in any amount of sodding danger just to ensure that Francis was found and dealt with. Jasper's chest squeezed disconcertingly. She cared for others far too damned much.

The carriage jolted, and someone shouted. Jasper's stomach churned.

Francis was hungry enough for the dukedom that he would not simply murder those who posed a potential threat; he would eviscerate them with excruciatingly slow assaults on their sanity. The man had already made attempts on Jasper's life, for pity's sake, took pleasure in inspiring fear in others and would, therefore, use any means to frighten Jasper.

During the trial, Francis and Miles' smug determination to prove Francis' legitimacy and—outrageously—to assert that Jasper's father was somehow responsible for their sister Jean's death was unhinged.

The fact remained that while Jasper's uncle—Francis and Miles' father—was older than Jasper's pater, he would never have become duke. And, therefore, *Francis* would never become duke.

Even skewed as the judicial system was when it came to the peerage, Francis' father was illegitimate, and couldn't benefit from such inequality. So what could possess Francis to believe that, after all he had done, he could still attain the dukedom?

The man had never truly been logical when it came to his wants and desires, but this...

A grunt of irritation escaped Jasper.

Now that Miles had been hung, Francis was alone in the world. And more dangerous than ever.

The carriage pulled up to his house, and he disembarked before it had completely rolled to a stop, his senses on high alert. The sky overhead had darkened, threatening a sudden spring rain and casting disquieting shadows along the streets of Grosvenor Square. A thread of unease tightened his gut, propelling him toward his front door. Which failed to open as he approached.

With a frown, Jasper pressed the latch and entered. "William?" His voice echoed in the stark, grand foyer.

There was a moment of absolute silence, then with crisp finality, the door slammed shut behind him. *"Sodding hell!"* Jasper exclaimed, gripping his chest as he spun.

His butler's clipped footfalls approached from the kitchens before the man appeared at the far end of the foyer. Jasper's pulse gradually returned to normal as he noted the shuffle of movement from his maids and footmen abovestairs and the off-key humming of his housekeeper.

"My humble apologies, Your Grace," William breathed as he accepted Jasper's hat and gloves.

"Not at all." Jasper's lips quirked in a tight smile. "I'm to pen an urgent missive to the magistrate then call on the Marchioness of Livingston. Please have the carriage ready." He stepped away, but turned back to the man. "And do not permit callers, William. My cousin has escaped the noose, and I'll not risk the safety of the staff."

"Of course, Your Grace."

With a nod, Jasper crossed the foyer and strode to his study. A fire was lit in the hearth but, despite the warmth to the room, a chill danced down his spine. He turned to close the door and his heart all but stopped in his chest.

There, jutting from the wood of the door was a dagger piercing a folded piece of parchment with his name penned on the front.

His pulse tripped, and he leaned forward to inspect it. He knew that slanted, untidy penmanship.

Inhaling deeply, he prepared to call out for his butler. But an odd fragrance stopped him. Cautiously, he sniffed at the paper. *Bitter almonds.* Jasper reared back in alarm and hastily retrieved a spare set of gloves from the drawer of a side table.

With a muttered curse and trembling fingers, Jasper donned the gloves and tugged the note free, striding toward the hearth.

*THOU A**R**T A BOIL,*
  A plague-sore or embossèd carbuncle
  In my corrupted blood.

JASPER'S SKIN GREW COLD. Francis had been inside his sodding house. And damn, but the quote was familiar, but he couldn't bloody well place it. It sounded like Shakespeare...

With a slight hiss, the parchment caught as he tossed it upon the fire. Then Jasper looked at his leather gloves. If Francis had meant to poison him through contact with his skin, his gloves were unquestionably soiled. He sighed. Damnable loss. Carefully, Jasper plucked at the fingertips of both gloves until he was able to flick them into the fire.

Whomp. Bright flames warped the leather, curling and distorting them until naught was left but a charcoal mass.

With a final scratch of her pen, Maria sat back in her chair and revelled in the success of completion. Warmth spread across her chest and a little bubble of happiness filled her abdomen. It did not matter how many articles she had written over the past years, she still felt the same upon their conclusion.

Someone rushed past, the movement rustling her parchment. Maria glanced up. The newspaper offices were bustling with activity. Some men sat writing news articles behind three neat rows of two small desks, while others went about their business, hurrying between the desks or out to the main corridor.

The wood-panelled walls were dark and confining, but two large windows along one side of the room flooded the space with natural light.

"Is that the article for this week, Mr. Robertson?" a young paper boy asked, suddenly appearing at her side.

Maria nodded, and replied in her practiced deepened voice. "Just finished." She handed the parchment to the lad with another nod, and he scampered to her superior's office.

With a flourish, she rose and lifted her coat from the back of her chair, smoothly sliding her arms through the sleeves before straightening the cuffs. It was her final day in the office that week, and she could scarcely countenance another moment away from her apartments.

How does Juliana fare? The thought ran through her mind, as it had all day. Juliana's cousins had been hanged that morning; Maria could only imagine that Juliana would need comfort at such a time. Mayhap she ought to fetch Heather, and they three could sit for tea. Although, she supposed Juliana *did* have her husband now.

Raised voices came from the building's foyer, causing Maria to pause in the act of putting on her hat. She trained her ears.

"...wasn't the right man!"

"This is a story; someone start writing!"

"Fetch Mr. Balfour; this ought to be tomorrow's headline!"

Along with several of her fellow writers, Maria rushed to the foyer.

"What has happened?" one man asked.

"The hanging!" a man replied breathlessly. "Francis Sinclair was not there!"

A shard of ice lodged itself in her chest, and tingles of unease raced down her gloved fingers.

Her colleagues dashed about, no doubt preparing an article for tomorrow's paper, but Maria was stuck. Francis hadn't made it to the hanging. Lord, but the man was vile, capable of any number of cruelties, and he would undoubtedly seek revenge on Juliana and Jasper.

No, indeed, she reminded herself. He would no longer come for just Juliana and Jasper. After the events of the past months, Maria knew the bestial, brutish games of which Francis was capable, and he would not limit himself to just his cousins. He would target anyone with whom they associate. That put Maria squarely in the line of his ire.

"Oh! Duncan—er, Mr. Robertson—I've a missive for you."

Maria blinked, the secretary's voice jolting her out of her reverie.

"Good day, Cordelia," Maria said, doffing her hat and offering a short bow at as she neared.

Maria felt a connection to the woman, who regrettably knew only one side of Maria. She grinned and accepted the folded piece of parchment. "Thank you. How was your day?"

Cordelia's auburn eyebrows bunched together in consternation, and she lowered her voice to a whisper. "I fear our superiors must be displeased with me. I'm absolutely certain that I've done nothing incorrectly but, as you know, they've recently requested that I replace Higgs in bookkeeping—in addition to continuing my position here." Her lips thinned and she leaned closer. "Well, I was double-checking the cost of ink—to ensure we weren't overcharged in our recent order, you see—and I happened to note that Higgs had been paid thrice my current wages, for just the one job."

Maria's heart sank as she watched worry and dejection swim in her friend's green eyes. While Maria knew about the disparity in men and women's wages, it hurt to know just how much it impacted Cordelia.

Perhaps...

"Have you considered," she began in an undertone, "an alternate vocation?"

Cordelia shook her head with a pained grimace. "I wish that I could, but I can ill afford to lose this position."

Tapping her gloved index finger on the desk, Maria made a swift decision. "Allow me to think on it. I might be able to offer my assistance."

"Truly? Oh, thank you!" A bright smile lit Cordelia's features as she waved Maria off.

Stepping out onto the sidewalk outside *The Morning Herald* offices, Maria lifted her arm to hail a hack, the motion pulling on the binding tightly wrapped around her breasts. By the end of the work day, the blasted thing grew tiresome. But it was necessary.

A gust of cool wind tugged at her coat and her queue, the darkening grey sky threatening rain. With a hearty *clip-clop* and the clatter of wheels on cobblestone, a hack stopped. Maria gave the driver the direction, and entered, more than content to finally be on her way home.

Flipping over the parchment in her hand, she glanced at the direction and instantly recognized the halting scrawl. Eagerly tearing open the seal, she scanned the first sentence.

. . .

THE LAGOON WAS warm and deep, the water an almost opalescent blue, somehow reflecting the sun even from within the cave...

SHE SIGHED. It was perfect. Her friend had answered her question and confirmed her research. They'd met at the opera years ago, when the woman and her brother had journeyed from Gibraltar to visit a Spanish uncle who had purchased a home in London. Before they returned home, she and Maria had exchanged directions and frequently corresponded.

But *this*. This information was precisely what she required to conclude her next chapter. Despite the dangers—and the tides—her principal character would secret treasure away deep in a lagoon... Her next chapter, however, would have to be delayed until Maria had spoken to Juliana and sorted out the business of Francis' escape from custody.

Her abdomen buzzed with trepidation, and she silently urged the driver to increase their pace.

Undoubtedly, their offices on Bow Street would hear the news of Francis Sinclair before the article was printed on the morrow. Maria had been welcomed in by Grace Huntsbury— the woman behind the business—but had not yet been given command of her first assignment. Would capturing Francis and returning him to gaol be her first? What would Jasper think of her involvement?

She clucked her tongue, the sound scarcely audible over the thundering of horses' hooves and the rattle of the hack's wheels on the cobblestones. Jasper would berate her, as usual, but beneath it all, he would be frightened. That underlying concern for her safety, and the safety of others, was what redeemed him during those irksome moments. Drat the man.

Another deep sigh escaped her. He'd surely been there to witness the hanging of his cousins and secure himself a sense of conclusion. How had he taken the news of Francis' escape?

The hack jostled around a corner, and Maria put a hand out to stabilize herself. They turned off Wafting Street onto Bread Street, and she drummed her fingers on her thigh. It was at this time that she ordinarily felt the buzz of anticipation in her middle, but today was different.

Voices rang out around her: the bartering of goods, tittering of young women, trotting of horses' hooves, rolling carriage wheels, and the faint wails of newly born babes.

Upon rocking to a halt, Maria quit the hack and paid the driver, breathing deeply the scent of horses, coal smoke, and manure. The buildings lining the street were coal-darkened and ever so slightly crooked. And she adored it.

Home.

Her apartments were on the third floor of a building with a cobbler as its ground floor shop front. Maria did so adore her home in Cheapside, and she rather lamented the fact that she had to return to her parents' house every eve. Would that she could live here with Thomas, regardless of the perils of Cheapside at night.

Snick. The lock slid open, and she burst through the door into her familiar space. The door opened onto their large sitting room furnished with overstuffed armchairs, a settee, and a chaise, all upholstered in rich purples and blues. A fireplace was set into the wall on the left side of the room, while the entire back wall was covered with custom-built bookshelves that wrapped around their tall windows. The door nearest the fireplace led to the kitchens, and on the right wall sat her writing desk, a piano, and the corridor that led to their bedchambers.

Pride swelled in her chest—as it did every time she entered her home—even while urgency flooded her.

"Thomas," she breathed.

"Maria!" Thomas Roberts rose from his armchair by the fire and set his book aside. "You're home earlier than I'd expected."

"The news has not yet broken, brother." Maria locked the door and rushed through the sitting room to her bedchamber. "Francis Sinclair did not appear at his execution."

"No?" he called through her slightly opened door. "Blimey. What does this mean"—he paused to release a throaty grunt—"for the duke and Juliana? And for you?"

Maria laid the walking dress that she'd worn that morning upon her never-used bed, then swiftly unfastened her waist-coat buttons and cravat. "I imagine that the duke's cousin will seek revenge."

Grunt, click. Another of Thomas' habitual spasms echoed down the short corridor. The spasms were as much a part of him as the colour of his eyes. But far too many people couldn't see past his uncontrollable sounds and movements and recognize the kindest, dearest man in London.

"You'd best act fast," he said. "Francis must be brought back before the magistrate and—*grunt*—pay for his crimes." He paused, and there was a muffled *thump* before he continued. "The duke, Juliana, and her new family must be protected. And no doubt *you* will be a target now, as well."

"In that you're correct." She stepped into her frock and slid her arms through the sleeves. "But I daresay we've bested the man before, and we can do so again."

Grunt.

"Please lace me?"

He strode into the bright lilac-and-white bedchamber, his face in a contorted grimace.

Maria laughed softly as she reached to smooth the hair over his furrowed brow. His spasms came more frequently when he was under stress. "How was your day?"

Grunt, grunt. "Well enough."

He rounded behind her and tugged at the laces of her stays.

"Did Mrs. Fredrickson—dear me, not so tight, please!—come to prepare meals?"

Thomas sighed. "Yes—*click*—she did."

"And the maid? Did she—"

"For pity's sake, Maria," he groaned, moving his attention to her walking dress. "You're less than a year younger than me and yet you flutter about—*grunt, grunt*—l-like—" He huffed in agitation as he struggled to get the words out. "You needn't —*grunt, click*—worry about me."

"It isn't worry; it is love," Maria assured him.

He groaned again, and fastened the last hook on her frock. "Are you intentionally trying to guilt me, sister?"

Maria spun to face him with a small laugh. "I am doing whatever you wish for me to be doing." She pressed a light kiss to his whiskered cheek. "Thank you."

"What would you do if I was not here to attend you while you changed personae?"

In her early days of embracing the side of her that was *Mr. Duncan Robertson*, she'd discreetly paid a courtesan to aid her, but that had not lasted long. Almost immediately after securing work and a home for *Duncan*, she had posed as a distant relative of Thomas' and removed him from Bedlam. They had been so close as children; it had nearly broken her when their parents sent him away.

A wave of sorrow swept through her, but she disguised it with a smirk.

She moved to her dressing table and removed the tie for her queue. "I would scandalize the general populace by walking about half-dressed, for certain."

Making swift work of her brushing, Maria hastily knotted her hair at the base of her head and began applying pins.

"Ah." Thomas caught her gaze in the mirror while he thumbed her missive. "You've received—*grunt, click*—word from your piratical friend."

Her grey eyes lit with anticipation. "I have. Right now, however, there is a more pressing matter at hand."

Grunt. "Correct. You must aid in the tracking and capturing of a madman." Thomas leaned a hip against her chest of drawers and crossed one ankle over the other, his face twitching into a grimace. "You've been among the ranks of the women of Bow Street for above a month but have yet to take charge of your own assignment. Tell me, h—" *grunt.* "—how do you plan to undertake such an ambitious task?"

CHAPTER 2

Muffled voices carried up through the building to reach Francis Sinclair's ears. The voices would soon turn to alarm and excitement as the news broke that he had not attended his own hanging. Miles had, though. And it was Francis' duty to ensure that his brother's death had not been in vain.

Not only was Jasper, the bastard, responsible for Miles' death, but the man's father had been responsible for Jean's. Francis was alone in the world. So Jasper would be the one to pay. Him, and everyone close to him.

Francis and Miles' tactics thus far—written threats and feigned attempts on Jasper's life—had been child's play. Enjoyable, to be sure, but they had not yielded the hoped-for results. Francis wanted Jasper to feel afraid. To feel pain. For that reason, Francis' efforts must be redoubled.

The door to his little home opened, admitting his woman, Sarah. Her blue dining gown accentuated her slender frame and small, pert breasts. The smile she always wore was pleasant enough, but it was her merciless nature that he so enjoyed. It fed his own.

She sat beside him on his cot. "My husband just left for his country seat—some emergency with his steward. And I had to come and see you. What a shame about your brother." Her soft voice failed to echo in his secret, diminutive quarters with its roughened wood ceiling and damp wood-panelled walls. Only a small dormer window allowed a thread of light.

Francis nodded. "I haven't time to feel the devastation that threatens. Instead, I shall focus on ways in which Jasper will suffer the consequences of Miles' death."

A smile quirked the corner of Sarah's mouth, and her eyes gleamed. "That's right, dove. You'll get him."

And he would. He wanted Jasper weeping and pleading for mercy before he killed the blackguard and took his rightful place in the ducal line.

Indeed, the dukedom was within his grasp, for with the correct alliances made and the seamlessly forged documents in his possession, he'd been assured success.

Francis spread his bare toes over the moth-eaten once-blue rug that covered a small portion of his floor, letting his hatred of his cousin—and his anticipation of what was to come— sink deeper into his soul.

"Don't be silly, Jasper. We simply *must* report this to Grace," said Jasper's sister, Juliana, the new Marchioness of Livingston. Her green-and-slate-coloured eyes—that very nearly matched his—were shadowed by worry.

Jasper had just sent a footman to the magistrate with an urgent missive when Juliana, her husband Leonard Notley— the Marquess—and the man's shadow, Mr. Percy Baxter, appeared in his foyer to discuss the news.

Jasper's stomach lurched with trepidation. "Who is Grace, and why is she privy to my—"

Juliana's gaze turned scornful. "You mightn't approve of my new profession, brother, but you could at least deign to listen when I speak of it."

Sodding hell.

"Grace Huntsbury is the founder of our runner offices," Juliana continued, "and my superior. She oversaw the handling of my first assignment, and I daresay she will do much the same now that Francis has slipped the noose."

"Very well, then," Jasper capitulated. "If this meeting is to take place in your runner offices, and will deliberate over what we might do to solve my family's quandary, will I be privy to what is discussed?"

Juliana narrowed her eyes at him. "Of course."

"What will you have us do?" Leonard asked. "Percy and I are at your disposal, should you desire aid."

Percy nodded. The former pirate was one of few words, often communicating with Livingston without speaking at all. He was tall, lean, and muscular, his face one of sharp angles and dark eyes that held pain, experience, and what was sure to be a wealth of knowledge.

"I've already sent word to the magistrate—"

"Are you privy to Francis' haunts?" Juliana asked, cutting over Jasper. "Surely he hasn't ventured out of town if his intent is to torture us."

"Indeed," Livingston put in. "Percy and I could conduct a search."

The fictional blade in Jasper's gut twisted. "Before this assault on our family began, I hadn't seen or heard from our cousins since our youth. Truth be known, I do not know if he has any vices at all, let alone places that he might frequent."

"What do you mean?" Percy inquired, his dark eyebrows furrowed. "Surely the man must do *something*."

Jasper shook his head and shifted his stance. "After Juliana fled our country seat and I journeyed to London, I had men searching for Francis and Miles as well as Juliana. We scoured every louche and squalid establishment—in addition to the reputable ones—but found no sign of them. I was left to conclude that they either hadn't any vices or had sequestered themselves out of self-preservation."

"And yet," Juliana put in, placing a hand upon her husband's sleeve, "I'm certain that an additional search would do no harm. I will accompany Jasper to Bow Street and see you both at home." She lifted a brow at Jasper. "Come along, brother."

Knowing when he was beaten—at least for the moment—Jasper accepted his gloves and hat from his butler and strode through the door. And into Maria.

Jasper's pulse jumped, and he scowled.

"Maria!" Juliana swept forward to embrace her friend.

"Miss Roberts," he said, doffing his hat.

"*Duke*," she replied with a sardonic smirk that tightened his stomach.

"Oh dear," Juliana fussed, glancing past her friend. "Is it raining?"

Indeed, the dark sky was heavy with clouds, and rain had begun to fall. Wisps of Maria's dark hair were damp around her ears and at the base of her neck. Jasper itched to peel them from her skin and feel their silkiness. Then he would press his lips to the soft skin of her neck and kiss it until her chilled skin had been heated from within. He would—

Damnation. I must stop thinking this way.

He cleared his throat. "We were just leaving."

"Do accompany us, Maria. This pertains to you as well."

With efficient movements, Juliana ushered her friend into Jasper's awaiting carriage and bid farewell to her husband. She called out the direction to the coachman, and they jolted into motion.

Despite the spaciousness of the equipage, the air felt close and tight as he settled across from the women...from *Maria*.

Rain fell in rivulets over the roof of the carriage, the sound a nigh-deafening against the discomfited silence within. The women bumped together as the carriage turned away from Grosvenor Square.

Jasper shifted in his seat across from them, his chest welling with dread.

"Tell her, Jasper," Juliana prompted.

His eyebrows lifted and his belly dipped. "I beg your pardon?"

Ignoring him, Juliana clasped one of Maria's hands. "This morning, my brother returned home to find a poisoned note impaled by a dagger in the door of his study."

"*Poisoned*?" Maria's concerned grey gaze fell on Jasper. "How do you—"

"It smelled of bitter almonds," Jasper interjected. "It is the same aroma of laurel water. I know not if he intended to actually poison me or if he merely intended to amuse himself with a game of mental torture."

Juliana nodded. "When our uncle and cousins would visit our estate, Francis would use laurel water as one of his means of killing our pets. Though I daresay it shouldn't do you harm if you touch it."

"How horrible," Maria whispered. "And your staff? What of them?"

Jasper shook his head and braced himself as they turned onto New Bond Street, his lips set in a determined line. "I had my butler make inquiries among the others, but no one seems to have noticed a thing." He pinched the bridge of his nose. "I checked the windows in my study, and all were locked."

"Mmm," Maria hummed. "If Francis has access to your home and continues to issue threats, do you imagine we could—"

"If we wait until he attacks one of us, then it is already too late to act. Is that not what we are attempting to avoid?" The dread in Jasper's chest spread as his mind worked. Maria had wit. And while she might have aided in Francis' previous capture, she could scarcely be expected to know what to do when confronted with such an odious man fighting for his freedom. His *life*. "I'll not have anyone face the danger of Francis on my behalf. You have all already done enough; it is time to set aside our pride and allow the Home Office and our local magistrate to handle this matter."

Maria balked. "We are doing nothing to encourage Francis' wrath, but he is well aware that we aided in his capture and Miles' execution. I'm afraid that we are already within his sights, and whether or not we search for him, the threat is there. Currently, the most sensible course of action is inaction, caution, and preparation while we conduct a discreet search and formulate a firm plan."

"It would be prudent for you and Juliana to seek shelter at the estates in Derby or Nottingham, and leave this matter to the professionals," Jasper argued. "By morning, Francis' likeness will be in every newspaper and magazine in the country; if anyone sees him, they'll surely summon the magistrate."

Juliana scoffed.

"I very much doubt that fleeing London would make any of us any safer," Maria supplied, her eyes flashing with indignation. "As experience has taught us, Francis has no compunction about following his quarry, and I daresay he's managed to secure some help to keep himself hidden."

A huff of frustration found its way out of Jasper, and he attempted to cover it with a cough. He hated that she was right. Why it bothered him, he couldn't be certain, but it bloody well did.

"I concede that point," he grudgingly admitted. "It would be best, however, to—"

"I have sent a missive to Grace and Heather," Maria cut over him, "alerting them to the situation. Grace will be awaiting our arrival, and no doubt Heather will join us directly."

MARIA'S BELLY quavered as she watched the play of agitation over the duke's features. The man was frightened and, naturally, concerned for his sister, but he needn't be an arse as well.

"I and the Home Office are capable of dealing with Francis on our own." Jasper frowned at them, his beautiful two-toned eyes glittering with apprehension and distress. "You needn't put yourselves in undue danger. Your positions as runners might see you searching for a wayward youth or retrieving some woman's baubles from thieving maids, but you're not prepared for what Francis will—"

"Your pomposity and contumely notwithstanding," Maria fumed, "you are welcome to join our meeting with the understanding that Juliana, Heather, and I will take part in bringing Francis to justice. Again. And I would suggest, Your Grace, that you accept our aid rather than fight us, because I can assure you that we will be the proverbial scuff on your Hessians until Francis hangs."

The rush of Maria's pulse filled her ears and drummed against her chest. Lord, had she just done that? It felt...good.

Juliana covered a snort of laughter with the back of her hand.

Jasper's dark eyebrows rose toward his hairline, and his lips turned down in one corner. Had the man ever been spoken to in such a manner? She rather doubted it.

"Very well," he drawled. "I surrender."

With Maria's nod of acceptance, they lapsed into silence

once more. The carriage's wheels splashed into puddles and rattled along the cobblestones until they rolled to a halt in front of the Bow Street offices.

Maria sent Jasper a warning glance. "Miss Grace Huntsbury is an excellent woman. I'll not have you impugn her—"

"Gads, Roberts, what sort of a man do you think I am?" Jasper gave a haughty sniff, swung the door wide, and stepped out, offering his hand to Juliana.

Maria glared at his profile before accepting his hand, descending into the rain—and determinedly ignoring the sudden stirring of heat low in her belly.

SHIFTING UNEASILY in his seat under the scrutiny of the four women, Jasper cleared his throat. "I'm certain. Francis will not show himself unless he has no other choice. He will, instead, toy with us from afar. We oughtn't, however, become insouciant."

The sound of rain against the tall windows of the small drawing room filled the space. They were in one of the few rooms on the main floor of the building, the space appearing to have been decorated to conduct business.

On one side of the room stood two wide desks, behind which was a wall of bookshelves. The remainder of the space was filled with cream-and-green upholstered chairs and chaises and inviting white-painted wood tables. It was an attractive sitting room by all accounts. It might even be pleasant, under other circumstances.

"Then you shall be prepared," Grace Huntsbury said. "Maria, it makes the most sense for you to oversee this investigation. You are already familiar with Francis and his approach. It is a rather perilous and delicate situation, but you have my full support. You will need to work closely with your client—I assume you are comfortable enough sharing confidences with His Grace, given your long acquaintance."

"Of course," Maria returned.

"Oh." Jasper sat forward. "I had not intended to—"

"We'll not accept payment from you, Your Grace," Miss Huntsbury said in a smooth, placating tone. "Miss Roberts requires investigative experience before taking on stipendiary clients, and you are closely acquainted. It is rather ideal."

Words failed him. Maria being in charge of this *investigation* meant more time in her company. More hours attempting to refrain from watching her graceful movements beneath her frocks, from inhaling her spicy citrus fragrance. It also meant that Maria would be directly in Francis' path. But was she not there already?

Christ, this was not to be borne. He cleared his throat. "Very well."

With a tight nod, Miss Huntsbury turned her attention to his sister. "Juliana, though you have a current assignment, do you believe that you are able to lend your aid to this as well, should Maria require it?"

"Yes, of course." Juliana straightened her spine.

"I would be glad to help as well," Miss Morgan offered.

"Excellent." Miss Huntsbury nodded. "I've already sought associations among the local magistrate's staff. I shall connect them with you, Maria, to begin your investigation into Francis' escape. And *I* shall confer with my acquaintances in the Home Office regarding His Grace's staff—"

"What of my staff?" Jasper interjected.

"Well." Miss Huntsbury's gaze fixed on him. "Your staff were present when Mr. Sinclair infiltrated your study, leading one to conclude, at the very least, that your cousin has influence over one of them. For your safety, and with the intent to capture Mr. Sinclair should he return to your home, we will arrange for your staff to be temporarily replaced."

Jasper's mind raced as the four women awaited his response. He ought to have immediately considered the implications of Francis' entry to his home. The blighter could have done something to the food in his larder, for Christ's sake, could have persuaded more of his staff to join his cause.

His gut dipped, and disquieting prickles of unease raced up the backs of his legs, at the thought of any member of his staff betraying him in such a way. He'd known them for years —some since he was a lad in short pants! And now he was expected to trust his home—his *life*—to strangers, at the behest of a woman he scarcely knew.

"They're lovely people," Miss Huntsbury hurried to add. "And while their number might be fewer than to what you are accustomed, they are efficient at their household duties while also being excellent at keeping a person safe."

Jasper nodded slowly. "You are acquainted with those in the Home Office?"

Miss Huntsbury's lips tightened. "I am. But"—she cut him off before he could ask the next question on his tongue— "I shan't discuss the matter further, I'm afraid. I will, however, have Maria introduce you once your temporary staff becomes available."

"I would be delighted to," Maria put in. "Additionally, Your Grace, I would like further consideration regarding the note Francis left for you. What, precisely, did it say?"

The tea Jasper had consumed sat heavily in his stomach as the quote drifted through his mind. He cleared his throat and recited: "*Thou a**R**t a boil / A plague-sore or embossèd carbuncle / In my corrupted blood.*" He lifted one shoulder in a shrug. "I can't place the quote, but it is familiar. I daresay he simply wished to frighten me."

A pucker formed between Maria's brows. "And while I don't disagree with you, Your Grace, we must consider all possibilities." She strode to one of the desks and withdrew a pen and a piece of parchment. "Could you please repeat the quote once more?"

He did, rather enjoying the sight of her features scrunched in thought while she wrote.

"Was there a signature?" she asked. "Any distinguishable markings, such as smudges or ink droplets?"

Miss Huntsbury hummed in approval over her teacup.

It was Jasper's turn to frown. "There was no signature, but one letter was slightly larger than the others in height and girth—as though it was capitalized, or the pen released too much ink."

Maria's gaze sharpened on his. "Which letter?"

"R." He cleared his throat. "It was the *R* in *art*."

With a nod, Maria jotted another note on the parchment, then resumed her seat among their group.

"I shall look into the quote and report back," she announced.

"Thank you, Maria," Miss Huntsbury replied.

Juliana sipped at her tea and returned the cup to its saucer. "The news of Francis' escape will break on the morrow, if the gossip mill has not already seen it spread through every home in London."

Miss Huntsbury took a moment to look each of them in the eye. "And we shall be ready."

CHAPTER 3

The rendezvous with Grace had gone rather better than Maria had anticipated. Grace had swiftly put Jasper in his place and taken easy control of the discussion. Maria rather envied her ability to command the room in such a way. Although she herself *had* managed Jasper in similar ways in the past, her emotions in the moment had always been too involved. She must learn to disengage herself.

"But they are *my* boots, Caroline!"

Augusta's screech filled the familial foyer as Maria stepped through the doorway.

Her youngest sister at eighteen, Caroline, snatched the boots out of Augusta's reach, her perpetual stubbornness flashing in her lively brown eyes. "They don't fit you any longer. Mama said that *I* could have them."

"*Mama*!" Augusta's shriek, Maria was certain, could be heard from across town.

Maria handed her pelisse, gloves, and bonnet to the awaiting footman, and stepped toward her sisters.

"When was the last time you wore the boots, Augusta?" Maria inquired.

Her sister's grey eyes narrowed, and she gave a mulish pout that wrinkled her hawk-like nose. It made her appear younger than her nineteen years. "I don't recall."

"Have you attempted to try them on?" Maria asked. "Mayhap they *are* ill-fitting."

"Well, I suppose—"

"What is all this shouting?" their mama questioned from the top of the stairs.

Augusta and Caroline erupted into protests, their argument increasing in volume. With a resigned sigh, Maria ascended the stairs.

"I shall be in my bedchamber, Mama," she said as she reached the top. An evening of writing was just the thing.

"I'm afraid not, my dear," Mrs. Roberts returned. "Your father and I wish to speak with you in his study."

Maria's heart squeezed as she turned around and slowly bypassed her sisters' conflict. Whatever the reason for the discussion, being summoned boded ill. Had her parents discovered that she did *not*, in fact, volunteer for various charitable causes every day, and instead became Duncan to fulfil her dreams and support the brother whose existence they denied?

Despite her stiffening spine, her stomach wobbled.

The scent of parchment and brandy filled her senses as she entered; her father kept his diminutive study organized to the point of obsession and completely devoid of literature. The room was used only for writing letters, managing properties, communicating with his steward, and arranging his children's futures.

"At last you've returned home, daughter." Her father lowered the letter he'd been reading to his desk and leaned back in his seat.

The door closed with a portentous *click*, and her mother strode past Maria to sit near her father opposite the desk.

"I have," Maria confirmed, stiffening her spine under her parents' scrutiny.

"I've no wish to endure your company any longer than strictly necessary, so I shall get right to it," her father said with a superior glint in his grey eyes. "If you do not find a match and agree to marry the man within a fortnight, you will first become a chaperone to your cousin Gertrude in her come-out year, and then you shall either take a position as a governess for your cousin Frederick's two children or you shall be a companion and nurse to your great-aunt Sylvie. I daresay you have enough experience by now to do an adequate job with Sylvie."

Alarm spread through Maria's chest and tingled distressingly behind her ears. "A *fortnight*!"

She was a wallflower at the age of six-and-twenty who deterred men with her "masculine" bone structure and the "madness" in her family, and she had no dowry to induce a potential suitor to see past their prejudice. She'd thought her parents knew this already and had come to accept her spinsterhood.

"A fortnight is plenty of time in which to find a suitor, Maria," her father intoned, his eyes narrowing with ire. "I've indulged your soft heart for charities long enough. But we will no longer house you here."

"Why now?" she asked, her voice turned pleading and her pulse rushing with panic.

"Come, Maria," her mother interjected, her voice dripping with distain. "You must know that you are a burden upon us. And Lord knows having an aging spinster of a sister is damaging Augusta's and Caroline's prospects."

Maria blinked, taken aback by the sudden, sharp stab of pain in her chest. "I ask for nothing from you."

Her mother waved a flippant hand through the air. "And yet you cost us more every year. Have you no notion of the cost of your attire? Of your *food*, for pity's sake? And what of the servants that must clean your rooms?" She scoffed. "A daughter's position in life is to wed someone wealthy and bear him his heir and spare, not to do *charity* work." She spat the word as though it tasted ill.

Maria's chest constricted, and a wave of dejection spread like frost through her veins.

"But I *enjoy*—"

"I do not care what you *enjoy*," her mother hissed. "You are our eldest child; your actions impact the family. You *will* do as you're told."

Anger flushed hot in Maria's chest, swiftly replacing her sadness. "I am not the eldest."

Her mother's eyes flashed. "Yes, you are."

Maria's voice rose with her anger. "You would dismiss Thomas so easily—"

"*Enough!*" Papa boomed. "We pay very well for him to be both cared for and kept secret from those who would use his madness against you and your sisters. It is for his protection *and* yours that he is locked away."

"Everyone knows of him, Papa, and he is discussed often. His name is spoken behind hands and fans at every mention of this family. Additionally, he is not mad and does not belong in Bedlam. If you would but speak to him, you would see that he is—"

"I'll not hear another word on the matter." Her father's tone lowered in warning, the deep baritone rumbling in Maria's chest. "And you'll not visit him again. Bedlam is no place for a gentleman's daughter."

It is no place for a gentleman, either. Maria bit the inside of her lip and nodded.

"Tomorrow night is the Weatherby ball," her mama said coolly. "I expect that you will find yourself off the wall and dancing with some eligible men." Her dark glare was severe and biting. The woman had the appearance of a doting mother but, in truth, she only desired the good opinion of—and a high position in—society.

Mrs. Roberts would never be satisfied with her life as the wife of a second son to an earl. She ought to have set her sights higher when she was on the marriage market, but Maria preferred to imagine that no man of dignity, wealth, and position would have her.

Maria gave her mother a tight smile and fisted her hands in her skirts. "Of course, Mama."

THE LOUD *CREAK* of aged wood settling under her weight briefly disrupted Grace Huntsbury's thoughts as she dropped a missive to her desk and leaned back in her armchair. The bill on which she'd been attempting to focus couldn't quite penetrate her mind. The predicament of Maria's assignment took precedence.

Grace sighed. She'd been in contact with her friends both in the Home Office and at their other runner offices, and while they'd agreed to help, she lamented the fact that she hadn't yet any foot staff of her own. They would come in time, of course, but men willing to work for hire were more inclined to take a position from a man, no matter her history as a spy.

"Grace." Maria swept into the room, her smile tight and hair damp around the edges from the rain.

Standing, Grace smiled at her friend and gestured toward the chair opposite her desk. "Good afternoon, Maria."

The low murmur of voices echoed in the room as Maria closed the distance between them. Another runner was interviewing a tearful woman in search of her daughter. Sadly, the assignment would take the runner into the depths of a gaming hell, where the woman suspected her daughter was being forced to sell her wares. It was a case all too common among their clientele.

Maria sat in the chair opposite and leaned close while Grace took her seat.

"Is Mr. Greene not available for instruction this afternoon?" Maria asked. "I ventured belowstairs, but he was nowhere to be found in our training rooms."

A regretful frown puckered Grace's brow. "I'm afraid Mr. Greene will be absent for some time, as he has been called away on his own assignment. I'd not intended for him to be a permanent fighting trainer, but I'd hoped to have a replacement for him by now." Her lips tightened in self-recrimination. "For the moment, I shall instruct our runners."

Requesting assistance and additional men from her friends and former fellow spies had been ideal at the beginning of this business venture, but it was time Grace found some men on her own. Mayhap she would visit the pugilist's.

"Thank you, Grace," Maria replied, her shoulders slumping fractionally.

"Are you well, dear?" Grace leaned her forearms on her desk.

Maria's lips pursed. "I'm facing a quandary, I'm afraid. I'd simply hoped to expel some frustration with Mr. Greene."

"I am at your disposal; do you wish to spar?"

"Thank you again, Grace," Maria said, shaking her head, "but no. I've a ball to ready myself for anyway, so I mustn't tarry."

Grace nodded, disappointment swirling through her. "Very well. I am here should you have a change of mind. In the meantime, have you the opportunity to acquaint yourself with Miss Isabelle Hill in the magistrate's office?"

"I have, indeed." Maria inclined her head. "She was reticent in her response, however."

"As would be expected from someone employed by the

magistrate," Grace mused. "I would suggest you spend a little bit of time establishing a *rapprochement* with her. Prove yourself as a person worth her trust. Do keep in mind that an association between you poses significantly greater risk to her than to you."

Maria nodded. "I understand. Thank you."

A smile tugged at the corners of Grace's lips. Maria was an eager and swift learner, and would undoubtedly prove an asset as a runner.

"Now," Grace added, "I should like to discuss our quarry. Have you formed any suppositions with regards to Francis Sinclair's motivation?"

The woman shifted in her seat as she thought. "By all accounts the man enjoys torture. And I daresay the deaths of his family urged him further toward insensibility." Her brow furrowed. "In fact, when Juliana lured Francis and Miles into our trap, they mentioned their sister Jean's death and alluded to their uncle's culpability. They were also insistent that the dukedom belonged to Francis."

"Mmm." Grace tapped her fingertips on her desk as thoughts raced through her mind. "The man might be rancorous, but I don't imagine him entirely devoid of sense."

"Indeed. He must know that Jasper's demise alone would not grant him the title."

"I believe you're right." Grace grinned in approval at her protégé. "He must be getting help."

A CHILL TRAVELLED up Jasper's spine, and he lifted his cloak's collar in an attempt to warm his rain-dampened skin. It was a damned ill idea to attend the Weatherby ball that evening, but he'd foolishly agreed to Maria's plan to behave as though nothing untoward had occurred.

How was he meant to do such a thing when someone among his staff might very well have permitted Francis access to his home? Hunger gnawed at his gut. For Christ's sake, he'd been too wary to even eat his sodding evening meal.

Bloody foolish.

He ought to be out, scouring hovels and dens of ill repute. It hadn't served him well before, and Leonard and Percy hadn't yet yielded results. But mayhap Francis would, with this month of liberty, become overly confident and make a mistake. Francis did not—*would* not—simply disappear. The man had taken his time, but he'd made his intentions known with that note on Jasper's door. Why allow Francis the freedom to do whatever he wished, to make plans for—

Halting his inner diatribe, Jasper reassured himself that the Home Office would have this well in hand. And, of course, Maria was assigned to help...

The carriage hit another rut in the road, and the shock of it jolted up Jasper's spine. "Bloody hell," he murmured. Turning his gaze out the window, he noted the slight tilt and the coal-darkened exteriors of the buildings they passed.

Wait a damned minute. They were going the wrong way.

"Oi!" Jasper rapped on the carriage's ceiling. "We're in Cheapside!"

Jasper's back abruptly slammed against the squabs as the horses started at a run. Alarm hit him full in the chest.

Shouting erupted between the coachman and the footman hanging on the rear, before a loud *crack* echoed off the close buildings around them. Jasper's heart leapt into his throat. Damnation, that was a pistol firing! Had someone shot at them?

They slid in a turn, rattling and bumping on the cobblestones, and Jasper put his hands out to steady himself, his breath nigh caught in his throat. When they straightened, he moved to the rear-facing seat and knelt on the cushion as he slid open the small partition window.

"Stop, man!" Jasper shouted at the coachman.

A wet, grizzled, and entirely unfamiliar face appeared in the small window, a sneer on his rain-slick lips. "Francis wishes you to die well."

The man shoved a wrinkled bit of parchment through the partition, then, with a maniacal laugh, leapt from the moving carriage and out of Jasper's sight.

"*No!*" Jasper pressed his hands to either side of the small window, stupefied by the man's actions.

His heart drummed against his ribs, his pulse beating a staccato rhythm through frozen limbs. Fear, icy hot, blazed in his gut as he considered his options: perish in a horrible crash, or find a way to stop the carriage.

He spared the parchment nary a glance as he turned toward the door. With a deep groan and trembling fingers, he pressed the door's latch and pushed. The carriage slid in a wild turn as the terrified horses ran down the crowded streets of Cheapside, and Jasper gripped the door's edge for his life.

Rain splattered his face, each droplet stinging his windswept skin. Buildings sped past, and the sound of screaming onlookers, huffing horses, thundering hooves, and carriage wheels filled his ears.

With slow, cautious movements, Jasper stepped out onto the outer trim of the carriage. A gust of wind rushed past him, and rainwater splashed his coat. His pulse fluttered, and terror rippled in waves up and down his limbs, dampening his palms.

All at once, his feet felt too large for the narrow ledge, his gloved hands too slick to keep purchase.

"What am I doing?" he breathed, his pants rapid and shallow.

He inched his feet forward.

The horses' manes flopped wetly as they ran hell-bent through Cheapside, and his heart clenched. A hoarse cry escaped him as the leftmost horse knocked over a table, spilling a vendor's wares upon the ground. If Jasper could but reach the driver's seat...

He shuffled himself ever closer, his fingers growing numb through his gloves from the strength of his grip. What a ludicrous circumstance in which he'd found himself. Of all of the games that he'd imagined Francis would attempt to play with him, he'd not thought of this.

"Maria and her bloody plans..."

He reached the edge of the driver's perch, and with his muscles screaming in discomfort, Jasper pulled himself to the seat and retrieved the flopping reins from the floor. The horses whinnied, their eyes wild as he tugged.

"Sloooow," Jasper urged, drawing out the word.

The frightened horses flipped their heads in rebellion, the rainwater flicking Jasper in the face. He held firm, the reins fisted in his hands until, at last, they gradually drew to a stop.

Residents of Cheapside shouted their displeasure at his reckless display from their places of shelter.

"Sodding hell," he gasped between heaving gulps of air.

He'd almost fucking *died*.

And who had been shot?

Glancing back, Jasper caught the wide, terrified gazes of his footmen clutching the handles at the rear of the carriage, their knuckles white. All while chaos surrounded them.

"THEY ARE RATHER LIKE BIRDS," Maria remarked, gazing dispassionately at the throng of London's *finest* moving about the Weatherby grand ballroom.

"Mmm," Heather agreed. "Ravens and tits waggling and preening at each other."

Beside them, Juliana smothered a laugh with the back of her gloved hand.

Maria snorted, a smile tugging at her lips. "They're fascinating, really." Indeed, in observing *polite* society, one could easily conclude that they were anything but polite. The garish dance of popularity, the desire for favour and admiration and, beneath it all, the stifling fear of rejection were apparent in every stiff back, squared shoulder, and pained eye among most members of the *ton*.

Then there were the few of the highest societal standing, the few that took delight in controlling the behaviour and opinions of those they deemed below them. Heaven forbid someone cross them, or the gossip mill would see them barred from every shop and home in good standing, leaving them to either live their lives shunned or quit London entirely.

Everyone in attendance was performing for their peers—even Maria. But while others in society merely sought esteem or marriage from their act, Maria was hiding part of herself. A part that could ruin not only Maria but all those among her acquaintance.

Her stomach wobbled as the strains of another quadrille filled the space and dancers gathered. This evening, she had an even greater performance to enact.

Among the spectators, young ladies tittered behind their fans and young men put their names upon dance cards, while everyone else engaged in lively conversation. Ordinarily, Maria would have remained against the wall with her friends and enjoyed observing human behaviour, but one glance across the ballroom would have her no doubt gazing into the disapproving eyes of her imperious mother.

"Such a pity that I must join them," Maria whinged.

"*Must* you?" Heather asked. "Surely there is some other solution."

"If I do not comply with my parents' demands, my positions at both the paper and Bow Street will be forfeit. I'll no longer be capable of housing Thomas."

Dancers swirled past, wafting the heavy odour of perfume and sweat in their direction.

Juliana wrinkled her nose. "Surely they would be forfeit anyway if you took a husband. I'm fortunate that Leo is a radical in his own way. Most men of the *haut ton* would not be receptive to their wife engaging in work—even under the assumption that her endeavours were charitable."

"The right man, however," Heather added, "should not impose too much upon your life."

Juliana leaned closer. "Additionally, they're rather enjoyable in the evening..."

"We've heard all about what a vigorous lover your marquess is," Heather interjected. "And as salacious as that information is, it does not help Maria in this moment."

Juliana sighed. "Very well."

Maria stifled a groan. "The thought of partaking in tedious, meaningless conversation is not to be borne. A man oughtn't be the answer to my predicament."

"Mmm," Heather hummed. "Have you considered *being* that man?"

"I—" Maria blinked. "No, I have not. Is that *possible*?" She tapped at her chin, then shook her head with a sigh. "That would not work. My parents will expect to not only meet a potential suitor, but to also attend a wedding. I cannot duplicate myself."

"Too right." Heather nodded.

"Perhaps we could find a solution such that your parents will be satisfied but you needn't alter your life to accommodate a man," Juliana murmured.

The music swelled, then concluded, and the dancers separated before new pairs joined for the next set. Maria sighed. Would that she could simply abandon her marital obligation and *become* Mr. Duncan Robertson. Though she did not particularly enjoy womanhood, she had no true wish to become a man. But a life free of restrictions, and the ability to control one's own finances—or *future*, for Christ's sake— would be just the thing.

"Indeed." Heather leaned closer. "Simply find someone biddable—"

"And beddable."

Maria lifted an eyebrow. "I cannot go about sampling suitors' sexual wares. How, precisely, do you expect me to judge his abilities in the bedchamber? How do I even encourage one to ask me to dance? I've been on the shelf for so long, I daresay the men in this ballroom know nothing of my existence."

"Hush now. Jasper is here, and—*blimey*—he's sopping wet!"

Maria followed Heather's gaze toward the ballroom's entrance. There he was. Wetness notwithstanding, he cut a dashing figure in his black trousers and tailcoat, green striped waistcoat, and starched white cravat. His dark brown hair, normally quaffed and appearing soft to the touch, was flattened to his scalp, the thick spikes dripping down his chiselled features.

Her pulse sped treasonously at the sight of him, and the underside of her breasts grew abruptly damp.

"Goodness, but he's a frightful mess," Juliana breathed. "What could have happened? Oh dear. He's spotted us, and he does not appear pleased."

CHAPTER 4

With an awkward *honk*, the musicians halted the music, and every curious and appraising eye in the ballroom turned Jasper's way. Unease rippled up the backs of his legs and wrapped disquietingly around his gut.

As the son of a duke, he'd been raised to live in society's gaze. Naturally, he'd relished the attention and adoration as a young man, but as he'd aged—and particularly now, at four-and-thirty—he felt increasingly disinterested and often smothered.

The butler, belatedly recalling his duty, stammered, "H-his Grace, the Duke of Derby."

Jasper scanned the throng, his heart leaping alarmingly when he caught sight of Maria. His blood thrummed—Lord knew why—before he shook the feeling off.

Whispers surrounded him as he made his way through the crush, his sleeves dripping on the polished floor and his once-shining shoes sloshing with each step. In an attempt at civility, he offered tight smiles and murmured greetings to the throng as he passed, until he reached the far wall and cut a brusque bow in front of his sister and her friends.

The musicians took up their quadrille once more, and the dancers slowly resumed. The tightness in Jasper's shoulders loosened ever so slightly.

He greeted the women in turn, then set his sights on Maria.

"Good heavens, Jasper," Juliana whispered loudly. "Why are you so wet?"

Ignoring his sister, he attempted a smile, but very much feared that it took on a predatory gleam. "Miss Roberts, will you do me the great honour of joining me in the next waltz?"

Maria's grey eyes sparked with—*indignation?*—before she flicked an apprehensive glance over his shoulder.

"I'm afraid that I am already engaged, Your Grace, but even should I not be, you're in a state."

Something cramped in his gut, and Jasper suppressed a grimace. Their exchange was expected, of course, even habitual, but whether it was his pride or something else altogether, he detested hearing her say those words each time he asked her for a dance.

His gaze flicked sideways to Maria before he turned to his sister. "An incident with my carriage."

Feeling entirely out of place, Jasper glanced out at the dancers. And the breath all but left his lungs as fear swept in. A flash of brown hair and glaring blue eyes caught Jasper's gaze through the crowd but was gone as swiftly as it had arrived. And for a moment, he was certain that he'd seen... But no, it couldn't have been Francis. He would surely never venture into so populated a place as this. The man was toying with his mind.

"Good Lord," Miss Heather Morgan put in. "Did you walk here?"

"No." Jasper's brows drew together as he eyed the shorter, ample woman with red-blonde hair.

"You seem reluctant to discuss matters, brother. Mayhap we ought to move to a more private setting?"

As discreetly as they could manage—which was entirely indiscreet, with everyone in attendance now acutely aware of them—the four of them wove through the throng and out the doors to the balcony. The evening air was cool and humid, the rain falling on the overhanging roof a delicate hum.

"Francis had my coachman replaced," Jasper said without preamble, raking his fingers through his wet hair in an attempt to tame it.

"How could he accomplish that?" Miss Morgan asked.

Another jolt of panic shot through Jasper's chest. "My footmen informed me that the hired man knocked my coachman to the ground and overtook the driver's perch after I enclosed myself within. He drove like a madman, then leapt from the carriage after shooting one of my footmen. I was forced to drive it, myself."

"Blimey," Miss Morgan breathed.

"And your footman?" Maria prompted. "Did he survive?"

Jasper jerked his head in a nod. "Merely a graze. I brought him to the physician."

"What do you suppose Francis' intentions were?" Miss Morgan asked.

"The driver said that Francis wished me dead, but he could have meant to injure me instead, for why else would he hand me *this*?" He withdrew the damp and wrinkled bit of parchment from his inner breast pocket and unfolded it.

"Is that—?" Maria began.

Jasper nodded. "*As **Flies** to wanton boys are we to the gods / They kill us for their sport*," he read. "The *F* in *flies* is emphasized. And"—he sniffed the damp parchment—"it smells of laurel water."

"Lucky you're wearing gloves, then," Juliana murmured.

"I don't even understand what it means." A growl escaped

him, even as a shiver borne not only from cold, but also from nerves, wracked his frame. "I grow weary of this emotional torment."

"I'm glad that you're well, brother," Juliana put in.

Maria nodded. "All the more reason for us to remain alert."

Jasper wanted to once more protest their *plan* of going on as normal, but he knew that it was futile. These women were rather too intelligent for any sort of underhanded game. Despite the local magistrate and the Home Office doing their part, his sister and her friends were determined to see this through. And while above all he wanted them safely away from any danger, they'd proven themselves incapable of leaving things well enough alone.

A month before, he'd attempted to avoid Miss Roberts and Miss Morgan's aid in dealing with Francis and Miles and finding Juliana. But he'd done abysmally, and his lack of trust in them and their abilities had rather cost them all valuable time, not to mention the strains it put on their relationships.

"Indeed," Jasper agreed, his jaw tightening. "Alert."

Another shiver travelled down his spine as a gust of warm wind blew past. He ought to have returned home and changed his clothes before attending. Christ knew the gossip mill would be busy on the morrow. He sodding hated that.

Glancing toward the balcony doors, he caught the watchful gaze of onlookers, and Lady Weatherby herself gestured toward him while in discussion with other guests. Her flushed cheeks and upturned brows implied concern and uncertainty, and he knew his time of private discussion would soon be over; the woman would surely join them to offer some sort of assistance. Hell, but he hoped she didn't do that.

"Your Grace, would you believe me if I informed you that Miss Roberts spends the entirety of her days doing charity work?"

Jasper narrowed his gaze on Miss Morgan, curious about her intentions and entirely nonplussed by the abrupt change in topic. "What sort of charity work?"

She shrugged one shoulder. "Does it matter?" He arched a brow, and Miss Morgan sighed. "Finding homes for orphaned children."

Turning his narrowed gaze on Maria, he twisted his lips in thought. The woman had the uncanny ability to command attention and obedience, and to encourage people to *feel* things...sometimes against their will. But to convince wealthy gentlemen and gentlewomen to adopt foundling children? Something inside him eased at the thought. Maria was caring —almost to a fault, inserting herself into the lives of others in order to aid them. She certainly had the soft heart for it.

"I would believe that, yes."

"Aha!" Heather exclaimed jubilantly, turning to Maria. "Gullible! Most men are utter fools and will believe any nonsense that doesn't challenge them. I believe you may safely choose any man to marry, and he should care nothing for your daily activities."

Jasper's heart nigh stopped. *Marry?*

Maria lifted an eyebrow at her friend. "Marriage that must first begin with a dance. Please excuse me; I must flirt my way into the life of some susceptible sod."

With a swish of her skirts, she returned through the doors to the ballroom. But Jasper's mind was stuck on that one word. *Marry.*

Something alarming was happening in his chest. There was a nervous tingling sensation. No, not nervous... Damnation, he couldn't name the heart-twisting feeling. Whatever it was, it made him want to return to the overheated ballroom.

"...It is so unreasonable of Mr. and Mrs. Roberts," Juliana was saying.

"No more unreasonable than any other society parents, I

assure you," Miss Morgan returned. "As a matter of fact, many would have forced her into a marriage long before now."

"I beg your pardon?" Jasper asked, entirely perplexed by their discussion.

Juliana put a hand to his damp sleeve and gave it a gentle pat. "Maria's parents have stated that if she does not surrender to their demands, she will be forced to become a chaperone to her cousin for a season and then a companion to her elderly aunt thereafter. They expect her to accept an offer of marriage within a fortnight and be married before Michaelmas."

"So little time," Miss Morgan moaned pityingly.

"She had more of a choice than I," Juliana said, narrowing her gaze at Jasper. "Gratefully, I had the presence of mind to run away."

Guilt suffused him, and he suppressed the scowl that threatened, focusing instead on the information at hand. A fortnight was, indeed, very little time in which to secure a match, especially for a woman already on the shelf, according to the *haut ton*. But Maria...*married* by the end of the summer?

Before he was aware of his actions, Jasper was through the doors and scouring the ballroom for any sight of her. He caught a glimpse of brown hair, but it was not the right shade, then saw a flash of lavender, but the dress was wrong...

Conversations increased in volume around him. One group of women discussed the *ton*'s newest favourite author, Mr. Mystery, and his upcoming novel. Juliana's and Miss Morgan's voices floated up to him from several paces behind.

"Mr. Mystery is truly a superior option for Maria," Miss Morgan was saying.

Juliana made a noise of agreement. "Your suggestion is excellent, but I do see Maria's point about it not working between them—"

Jasper halted and spun around, forcing the two women to

draw up short. Unreasonable anger burned in his belly and fisted his hands. "What do you mean?"

With a glance about for eavesdroppers, Juliana leaned close and whispered, "Maria is...*close* to Mr. Mystery. Heather merely suggested that Maria come to an agreement with the man, but Maria made the excellent point that, er, Maria's parents would not approve. Heather disagrees."

Words wanted to spill forth from his mouth, but he clamped his lips together and spun on his heel to prowl through the throng once more. *Jealous*. The word buzzed around his head as he moved. He was sodding jealous. But *why*, for God's sake?

Another flash of lavender caught his eye, and he turned his attention to the dancers. There she was, smiling charmingly at some prat as they danced the waltz. How in the bloody hell had she gotten a man to seek her hand so quickly?

Keeping her smile as genuine as possible, Maria clasped the baronet, Sir Asham, by the forearm and allowed him to guide her to the refreshments table. Despite the man's unfortunate name—it reminded her dreadfully of burnt supper—he was an entirely acceptable, if tiresome, companion.

The poor man was known to seek the hand of at least one maiden per season, but he had been spurned by all of them. Nearing his fiftieth year, he was still youthful enough to sire children but old enough that he would not be overbearing in their rearing. He had a pleasing—if perpetually confused— disposition, but was appallingly incapable of carrying on a conversation. His complexion was enduringly ruddy, but he had a full head of dark hair and pleasing brown eyes.

She'd never considered the man as a potential suitor before, and likely never would have if her parents hadn't demanded that she marry. But Sir Asham had responded to her brief flirtation, and she was very nearly guaranteed a proposal from the man if she gave him any sort of encouragement.

Her heart gave a squeeze and her stomach a sad wobble, but she brushed the feelings aside. She hadn't a choice in this matter, drat it.

But surely there is someone more fitting *with whom to spend my time?* her inner voice whispered. Despite herself, her gaze slid across the ballroom to where Jasper stood with Heather and Juliana, his darkened gaze catching hers...and his attire still alarmingly damp. His eyes looked troubled. *No. Angry?* Whatever the emotion was, it sent an inappropriately heated quiver through her middle.

He'd nearly died that very evening. *I almost lost him.* But no. He wasn't hers, and yet...

Her stomach twisted, and nerves danced up her arms and down her legs. She and Jasper had faced danger before—both together and separately—but what if Francis' intent was no longer just emotional torment? What if the next time they crossed paths, Francis followed through on his threats?

No. She couldn't countenance such a thought. Their replacements for his staff were, even at this moment, assembling and would soon be securing his home as a safe space.

Sir Asham patted the hand that rested upon his arm as they navigated the crush. *Marriage.* She suppressed a sigh, her thoughts drawing once more to Jasper.

Her unruly heart fluttered. *I cannot pursue Jasper,* she reminded herself.

While ten years was indeed a lengthy time to hold a grudge over his wager, it was not the only indiscretion of the duke's that prevented her from allowing her obstinate feelings to flourish. His initial handling of the concern over his cousins, his rush to see Juliana married—which had forced her to flee him entirely—and his subsequent lack of confidence in the women's capabilities with regard to this assignment were disheartening indeed.

And yet her pulse still quickened whenever she was near him...or saw him...or indeed whenever she *thought* of the dratted man.

And I almost lost him. Her heart squeezed painfully once more. The man might be irksome, but he was also... She sighed. He was also *Jasper.*

They reached the refreshments table, and Sir Asham thrust a cup at her. "Punch."

Maria smiled graciously and accepted the proffered drink. "Thank you for the lovely dance."

His ears pinkened. "Yes, thank you. Er, you as well. To be sure." He rose up on his toes, his ears increasing in redness. "Quite right."

"I do hope that the weather improves." She took a sip of the punch. It was nearly tasteless it was so watered-down, but it was a relief from the heat of the room.

"Uh, yes. Quite. I bought a new curricle that I'd hoped to drive."

"That sounds rather lovely."

"W-would you care to join me? Wednesday, perhaps?"

She smiled at him. *No.* "I would, thank you."

He beamed, his ears a full tomato red.

The strains of a quadrille began, and his eyes bulged. "Oh! I had better— I must seek my dance partner."

"And I shall return to my friends. Thank you again, Sir Asham." She grinned, watching him fumble his way through the crush as she steadfastly resisted the urge to tug discomfitingly at her bodice. The man was hopeless, but perfectly ideal for her purposes.

❦

SIR ASHAM, Jasper spat in his mind. The man was a fool, and entirely beneath Maria's notice. Why would she bother to entertain the baronet's attentions?

Marry... The word glided through his thoughts once more, and he bit back a growl. *What the devil is happening to me?*

Hell, he was still damp and chilled, it made no sodding sense that he'd remained at the Weatherby ball. *Maria.* His gaze floated away from blasted Asham and back toward Maria, and something in his chest squeezed. He couldn't leave now. Indeed, since the moment he'd learned of her intentions, he couldn't pull himself away. But *why*, curse it? The woman held too much power over him.

"I see that you've become friendly with Sir Asham," Heather drawled as Maria reached their group.

Maria hummed her confirmation. "He's asked me to join him for a ride in his curricle on Wednesday."

Jasper huffed. She'd never joined *him* for a drive. To be fair, he hadn't asked. But she was always off with Juliana at some event, or having tea for Christ's sake, and he'd never been included in their activities.

Fuck. I've missed my chance.

He blinked. *That* was an alarming thought. Maria had always just *been* there; when had he begun to desire more from their acquaintance?

"And did you accept?" Juliana asked.

Maria's gaze flicked sideways to meet Jasper's, and a bolt of awareness skittered down his spine.

Maria shrugged one shoulder. "Of course. He's charmingly biddable."

"Though not beddable," Heather put in.

Jasper's gut clenched, and his throat nigh closed. *Hell's tits.*

"Sadly not beddable, no," Maria agreed. "But certainly virile enough to give me a child, which should be pleasing."

"His virility?" Heather asked.

Jasper's jaw clenched as an unreasonable tide of anger swelled in his chest. How could gentlewomen speak thusly? Surely this was not the norm. And surely Maria didn't truly imagine herself and Sir Asham in such a way.

Maria gave one short, breathy laugh. "I should say not. I meant the child."

Hell. The thought of Maria being *intimate* with Sir *sodding* Asham, of having a child with him, was unconscionable. Without Jasper's consent, a low growl emanated from his chest, garnering the attention of the women at his side.

Shite.

"I beg your pardon," he muttered, forcibly shaking the tension from his hands, though the devil knew his body was teeming with it.

They stared at him silently for a long moment as the cheerful music, shuffling of feet, and animated conversations around them filled the void. The skin at the back of his neck began to prickle at their scrutiny.

"Shall we come to yours for tea on the morrow, Maria?" Juliana inquired.

Jasper shook himself internally, relieved by the sudden change in topic.

"Of course." Maria grinned at her friend. "But let's schedule for the afternoon at my alternate rooms; I have a standing engagement in the morning."

Jasper frowned in puzzlement. *Alternate rooms?* "What sort of standing engagement?"

Maria and her friends replied simultaneously, "Charity."

CHAPTER 5

Milky moonlight shone in through the master bedchamber's window, illuminating the large bed and the sleeping form within. Francis glowered at his cad of a cousin.

The man's mouth hung slightly open, his brow clear of worry—the bloody rotter—and soft snoring came from his bared chest. If Francis but wrapped his hand around the cur's throat and squeezed hard enough, or pressed a pillow into his face...or fetched a knife from the kitchens and slit his throat, or tied him to the bed and cut—

He shook himself. He could be rid of his infernal cousin right then, as could he have been countless times before.

But where's the fun in that? While he wished his cousin a great deal of pain, he intended for the man to suffer for some time. A slow smile curved his lips. *Indeed.* He would play with this mouse. And in the end, Francis would prevail. The dukedom would be his.

56

THE LIGHT of predawn peeking between Jasper's bedchamber curtains cast shadows along the walls and ceiling. His gaze idly traced the lines, stretching over every imperfection.

It was nearly time to rise, and while he'd been to bed early enough, he'd struggled to remain asleep after his clock chimed three. He blamed Maria. Maria, and her determined search for a *biddable* and sodding *beddable* husband...and his body's bewildering reaction to the revelation. He'd never felt such a disagreeable mix of boorish possession and irrational ire in his life. It was impossible for him to truly *possess* the woman—despite what many men of his station were wont to believe—but his body hadn't considered that fact when it reacted so viscerally the previous night.

The pre-dawn light shining through his curtains grew brighter as he pondered his impossible feelings. Why did the thought of Maria Roberts finding a man to marry cause him such revulsion? They'd maintained a mild flirtation, and ever since she'd first rebuffed his request for a dance all those years ago, he'd noted a desire to learn more about her. Surely that was naught but idle curiosity.

There was no denying that she was a beautiful woman with a fiery passion for justice. Since they were young, Maria had frequently been the arbiter of his and Juliana's disputes. Of course, a great deal of her admirable courage and determination was inopportune, which often put them at odds.

His chest squeezed. She clearly detested him—or at the very least considered him the irritating elder brother of her close friend. For she'd never hidden her distaste.

Perhaps it wasn't jealousy at all that he'd felt the previous night. She was a dear friend of his sister; mayhap he merely wished her well, and he knew that Asham wouldn't be the man she deserved. But he rejected the thought with a frown. If she were another woman, Jasper would not object to Asham's pursual—he likely wouldn't even take notice. It was that she was Maria, that she was strong and vibrant. And he'd begun to find himself attracted to her.

The allure of her striking physical attributes, however, was not alone enough to inspire such feelings, for he'd known many a handsome woman and had never before experienced this.

A gusty sigh escaped him as he ran a hand over his face.

After his abysmal attempt at protecting Juliana—damn, but that truly was an ill-conceived plan—had led her to flee through the English countryside while being pursued by Miles, Jasper could not abide being responsible for another person. And that was exactly what marriage entailed. Hell, even the thought of it put a pang of anxiety in his chest.

He had tenants and staff, of course, but relied heavily on his steward to manage those properties. His father had raised him to be a duke but had been negligent in his own role, leaving Jasper with debt and concerns that he was ill-equipped to bear.

Of course, he and his new steward had worked tirelessly with his tenant farmers to recover their crop and cattle yields. And, even now, the dukedom's coffers were beginning to see growth. But, *hell*, someone among his household staff had permitted Francis access to his home! His gut sank. It was proof that he oughtn't be responsible for others, for he couldn't even maintain loyalty within his own household.

He heaved another sigh.

Even should he make the attempt with Maria, he might make the same mistake with her that he had with Juliana. She, of course, wouldn't stand for his being high-handed. Given their long-standing acquaintance, Maria knew him better than any other woman of the *ton*—aside from Juliana—and even she found him lacking.

Nerves and uncertainty fluttered low in his belly. If she

was bound by duty to marry anyway, would his offer be the superior choice? Or would she feel as though he'd forced her hand?

Damn, but it was a terrible muddle. And entirely vexing.

The sunlight was now shining through his curtains brightly enough for him to watch the dust motes dancing along the air. Jasper tossed his bedclothes aside and stood. His yawn misted his eyes and he swiftly blinked the moisture away.

Turning toward the table with his washbasin, his breath caught and his heart jumped into a staccato rhythm.

"What the hell?"

Where his washbasin had been, there was now a pile of coats. His gaze travelled over the remaining furniture in his bedchamber, and his trepidation expanded like a balloon of hot air, rising until it would surely burst and send him falling to his death. Every book, penknife, bit of parchment, personal possession, and article of clothing had been carefully removed from its proper place and strewn over every surface.

His writing desk, wardrobe, chaise and armchair, dressing table, and privacy screen were entirely covered with his belongings. His chest of drawers, however, was bare but for one thing: standing erect from deep within its wood was a dagger, holding a note in place.

"*Fuck*." Francis had been *in his sodding room*! He'd moved everything about, and Jasper had bloody well slept through it. *Fucking hell*. Francis could easily have murdered Jasper in his sleep.

With sure steps, and dread pounding in his heart, Jasper searched his scattered belongings until he found and donned a pair of gloves—the third pair lost to these letters.

He couldn't tell the women about the intimacy of this incident. And he couldn't tell them just how terrified it made him. It was...jarring to be faced with his mortality not once but twice in less than four-and-twenty hours. And the women would no doubt find a way to put themselves in greater danger on his behalf. That, he could not abide.

With trembling fingers and a burst of force, Jasper tugged the dagger free and carefully slid the parchment from the blade. The faint scent of bitter almonds reached his nose, and he grimaced. The bastard had used laurel water again.

He opened the letter.

BUT I HAVE, sir, a sOn by order of law
some year elder than this...

A CURIOUS MIXTURE of anger and fear rushed through him. Francis had not only been in his home but in his private quarters. It sent a very clear message.

"AS YOU SEE, Sir Vaughan, my cousin has access to my home —could very well have *killed* me last night—"

"And yet here you sit, as well as can be," returned the local magistrate, Sir Ludlow Vaughan, tapping his index finger on his desk's surface.

Jasper frowned and adjusted his position in the seat across from him. "Well, yes, but—"

"The way I see it, Duke, is this man—Mr. Sinclair— somehow escaped the noose then fled the country. *Why* would he remain in London? What you're suggesting is illogical, I'm afraid." Sir Vaughan leaned back in his chair and folded his hands over his narrow abdomen. The morning light through the windows caught on the perspiration beading at his temples and upper lip.

Frustration sped Jasper's pulse. "While it may be illogical—"

"I'll have no more of this nonsense." The man waved a hand through the air in dismissal. "At this point, we are certain that Mr. Sinclair has meant to frighten you by hiring ruffians in town. My men are searching for those men, I assure you, and you shall be immediately notified with any updates."

Jaw clenched, Jasper muttered his thanks and left, striding swiftly from the man's office and past his secretary.

How could Sir Vaughan dismiss this danger so easily? His pulse rushed in his ears as he strode through the building and out into the street, where his carriage awaited him.

"You've made—*grunt*—the papers again," Thomas announced gleefully when Maria entered their apartments.

"That is hardly surprising. I write articles for them." She hung her greatcoat on her hook by the door and ambled toward the sitting area, her Hessians clicking on the polished wood floor.

"Ah." He waggled a finger at her, then grimaced and grunted. "But you do not write the gossip column."

She frowned at him, flopping down upon her favourite plum-coloured chaise and stretching her feet out on the threadbare rug. "And what have the gossips to say about me today?"

Thomas flicked the paper with mirth. "It would seem that our secretive, stormy-eyed, and slightly aloof wallflower—*grunt, click, grunt*—has peeled herself from said wall and deigned to dance with an aging—*grunt*—baronet." His lips twisted in a grimace before returning to a smug grin. "Was he a fine dancer, sister?"

A loud groan escaped her. "Would that I not be obliged to

dance at all, Thomas, but our parents gave me little choice. Sir Asham was kind enough. And he will most assuredly not inquire into my daily whereabouts, or my spending, and at the moment that is all I require."

He shook his head, his floppy mop of brown hair wobbling with the movement. "Of course I understand your reasoning, and our...constraints, but you must know that you deserve much more than Sir Asham. You deserve love, Maria."

"With you as the exception to the rule, men are largely contradictory creatures that offer praise and pretty words to one woman while carrying on an affair with another. You forget, brother, that I have lived much of my life these past years as a man, and have heard them discuss their wives and mistresses with detached disinterest or flagrant contempt. They drink and whore and find nothing iniquitous about the awful fact that they carry on infidelities while their wives are at home with newly born babes. Most women of the *ton* care not what their husbands do as long as they are discreet—while they themselves often carry out dalliances in response to their husbands' inattentiveness.

"I could never abide such dishonesty and immorality. I will, therefore, never marry for love. I could not allow a man to hurt me in such a way." An image of Jasper's face flashed through her mind's eye, but she forced it away with a sigh. "I'm afraid to say it, dearest, but a man is good for only one thing, and that is his seed."

There was a long moment of silence, broken only by Thomas' continuous twitches and spasms.

Being on the shelf had meant that she needn't consider any man; she could pursue her writing, move freely about London, and live a happy and fulfilled life, caring only for herself and Thomas. She would grant, however, that she *did* long for intimacy.

Previously, she had been content to satisfy her needs with

her own hands, but since Juliana had shared details of her intimacies with her "darling Leo," Maria confessed to be curious about—and perhaps desirous to seek—pleasure with a partner.

The image of Jasper the previous night—sopping wet and entirely too appealing—flashed through her mind's eye. And she blinked it away. To be sure, the notion of being pursued by the man had its attraction—and it *did* seem as though he was changing for the better—yet they could not possibly share the same beliefs when it came to matrimony.

"*Christ*," Thomas said gutturally, his eyes wide as he cut through her thoughts. "I never knew that you viewed my sex with so jaundiced an eye."

Maria nodded. "Sadly so. I'm certain that there are men who would not stray, such as Juliana's lovely new husband, but finding one would be such a chore, and I'm afraid that I do not have the luxury of time."

Thomas' lips thinned, and he gave her a sad nod. "Well." He heaved a sigh and forced brightness into his voice. "You know very well that I—*grunt*—disagree with your assessment. Men are delicious. If it didn't threaten my life to do so—and should it be legally permitted—I would gladly marry one."

A huffed laugh escaped her, and she matched his grin. "Of course you would. You're a romantic."

She rose to peruse her wall of books.

"And you're a cynic." He huffed a breath, turning his gaze back to the paper. "This column made note of another fascinating bit of gossip."

Maria's lips twitched. "I'm certain it did."

"Did the duke truly arrive sopping wet?"

"Indeed he did, but I'm afraid the reason behind it is not so amusing." Maria succinctly outlined the events of the previous evening as she inspected the spines on her bookshelves.

"Blimey," Thomas breathed, his face scrunching in a twitch. "Have you plans on—*grunt*—how to proceed with your search for Mr. Sinclair?"

She hummed. "I intend to search through my works of Shakespeare here for the quotes that Francis used in his notes to Jasper. I'll search through my collection at home should I not find what I seek. I've been introduced to a secretary in the magistrate's offices, with whom I must develop a friendship. I believe I shall write to her once I've concluded my search, and then work on my novel."

He grinned. "The timing is fortuitous, then. It would seem that you have quite the eager—*grunt*—group of readers awaiting the next Mr. Mystery novel." He shook the newspaper once more.

Pride raced through her, warming her briefly from within.

"The printing press has the next instalment. It shan't be long now." Smirking, Maria strode to her writing desk and arranged her notes and new manuscript before sitting. "It's *this* manuscript that is causing me grief. I cannot yet conjure a reason for Mr. Grayson to attend the country dance where the second murder must happen. He reviles dances and cannot tolerate large groups of people."

"Have the murder occur someplace else," Thomas offered.

Maria shook her head. "It cannot! The remainder of my plot depends entirely upon the murder occurring at that dance."

"I'll leave you to it, then." *Grunt.* He pushed off the arms of the chair and stood. "I have new fabrics to turn into waistcoats."

"Sounds lovely, dearest."

She returned to the bookshelves, withdrew a copy of Shakespeare's *Othello*, and sat down to read. Then a thought occurred to her. "Oh!" She glanced up at her brother's retreating form. "We have guests coming for tea this afternoon."

He nodded and waved her on, turning toward the corridor leading to the bedchambers.

Several long minutes went by while she scanned *Othello* before she returned it to the shelf and retrieved *Macbeth*, then *Julius Caesar...*

Nearly an hour and three more notable works passed before she froze. "*...In my corrupted blood,*" she muttered, darting out of her seat and hurrying to her desk to retrieve the quote.

Setting the parchment beside Shakespeare's *King Lear*, Maria read: "*Thou art a boil / A plague-sore or embossèd carbuncle / In my corrupted blood.*" She lifted her hands in the air with a cry of victory. She'd done it!

But why *King Lear*? Resuming her seat, she read through the play, then set it aside. *King Lear* had been forbidden since 1810—over seven years. Why quote it?

The play was full of family distrust, betrayal...and death. Rather a lot of death. A tremor of fear raced up her spine, spreading gooseflesh in its wake.

Francis meant to use *King Lear* as a threat—or promise— to kill to achieve his aim. Maria's spine stiffened against her chair's back, resolve steeling her nerve. She would not allow him to do so.

That thought, of course, brought her to her next task: penning a note to the magistrate's secretary. She set the book aside and swiftly jotted a friendly greeting and request for correspondence. It was light and brief, but she would write again on the morrow, perhaps, to begin exchanging tales and exploring shared woes, until their acquaintance developed into something of a friendship. The association would be invaluable, but the prospect of a new friendship was rather exciting, for it was not something she ordinarily pursued. This woman, however, would know Maria as a runner, which meant there was one fewer thing for her to hide.

Placing the folded and addressed missive on her desk's corner, her gaze once more caught on *King Lear*. Agitation crawled up her back and tightened her shoulders. Would that she had greater control over Francis' actions, and of their search for him.

A sigh escaped her. She *did* have control over her writing, however.

Adjusting her leather writing gloves, Maria settled in to her desk's chair and, within moments, was lost in her writing. Despite her troublesome plot, words flowed, the ink scratching along each piece of parchment, scarcely legible from the haste of her hand's movements.

"Maria, for God's sake!" A sharp, feminine voice broke through her writing fog.

Maria's back creaked as she turned to find her friends standing in her sitting area, watching her with amusement.

"Oh!" Maria placed her pen aside and stood. "My apologies; I was lost in my work." She strode forward and noted the mirth shining in her friends' eyes.

"You've got a little something..." Heather pointed at her own chin, and at once Maria became very aware of what they found so amusing.

Glancing down at herself confirmed it: she was still dressed as Mr. Robertson, with matching grey breeches and coat, a blue waistcoat, starched white cravat, gleaming black Hessians, and the shadow of a beard dusted lightly on the lower half of her face. "Drat."

"Handsome as ever." Juliana winked at her.

Maria shook her head. "Please excuse me while I change."

Several long minutes later, Maria swept from her bedchamber wearing a front-fastening blue paisley day dress with matching slippers, her hair pulled back in a tight knot and her face washed clean of her artificial beard shadow. She strode toward the sitting area, where Juliana, Heather, and Thomas had served their tea and sat conversing.

Heather had prepared sandwiches, which they'd displayed happily upon a decorative platter, and Maria selected two before sitting on her preferred purple chaise.

"Now," Heather said, turning her gaze on Maria. "What of your case? Have you spoken to your love to learn if he has heard once more from his scurrilous cousin?"

Thomas snorted, then attempted to disguise it as one of his twitches.

Maria frowned at her friend and brother. "The duke is not my love, and I—"

"But you wish that he was," Heather muttered over her.

"Here, here," Thomas put in.

The truth in their teasing sent Maria's stomach into knots and flutters. But she would never admit it. Even the thought of her feelings was not to be borne. She knew what sort of man Jasper Sinclair was, and he was most assuredly not for her...no matter what her heart thought of the matter.

Maria's eyes narrowed. "Damn you both." She shifted in her seat.

"You know," Juliana put in, "if you were to wed Jasper, we would become *sisters*."

"Not you as well," Maria groaned.

"Come, now." Juliana reached out to pat Maria's knee. "Wouldn't it be lovely?"

"That might be," Maria conceded, "but you know the man is not biddable."

"Mmm," Heather hummed. "Quite so."

Juliana waved a hand through the air. "I daresay it scarcely matters. He already knows of your position on Bow Street, so your absence from home will not be alarming."

For the briefest of moments, a spark of hope kindled in

Maria's chest. But just as swiftly, she doused it. If she were to pursue a romance with Jasper, she would undoubtedly fall in love with him. And she could not endure the pain of her feelings going unrequited.

She cleared her throat. "As you know, I have a new suitor."

Heather shrugged one shoulder. "That should not stop you from carrying on a deliciously torrid affair with the duke, I imagine."

Anger flared in Maria's chest. "That is *precisely* why I do not wish for a fashionable marriage! Most particularly not with a man for whom I might actually come to care." *Already do*, her conscience whispered. "No, indeed. When I marry, I will take my vows to heart. Additionally, you know that I am not an ordinary woman... As a duke, Jasper would require someone more suitable to exhibit before the *haut ton*." She took a deep breath. "As for the case, I discovered something of note—"

Knock, knock.

Their gazes swung toward the apartments' front door, and Thomas stood.

"I'll—*grunt*—get it," he said quietly.

They remained silent and still as Thomas answered the door, ensuring that his body blocked their newcomer's view of the room.

Maria's pulse sped. Who would come calling on *Mr. Duncan Robertson*? Not many knew of her shared apartments, and most of those were currently within its walls.

With a murmur of thanks, Thomas closed and bolted the door, then sauntered back toward them, a missive in one hand.

"From Grace," he said, before grimacing and squeezing the letter in a fist as a spasm overtook him. "Beg your pardon." He handed the bit of crumpled parchment to her.

"Thank you." She opened the letter and smoothed out the wrinkles. "It's a summons. We must leave at once."

CHAPTER 6

asper's carriage rolled gently along Bow Street, nearing the women's runner offices. Since his disappointing meeting with the magistrate that morning, the weather had turned for the better, the sunlight peeking through white fluffy clouds and warming the once-crisp air.

His mind, however, was rather occupied by the reason for this little drive. He'd been summoned. By Miss Grace Huntsbury. No doubt she wished to discuss his *case*, and for the first time since Francis had begun his assault, Jasper was glad to have the women's aid.

Maria's mien of heated determination sprang to his mind's eye, and his already-speeding pulse tripped in his chest.

Fuck.

When he'd arisen that morn to discover just how easily his cousin might have taken his life—and most particularly after the magistrate's abysmal response to it—Jasper knew something must change. And Maria and the other runners not only took his concerns to heart, but they had proven themselves once before. He'd just been too blinded by concern and, curse it, superiority, to openly embrace their contribution.

He detested the notion that he couldn't trust his own sodding staff. And yet, there he was, unsure who had granted Francis access. Miss Huntsbury had instructed him to behave as though naught was wrong so as not to frighten Francis into more drastic action. And yet...he couldn't help but worry that they were in error to set this glacial pace.

The conveyance drew to a halt and, with a nod to his driver, he strode toward the building's entrance. It was warm inside and smelled faintly of citrus. The small amount of comfort failed to calm his rattling nerves, however.

Following the sound of voices through the nearby doorway, Jasper found himself drawn to the sitting room.

"...She's a lovely woman, and I'm certain would be a fit for a position here," Maria was saying.

"Of course I trust your judgement, Maria," Miss Huntsbury replied. "Do have her come in to speak with me."

Jasper rounded the doorway, and the women stood, eyeing him with expectation. He bowed and offered a polite "Good afternoon," but he scarcely noticed the other women in the room. His attention was entirely captivated by Maria.

Her dress brought out the hint of blue in her determined grey eyes. Defiant wisps of brown hair flew about her head with the gentle movement of air in the room. Her lips were perfectly formed: plump and pink. He wanted so badly to taste them.

"Excellent. We're all here." Miss Huntsbury urged him forward.

Taking the proffered armchair, Jasper settled back and turned his gaze on the woman.

What would Maria's lips taste like? his inner voice ruminated. *Would she be receptive to a kiss?* His jealousy the previous evening came roaring to the front of his thoughts.

Was it really *fanciful nonsense and mild attraction that I felt?*

His gaze slid sideways. Maria was listening to Miss Huntsbury with rapt attention, and his gut gave a slight twist. *I want to have her in my arms and on my cock.* Damnation, the libidinous thought had come from nowhere, but once in his mind, he wanted it to stay. And he wanted to do something about it. He just didn't know what. For fuck knew he couldn't have anyone in his bed when Francis had access to it.

"...new stratagem for us to put into motion," Miss Huntsbury was saying.

Maria nodded and turned her gaze on him. "I've a question for His Grace."

Shaken from his lascivious musings, Jasper cleared his throat. "Yes, of course."

"When both of your cousins were in pursuit of you and Juliana, did they say anything that might imply a reason behind their actions? Surely this isn't *only* for the title and estate, as we'd first assumed. They must have known that Francis would not be able to enjoy his newfound title for long before he met his end after a trial."

"I confess, I've been struggling with this question. All I could glean from his letters was his desire for the title, and vague allusions to family and death." Jasper raked his fingers through his dark hair. "Prior to their previous capture, they'd inferred that Francis blamed my father for the death of his sister, Jean. I'm unaware of the circumstances of her death, but I know without question that Juliana, our father, and I were in London the entirety of that month. A woman named Marie Tussaud was showing an exhibit of wax death masks from the victims of the Reign of Terror. Surely Francis knows that my father could not possibly have had anything to do with Jean's death. All I can surmise is that the man is simply mad."

Miss Huntsbury hummed. "Mr. Sinclair is determined, and understanding his motives would be beneficial. We had best make the attempt to learn more."

"Before you continue, I have some news." All four women watched him with concern as he spoke. "Another poisoned letter from Francis was pinned to my door with a dagger." *It was my bedchamber chest of drawers, but you needn't know that.*

His sister gasped and...had Maria grown pale?

"Was it another quote?" Miss Morgan inquired.

Jasper nodded. "It was. And I have yet to learn where it is from."

Maria hurried once more to the nearby desk to retrieve a bit of parchment. "Do you recall what this note said?"

His jaw tightened. "I do. '*But I have, sir, a s**On** by order of law, some year elder than this.*'"

"I see." Maria's lips pursed in thought. "And, as in the previous notes, did a word or letter visibly stand out?"

Jasper's jaw tightened once more as he determinedly kept his gaze from her pinkened lips. "As a matter of fact, yes. The *O* in *son*."

Maria tapped her chin. "R, F, and O."

"Perhaps he has scrambled the letters," Miss Morgan offered.

"Forever, fortuitous," Juliana added. "There are countless words that it might be, but mayhap if we garner Francis' motivation behind the letters and his attacks, we might be able to decipher these quotes."

"As a matter of happenstance, I made a discovery today," Maria replied, returning to her seat with a swish of her skirts.

Jasper's heart hiccoughed as he leaned forward, eager to hear her discovery.

"The quotes you've received are from *King Lear*."

"Indeed?" His brows puckered. "Has that not been prohibited since—"

"Since 1810," Maria finished. "At that time, our monarchy feared members of society would see the similarities between King George III and the mad King Lear. Which is likely why none of us recognized the quotes directly we heard them."

"Why do you suppose Francis chose *King Lear*?" Juliana asked.

Jasper shrugged one shoulder. "I haven't the faintest."

"*Edmund*," Maria stated.

A gust of wind from outside rattled the tall windows, and Jasper suppressed a shudder.

"Edmund?" he repeated.

"Yes." She leaned forward eagerly, her intelligent eyes lit with enthusiasm as she spoke. "I imagine that Francis feels a connection to Edmund's character. Early in the play, he is determined to become the earl and will kill anyone that poses a threat to his pursuit. Francis feels much the same about the dukedom."

Damn, but the woman was clever. He ought to have seen the connection, as well, but it had been years since he'd seen the play. And hell if he could muster a clear thought with her face lit up as it was.

"Blimey," Miss Morgan muttered.

"Of course," Jasper grunted, raking a hand through his hair once more. "Yes, that makes perfect sense."

"And you say the note was *in* your home, as was the first, Your Grace?" Maria's face scrunched once more in thought.

"Yes."

"What of your staff? Were they in residence?"

"They were."

Miss Huntsbury's lips thinned, her young, round face growing increasingly grave. "Yet another reason why I must insist that we carry out this new stratagem. Someone within His Grace's household has allowed Mr. Sinclair access, whether by leaving a door unlocked or willingly opening it.

Whatever the method of his entrance, he is somehow going unseen."

Jasper cleared his throat. "I must confess, I spoke just this morning with the magistrate on this very topic. He and his men believe that Francis has, in fact, fled the country—perhaps by way of a merchant ship—and that the happenings here in town are being carried out by a band of paid individuals with instructions left by Francis." He tapped his fingertips on his thighs, his body fraught with unease. "The probability of a member of my household staff being among his ranks is entirely possible. And decidedly unnerving."

Miss Huntsbury's shrewd gaze flicked to Maria, as the others watched him with varying expressions of exasperation and aggravation.

Maria's lips pursed. "We've just been informed by Miss Huntsbury that the men and women she sought to replace your staff are ready and willing to accept their positions. They are to arrive at half-six at the staff entrance. As such, it would be prudent for you to meet with your housekeeper and inform her of the intended changes. Mayhap suggest a stay with their families or offer temporary lodgings at one of your estates.

"I imagine," she continued, "that this will bring some comfort to you, Your Grace."

"It is of some comfort, yes," he agreed.

"Thank you for letting us know," Miss Huntsbury said. "Maria will continue the lead role—working around her current schedule, of course—by taking a position as a maid. When she is not on shift, Heather will take on the role." She turned her attention briefly to Miss Morgan. "Are you amenable to taking on this assignment in addition to your other new case?"

Jasper's heart leapt, and his stomach all but flipped over entirely. *Maria. In my home. Every day.*

"Yes, of course." Miss Morgan beamed, clasping her hands and bouncing slightly in her seat as she nodded eagerly.

"Why maids?" Jasper inquired. "If my staff are to be removed from my residence and replaced by yours, what purpose does a disguise serve?"

"As a duke living on Grosvenor Square, your home is observed for a number of reasons, but largely for gossip. Neighbours' curiosity could mean devastating consequences for our runners if they are noticed arriving and departing your home at all hours, or if they're spotted through any of your windows."

"Right," Jasper murmured. "Noted." Another thing he hadn't sodding considered.

With a small smile, Miss Huntsbury continued, "Because your staff will be absent, Maria will direct the new staff. A potential source for the laurel water must be found—if indeed the letters have been left by someone in His Grace's household. Maria and the new staff will secure the house by keeping guard and inspecting all entrances for evidence of tampering. Both Maria and Heather have been given some training and are more than capable of aiding the new staff in defending the home, should it be required."

Maria has received combat training? He caught her profile as she listened to Miss Huntsbury, and his heart tripped over in his chest. Might she be capable of overpowering *him*? Hell, but that was a curiously arousing thought.

Heated images of Maria flipping him onto a bed and restraining him flashed through his mind...and his cock stirred.

A distinctly uncomfortable awareness of where he was sobered him, and he internally shook himself.

"...Cook is an assassin best skilled in archery, while the last three new members of staff are exceptionally skilled in espionage," Miss Huntsbury was saying.

Blast. He was sorry to have missed that last bit; it sounded intriguing.

"And they shall be at your disposal, just as your ordinary staff are, Your Grace."

Jasper nodded his understanding.

Maria shifted uneasily in her seat, her face crestfallen. "Your plan is an excellent one, Grace, but I'm afraid I'll not be able to continue my role in this plot. Mayhap my part ought to be given to Juliana?"

"Can you not?" Miss Huntsbury asked, her brow furrowed.

Despite himself, Jasper's chest gave a squeeze at the hopelessness and defeat in Maria's grey eyes.

"You see," Maria went on, "my parents have demanded that I accept an offer of marriage within a fortnight, and I am currently being courted by—"

"Why not marry *me*?"

The room went entirely still, and Jasper's heart nigh stopped beating. Had he truly just proposed sodding *marriage*?

Just that morning, he'd reminded himself that he did not wish to incur the weight of responsibility for anyone else's life, and marriage was just that. Maria would be in his home, in his care, and in his...bed.

He swallowed convulsively as his cock stirred once more. *That* was certainly an inducement for marriage to Maria. So long as she said yes. But truthfully, his stirring anticipation at the thought of Maria in his bed was secondary to the leap his heart gave when he considered the possibility of a future filled with her intelligence, determination, and kindness. The way she saw the world around her, the curious solutions that she always managed to find when faced with a problem, and her incredible—and often insufferable—penchant of outwitting him.

The notion of a future with Maria was tempting, indeed.

Gaze sharpening on the woman, Jasper shifted in his seat, his pulse drumming through his veins. Damn, but it was alarming just how much her answer meant to him.

The proposal might have been sudden, but he wanted to trust the instinct that had driven him to it.

SAY YES! Maria's heart screamed, while her mind said *absolutely not*. The internal battle had her incapable of coherent thought, let alone speech.

This was *Jasper*, for goodness' sake! The man who was capable of charm and affability as a means to win a wager. And, whose presence had the ability to speed her pulse and spread tingles of awareness throughout her body. Lord, but intimacies with him would be—

Stop that, Maria. Think rationally.

She took a slow, deep breath, acutely aware of her friends' penetrating gazes.

Consenting to marry Jasper would both satisfy her parents' demands and potentially give her a child. He was aware of her position on Bow Street, and would likely not question her frequent absences as a result. She could still maintain her apartments, and...

It would offer her the freedom that she so desperately required.

Hope buzzed through her, and yet just that morning, she'd told Thomas that she would not marry a man for whom she might possess amorous feelings. And this was *Jasper*, the very man to teach her such a mortifying lesson about his sex.

Logic—and hope—won out. Her reply was all but written already, no matter how painful the result might be. She simply must hold firm against any burgeoning feelings and guard her heart.

"Very well, Your Grace," she said, her voice hoarse and trembling. "I shall marry you."

Heather released an uncharacteristic squeal, and Juliana clapped her hands, but Jasper's eyes were what captured Maria's attention. The blue deepened to cerulean, and the spots of brown grew liquid as chocolate. The realization that she could get lost in those depths cooled her ardour. She mustn't allow herself to weaken in the face of his charm.

Jasper inclined his head. "Capital. I shall speak with your father this afternoon and post the bans on the morrow."

"And we shall be your chaperones!" Juliana cried happily. "For I am to be your *sister*, Maria!"

"Congratulations are in order," Grace said, a thoughtful smile on her face. "That certainly seems to resolve your concerns regarding time, Maria."

"Yes, it rather does," Maria replied, her voice still slightly rough.

Lord above, she would need to speak with Sir Asham to apologize.

"...To the matter at hand," Grace was saying, "Maria and Heather will alternately be stationed in His Grace's home. Your uniforms were commissioned after our first meeting and have been hung in the wardrobe near the door." She turned her attention to Jasper. "Do you have any questions, Your Grace?"

ACCEPTING the proffered hand of a man named Harris, Maria descended the carriage steps into the mews behind Jasper's home. She murmured a "thank you" and led the milling new staff—the hired guards on loan from Grace's spy friends—to the rear servants' entrance. Nerves skittered along her skin, creating gooseflesh in their wake.

Mindful of her precarious position, Maria retreated to the back of the group, careful to keep out of sight with her mobcap tugged low. For Lord knew Jasper's staff would recognize her on sight.

The servants' door swung inward to reveal Jasper's rosy-cheeked housekeeper.

"Oh!" she exclaimed, fanning her face. "I'll fetch 'is Grace. Do come in."

The housekeeper led Maria and the new staff through the bustling scullery and kitchens and into the corridor of service rooms, fussing the entire way.

"'Tis not often we 'ave visitors 'ere, let alone *new staff*. 'Tis a veritable gaff, it is! I adore the master—we all do, really—bu' sendin' us all about th' countryside t' make way fer new staff training... *Bah*! Oh!" She clasped her hands to her chest and her eyes welled as she glanced over her shoulder at them. "But 'e is so dear t' us. Do ensure 'e 'as piping hot coffee in th' morn —and 'e does so love 'is boiled eggs, cooked just so fer four ticks. And o' course, 'is bedchamber must be turned down at precisely eight-of-the-clock, and fires always lit in 'is rooms and study.

"'Ere y' are," the housekeeper finished with a rushed flourish. "The duke 'as instructed y' te await 'im in the servants' 'all, if y' please."

With a tear and a low sob, the woman hurried away, leaving Maria and the new staff to sit at the long dining table in the servants' hall. The housekeeper's distress seemed genuine, and compassion tugged at Maria's heart. There was, however, someone among Jasper's staff who had betrayed him, so needs must.

The servants' hall was a tight, unremarkable room with cream-and-white walls, a narrow sideboard, and no windows

—though the light from the long windows in the service corridor brightened the space.

The others engaged in easy conversation, evidently anticipating their new roles and the potential for a skirmish. But Maria...

She had been to Jasper's residence on countless occasions, and yet now she was fraught with unease. She'd agreed to be his wife. *His duchess.*

In the moment of his proposal, she'd considered only the fact that Jasper was aware of her absence during the day, not whether her new title might impede her normal activities. Society closely followed the lives of the nobility, and would no doubt include Maria among their ranks upon the announcement of their engagement. And while she would not lament the loss of her position at the newspaper—for surely she could keep Thomas comfortable in their apartments using whatever allowance Jasper gave her—being under the watchful eye of society would undoubtedly impact her position as a runner.

She frowned. Of course, Juliana had yet to experience an impediment in *her* duties...

Heavy footfalls preceded the shuffling and scraping of chairs as Jasper rounded the door's frame and the new staff stood. Maria's pulse throbbed at her throat, and she quickly made introductions.

"It's a pleasure to meet you all," Jasper rumbled. "The circumstances notwithstanding."

There was a murmur of agreement around the room.

Maria cleared her throat and turned to Jasper, perspiration beginning to gather under her breasts. "Everyone here has been briefed on their expected duties, Your Grace, but I thought to offer you the opportunity to make additional requests or ask questions, should you have them."

Jasper's gaze caught and held hers for a long moment, an array of emotions playing across his features, before he shook his head. "No." He cleared his throat. "My staff are preparing for departure, but you are all welcome to make yourselves comfortable. Maria has the lead on this investigation, and I trust her to ensure everything is in order. I imagine she has a plan in place for a house tour, so I shall leave that to her. There is no space that is off-limits."

"Thank you, Your Grace." Harris bowed and turned to Maria. "I will bring my men to the servants' quarters and await your instructions there." He bowed again before leading his fellows from the room.

Maria's heart tripped in her chest as silence descended upon her and Jasper.

"Thank you," Jasper whispered.

Her lips curved up in a half smile. "I'll gladly accept your thanks, Duke. But whatever for?"

"For consenting to being my wife."

There went her heart again. Heat spread across her chest and, she was certain, brightened her ears, but she refused to break his gaze.

"Thank you for asking."

THE CARRIAGE ROLLED to a halt before the home of his betrothed—*Christ, what a thought*—and Jasper stepped out. Maria's equipage stopped just behind his, and he watched as she descended the step.

She'd scarcely spoken a word after introducing his new staff and, despite himself, he rather missed her incisive, pithy commentary.

He gave her a grin while offering his arm. "Shall we?"

"I'm ready, yes." She returned his smile with a small one of her own. That quirk of her lips drew his gaze...and sped his pulse.

"Darling!" The shrill voice of a woman came from the opened doorway, and Jasper immediately noted the stiffening of Maria's spine and tightening of her jaw. "Come in, come in!"

Turning his smile toward Mrs. Roberts, Jasper made the first step, leading Maria into the warm house.

The foyer was small and decorated in a vibrant floral pattern that covered nearly every surface. It appeared as though they'd found a rug whose pattern they found pleasing, and spread it to the walls, upholstery, and stair runner.

"My, Your Grace, it is so delightful to see you again!" Mrs. Roberts squealed, dipping into a deep curtsey and struggling to rise.

Jasper sketched a short bow. "Indeed, madam."

Her grey-streaked brown hair was done elaborately with curls and ribbons, without the mobcap that most married women were wont to wear at home. Her cheeks were sallow and her jaw thin—not at all like Maria's—her nose narrow and pointy, and her skin tinged red, as though she'd imbibed too much sherry. Her eyes, however, were very similar to Maria's, though lacking in their depth and personality.

"My!" Mrs. Roberts' hand fluttered to her wrinkled chest. "We're honoured to have you pay us a visit. Won't you join us for tea in the parlour?" She gestured toward a hallway leading off the end of the foyer.

"As a matter of fact, Mrs. Roberts, I had rather hoped to speak with your husband. Is Mr. Roberts at home?"

Her eyes widened, and an unrestrained squeal escaped her. She flapped her hands about. "Of course, of course! Do come this way."

Maria offered him an apologetic glance as they strode through the corridors, presumably to her father's study.

The man stood at their entrance, and his brown eyes filled with avarice at their introductions. Jasper braced himself while simultaneously smiling and making pleasantries. This was the sort of man of whom he must beware. He didn't appear to be careless with his funds, but he clearly desired more, and saw Jasper as his opportunity for financial gain.

Little did the man know that the dukedom was only just recovering from being very nearly destitute. Maria was aware of the circumstance, of course, the truth having come out when they had faced off against Miles and Francis those weeks ago. As it happened, however, the reason for his family's misfortune was due to his father's steward's connection to Mr. Sinclair—Francis and Miles' father. The steward had been pilfering from the dukedom's coffers and lining his and Mr. Sinclair's pockets for sodding years. The problem, of course, had been corrected, and the estate was now paying for itself, but to recover fully and refill the entirety of his coffers could take years.

And still...even knowing the truth, Maria had agreed to his proposal. The rest of the *haut ton* saw him not as a man but as a title and money. But Maria saw *him*.

While his stomach erupted in sudden, absurd nerves, Jasper took his seat in front of Mr. Roberts' desk, and the man himself behind it. Maria and her mother hovered near the door, which struck him as odd. He would rather Maria sat at his side, though he supposed most fathers would hold the meeting privately. Would they not? Hell if Jasper knew; he'd never asked for a woman's hand in marriage before.

He took a deep breath, filling his lungs with the scent of old brandy and parchment. He noted, rather amazedly, that not a single book sat upon the bookshelves lining the walls.

"I'll not prevaricate," Jasper said, launching into the point of his visit. "I wish to request your blessing for Maria's hand in marriage."

A disconcerting choking sound, followed by another of Mrs. Roberts' squeals, came from behind him.

"Of course!" The man beamed triumphantly, his long face sharpening. "But, naturally, we must discuss her dowry. At her age, I'm afraid that it isn't much. We'd quite lost hope, you see."

Jasper put up a hand to halt the man. "That is not necessary, I assure you. Maria will want for nothing."

He leaned forward to shake the man's outstretched hand, and stood. That had been rather swifter than he'd imagined.

"Oh!" Mrs. Roberts fluttered. "Won't you stay for supper?"

CHAPTER 7

A maid and footman entered the dining room carrying plates of what looked to Jasper like braised pigeons and potato pie. It was rather similar fare to what Jasper had been able to afford of late.

The scent of savoury spices reached his nose, replacing the scent of rolls and cream, which had been their first course, and his stomach growled in response. The first course had scarcely grazed the surface of his appetite.

From her seat at his right, Maria murmured her thanks to the maid as her meal was placed before her. A ripple of awareness and heat travelled up his arm and along his chest, as it had repeatedly done since they'd taken their seats. She was still abnormally sedate, though he could understand why. Her family seemed to delight in monopolizing the conversation.

"This is not our usual fare, Your Grace," Mrs. Roberts was saying. "Nothing so homely. But our usual cook has taken ill and, well, we must accept what her replacement has prepared for us."

"Oh, how awful for Mrs. Wells," Maria breathed, her brow furrowed.

Mrs. Roberts sharpened her gaze on Maria. "Yes, well, she ought to take better care."

Jasper lifted his fork and turned his attention to his plate.

"Have you been married before, Duke?" a voice trilled. Jasper noted that it was the sister with the dark brown hair and hawk-like nose—Augusta?

"Augusta!" Maria chided.

The young lady scowled at her sister, evidently unaware of the impropriety of the inquiry and familiar address. She then preened as she turned her flirtatious gaze back on Jasper.

He resisted the urge to frown, swallowing his bite of sweet potato pie. "I have not previously been married."

Maria's sisters eyed each other meaningfully from across the table, then both turned to gaze adoringly at him.

"Why did you choose Maria?" the other sister—Caroline —inquired, her nose wrinkled. "She's dreadfully boring."

Maria stiffened in her seat beside him.

"And old," Augusta put in.

Jasper opened his mouth to refute their assertions, but Mrs. Roberts' rebuke cut over him.

"*Girls!*" Masticated food sprayed from her mouth, and Jasper cringed.

Mr. Roberts turned to him with a brandy-hazed smile. "How pleasing it shall be to have a son at last."

"You *have* a son, Papa," Maria said firmly. "He—"

"We have a guest, Maria." Her mother's frigid gaze had enough strength to send a chill down Jasper's back.

He'd heard something about her brother, but damn him if he could recall what that was. Had he been injured in the war? Hell, he couldn't remember. Would that he had paid attention when Juliana spoke of her friends, but for far too many years he'd shirked his role of brother and confidant.

This wasn't the first time that his past poor attentiveness had impacted his present, and nor was it likely to be the last.

But he now had the presence of mind to learn from his mistakes.

The servants swept through and removed his half-consumed plate. He wasn't finished, his hunger only minimally appeased, but if it would conclude the meal, Jasper was content to let the food go.

Under the guise of adjusting the napkin on his lap, Jasper brushed the backs of his fingers over the side of Maria's thigh in a show of unity.

Her breath caught, and his stomach swooped. He instantly wanted more of that delicious contact, but the moment was entirely inopportune.

He cleared his throat. "I look forward to spending more time in Maria's company."

Mrs. Roberts smiled at him. "I'm sure she feels the same."

"Yes, yes," Mr. Roberts added in between gulps of his brandy. "Perhaps she will spend fewer hours toiling away with her charity groups if she has a nice young man to dote on her."

Charity. The word rolled through his mind as Miss Morgan's words from the previous night came to him. *Would you believe me if I informed you that Miss Roberts spends the entirety of her days doing charity work? ... Aha! Gullible! Most men are utter fools, and will believe any nonsense that doesn't challenge them.*

He glanced down at Maria, who was suspiciously diverted by the silverware. With what, precisely, did she fill her days, if not charity and work as a runner? Was there *more*?

The longer he remained in the Roberts' company, the better Jasper felt he understood Maria. Her sisters, newly out, were young and vibrant but quarrelsome and contemptuous. Their mother, while loving in her own way, was vulgar and rather uncivilized, and Mr. Roberts was a greedy inebriate. Was it any wonder that Maria wished to seek employment as a runner?

Their meal concluded with a nauseatingly sweet fruitcake so dense that he struggled to remove it from the roof of his mouth. He swallowed it down with the remainder of his port, and smiled along with the Roberts' inane chatter.

Finally able to make his excuses, they said their farewells before the family allowed Jasper precisely what he'd desired all evening: a few minutes alone with Maria.

The strident voices of Maria's sisters and mother faded down the hall, followed closely by the lumbering footsteps of Mr. Roberts, and Jasper's shoulders relaxed slightly.

Maria watched him warily, her grey eyes troubled. "Might I speak with you in the parlour, Your Grace?"

"Of course."

He followed her across the hideously floral foyer and into an equivalently patterned parlour.

She spun to face him. "I must apologize for my family—"

"It's quite all right."

"No," she asserted, "it is not. I will understand if you should decide to jilt me once the assignment has concluded and Francis' trial has once again come to an end. As a matter of fact, I would be rather astonished if you didn't."

Bloody hell, she was offering him a way out. Something twisted alarmingly in his chest and tingled in his fingertips. "I'll not abandon our agreement."

"I imagine that your opinion on the matter will change after prolonged exposure to my family."

Her family, his mind whispered, once more piquing his curiosity about the moment of tension between Maria and her parents at the table. He wanted to ask her about her mysterious brother but, despite his tenacious interest, there was something more pressing on his mind.

He stepped close, the suddenly warm space between them growing thick with anticipation. His gaze dropped to her full lips and his stomach erupted with nervous buzzing. And hope.

Despite imagining this moment more times than he could count, he'd not once believed it would come to fruition.

Now was his moment.

He breathed deeply of her scent of ink, parchment, and soap, letting it drift through his senses. Maria was not a woman for the superfluous, and somehow the absence of bottled perfume was bloody arousing.

Heat warmed him just beneath his skin as he ran his fingertips along her jaw. Grey-blue eyes flickering, Maria's breath hitched.

"May I kiss you, Maria?"

JASPER'S LOW, hushed voice sent tremors of awareness through her and gooseflesh spreading across her skin. There was no denying it: she craved his kiss. She wanted to have him against her, to feel his skin on hers. Damn, but the man was maddening!

"Yes," she breathed.

She had only the time to blink before his mouth pressed gently to hers.

It was the softest touch of skin, but it spread waves of heat swiftly through her body. She gasped, and Jasper groaned, deepening the kiss. *Good heavens*, but his tongue! With long, languid strokes, he teased her senses and urged her to reply in kind. So she did.

Clasping his lapels, she flicked his tongue with hers, tasting and exploring. Lord, but he tasted like sugar and fruit. She wanted more.

His arms slid around her, his warmth seeping through the material between them feeling hot against her skin. He pulled her close against him, the hardening ridge of his manhood pressing insistently against the soft belly above her mons. He moaned deep in his throat, and Maria felt a surge of tingling pride. The knowledge that she was the one to cause his state of discomfort was more empowering than she could have imagined.

Just as swiftly as the kiss began, it ended. Jasper released her, retreating a step, and her body felt abruptly chilled by his absence.

She blinked, confusion and arousal tumbling through her.

"I shall make the announcement with the papers, and I shall see you on the morrow," he said, his voice thick.

She gave him a nod, and was only dimly aware of his departure. Lord, but the man could kiss!

"How could you *do* that to us?" Her mother's piercing voice came from the parlour's entrance, and Maria winced.

Turning, she watched her mother walk stiffly toward her, her curls bouncing.

"How do you expect us to make a favourable impression if you do not give us advance notice that we will have a duke join us for our evening meal? A *duke*, Maria!" She turned her face up to the ceiling and placed her hands upon her chest. "Oh, what he must think of us! *Braised pigeon and potato bloody pie?*" Her eyes fairly bulged as the volume of her voice rose. "And who shall become chaperone for your dear cousin and companion to your aunt? Whatever shall I say to them?"

Maria frowned, her heart pinching. "Were you hoping that I would not find a match? That I would be forced to—"

"Do not say such nasty things," her mother hissed.

"I'm merely stating my observations."

"*Hssst*! Watch your tongue, girl! I'll not have such insolence in my home."

As though popping a bubble, the fight fled Maria. It had been a trying day, and all at once, she desired the comfort of her bed.

"Please excuse me, Mama. I have the headache and wish to go to bed."

Abruptly, the scorn in her mother's eyes turned to malevolent delight. "I would advise you to get your beauty rest, but we all know that would prove fruitless. You're too much like your father's dreadful relations. But best keep up appearances if you wish to garner *some* attention this season. Lord knows the duke will likely jilt you before you reach your wedding day."

With a nod, Maria turned away from her mother. Fatigue and discomfort slowed her steps as she made her way to her bedchamber. Abruptly, the frock she'd donned no longer felt correct, her chemise and petticoats *wrong* against her skin. Would that she had some of her men's attire at home in which to sleep.

She expanded her lungs as far as her corset would allow and blew the breath out in a *whoosh*.

Tomorrow would dawn another long day, which included her first shift in Jasper's home. She had a task to accomplish. And...part of her hoped that he would find the opportunity to kiss her again. Warmth flooded her belly at the thought.

Have a care, Maria, she cautioned herself. She must remember to guard herself from the man's palpable charms, no matter how delicious his kisses.

Moving slowly through her bath and her ablutions, Maria allowed her mind to wander. Biddable, Jasper was not, but *beddable*... How long would their kisses have lasted had he not pulled away? Little prickles of delight warmed her from within. She ought to have run her hands through his hair. *Is it as smooth as it appears?*

Her bed had been turned down, the bedclothes crisp and cool against her flushed skin. She wanted nothing more than to return to Jasper's arms and lock her lips with his, their tongues entangled and her body pressed against his hardness...

and that was precisely why she mustn't ruminate on it for one moment more. She was on assignment now and had an important task at hand.

But although her determination was firmly in place, her last thought before she fell asleep was of the sweet taste of fruits upon Jasper's tongue.

"GRACE!" Harriet exclaimed breathlessly as she darted into the training room, nervously toying with the ties of her evening cloak.

Grace put up a hand to halt her gentle sparring instructions with Juliana. "Harriet? Whatever is the matter?"

The young recruit gulped air and gestured wildly with her hands as she drew near. "My client's estranged husband has followed our trail as far as the Swallow and Cross Inn. I cannot possibly risk her safety by continuing on with our plan—most particularly as the evening grows darker. We must have an alternate course."

"I see," Grace returned, her nerves calm and her mind racing with possibilities. "Fetch Isadora and return to your client's side; she mustn't be left alone from now on. Take the road north toward Leeds and ask for 'Black Bear' at the Goat's Horn Tavern. I'll send word to an acquaintance in Brampton who can arrange shelter for the three of you there. Additional funds are on my desk in a satchel with an embroidered *L*. Send word once you arrive."

Harriet huffed a grateful sigh and dipped in a shallow curtsey. "Thank you, Grace."

Grace nodded, and the woman dashed from the room.

"You've begun something wonderful here, Grace," Juliana remarked, resuming her position on the sparring mat. "I'm proud to be a runner for you."

Emotion swelled in Grace's chest, and she smiled, glancing around the room. Their sparring dummies were naught but burlap jute and hay surrounding a wood structure, and their wall of weaponry was sparse, but she had done a great deal with the space and was proud of the progress.

"Thank you, Juliana. There is much yet to accomplish before we will be in smooth working order, but I'm so pleased that even our smallest cases are impacting women's lives positively."

"Certainly." Juliana eyed her sympathetically. "I've sensed some frustration from you with regard to Maria's case. Are you well?"

"I am." Brushing a fallen lock of hair from her forehead, Grace grinned thoughtfully. "I trust Maria entirely. She's determined and, despite having multiple vocations, has proven herself to be an invaluable and intelligent resource for our offices.

"My concern lies with Francis," she continued, her heart giving a little *thwump*. "Finding and apprehending someone in London who does not wish to be found will prove a considerable task. There is danger in this assignment and, their willingness to face the risk notwithstanding, I worry over everyone's safety." Her lips quirked. "That said, I imagine Maria's greatest challenge will, in fact, be the duke."

A light laugh escaped Juliana. "Indeed. Maria has adamantly denied her love for my brother since we were children."

Grace's grin widened. "I daresay he feels much the same."

"'Struth!"

"Now, we resume." Grace adjusted her skirts and lowered her stance. "Copy my movements, and you shall learn what to do if an opponent attempts to strike you with a blade."

THE SUN FOUND its way into the narrow close beside the newspaper offices—*The Morning Herald*—warming Maria through her grey woollen coat and matching breeches as she descended the step of the hackney. The morning had gone precisely as usual. She'd eaten, dressed, and summoned the carriage with her favoured coachman and footman—whom she paid handsomely to keep her daily whereabouts secret— and rode to Cheapside, where she left them. Thomas had remained asleep while she changed for her day of work, and then she'd summoned a hack to bring her there.

She inhaled deeply as she entered, taking in the aroma of paper and ink.

The office was humming with activity, and she inwardly grimaced. Working at *The Morning Herald* was valuable for experience, and it provided a means to help Thomas, but she rather preferred silence when she wrote.

"Oh! Good morning, Mr. Robertson." Cordelia smiled at her in greeting, green eyes crinkling in the corners.

Maria returned her smile and touched the brim of her hat before slipping the secretary a piece of folded parchment. "Good morning, Cordelia."

The woman nodded, curiosity brightening her eyes as she accepted the note and hid it in the folds of her skirts. Maria winked at her and strode away.

Reaching her desk, she found three article requests from her superiors, as well as several leads on where to find information. She placed her hat on a nearby hook and settled in to do her work.

Despite the noise, she was soon lost in her writing, the words flowing swiftly from her, the gentle scratch of her pen filling her ears. Before long, two of her articles had been completed, and she was working on her third.

Loud murmuring broke through her focus and drew her notice. The men in the desks around her spoke softly to each other, their attention fixed on the office's entrance. There stood four men in conversation at Cordelia's desk. Two of them—unquestionably fellow writers—had their backs to her, and the other two men were obscured by a wall. They spoke animatedly until one of her fellows, Mr. Shoemaker, gestured one of the hidden men toward Shoemaker's desk.

Her pulse sped and shoulders tightened. *It couldn't be.*

They rounded the corner and strode into the room. Mr. Shoemaker's wide smile was bemused but genuine as he walked past. And following him was the Duke of Derby.

Maria's breath froze in her throat. If she did not draw attention to herself, perhaps she could take her leave without his seeing her. Surely he would be too preoccupied with his own business to trouble himself with the other workers around him.

She slowly released her breath and unclenched her fists. All that was required was patience, and she could—

No doubt feeling Maria's scrutiny, Jasper's head turned abruptly. His gaze, two-toned and penetrating, met hers as he stood immobile, poised to sit in the proffered chair across from Mr. Shoemaker. Hope fleeing and heart fluttering wildly against her ribs, Maria attempted to keep her expression neutral. Mayhap he would not recognize her.

Just as the thought occurred, his eyes widened.

CHAPTER 8

*I*t *cannot be*. Jasper's gaze was transfixed on the stormy grey eyes of a writer for *The Morning Herald*. But they were *Maria's* eyes.

"Oh!" the genial man across from him said. "Have you met Mr. Robertson?"

"I do believe I have," Jasper replied absently.

Without a conscious thought, he straightened, his feet carrying him toward *Mr. Robertson*. Panic flooded those grey eyes, and Maria stood, reaching for her—Mr. Robertson's—hat.

"Good morning, Mr. Robertson," Jasper said, his voice low and challenging.

Maria's lips thinned into a grim line and her shoulders dropped as she turned to face him, sketching a bow. "Your Grace. Mr. Shoemaker."

The woman had lowered her voice and painted the shadow of a beard upon her face, for Christ's sake. What in the hell did she think she was doing?

His gaze travelled over her person: starched white cravat, pale-green waistcoat, and grey coat and breeches over shining

Hessians. *Christ, those legs.* To his surprise, his cock twitched in interest and heat spread across his chest.

He cleared his abruptly dry throat. "I did not expect to see you here."

Mr. Shoemaker chortled. "Oh, but Duncan comes in to complete his articles nearly every morning, don't you?"

Every morning? Was *this* her "charity work"?

Maria gave a shaky smile, her cheeks growing increasingly pallid. "I do, indeed."

"I knew Mr. Robertson as a child, you see," Jasper explained to the man beside him. "I'm pleased to learn that he has found some success. How long would you say it has been since you've taken this position, *Duncan*?"

"Fancy you knowing a duke!" Mr. Shoemaker's eyes bulged at Maria. "I've known you for eight-and-a-half years, and you never said a thing!"

Eight-and-a-half years!

Eyes flickering with trepidation, she gave a rigid smile. "Our friendship was in the past. I did not think that the update on my life was prudent." She turned her attention back to Jasper. "What do you say we go for a drink at the pub to reflect on those pleasing times we had as children, Your Grace?"

"I rather think that we ought." He tapped the surface of her desk with his index finger. "I'll call on you this afternoon."

With Maria's murmur of agreement in his ears, he returned to Mr. Shoemaker's desk to commission his announcement. The announcement of his and Maria's betrothal.

Sodding hell. Never would he have fathomed that Maria had taken a job. And for eight bloody years! By working under a falsified name, she put not only herself at risk, but the newspaper as well, for hiring said fictional man. What was she thinking to do such a thing? And *why*? What could possibly require her to work *two* jobs?

His mind whirled with questions.

Duncan Robertson. Christ, but he'd read her bloody articles! She was a damned fine writer. But that wasn't the point, blast it.

Maria works at the newspaper! The thought burst through his thoughts at regular intervals, entirely derailing his concentration as his meeting with Mr. Shoemaker progressed.

On more than one occasion, Maria's lowered voice floated to him across the room as she conversed with others. And every time, the need to look her way clawed at him. *Christ*, but the beastly urge to simply sit and *watch* her wearing those sodding breeches had his cods in a vice. But he wouldn't.

His thoughts were a lust-filled haze as he concluded his discussion with Mr. Shoemaker. He stood, eager to see Maria as *Mr. Duncan* once more. And there she was, her hat in hand as she spoke quietly with the secretary.

Damn, but those legs.

Never would he have thought that a pair of men's breeches would arouse him so, but there was no disputing that Maria wore them exceedingly well and his body most certainly enjoyed the sight.

He wanted to bid her farewell but suspected she would not appreciate further contact at her place of employment. Instead, he strode from the building.

And into a sudden dense fog. The street was still and quiet.

A chill swept up his spine, and his body trembled with a convulsive shiver. *The London particular. Damn.* A cough wracked his frame, and a grimace distorted his face as he caught the acerbic scent of sulphur and soot.

Jasper withdrew a handkerchief and pressed it over his mouth and nose, attempting to keep the dense, poisonous impurities from reaching his lungs—it was known as the 'killer fog' for a reason.

He blinked into the obscurity, unable to even see his sodding hand in front of his face, then turned. The door had disappeared behind the fog.

He could not let Maria travel home without some sort of protection—for Lord knew blackguards took advantage of the London fog—and according to Mr. Shoemaker, she ordinarily left at about this time. He very much doubted that she would let the fog slow her, but the nauseating twist to his stomach would not abate. Most particularly knowing Francis roamed free.

With an outstretched hand, Jasper felt along the damp brick wall, until the door reappeared.

The door abruptly opened, and a soft curse found its way to his ears.

Maria.

The breath in his lungs froze when he spotted her. He wanted to call out, to alert her to his presence, but his body wouldn't respond to his commands.

Securing the hat upon her head, she put a handkerchief to her mouth and strode down the street, disappearing into obscurity.

Instinct moved him. Swirls of fog danced around them, whirling and chaotic, and entirely disorienting. The damp seeped beneath his coat, chilling him through to the skin. It was completely at odds with the weather a mere hour prior. Such was the London particular.

Maria hid the fact that she worked for the paper. Her family, while not particularly well-to-do, ought to be able to provide for all her needs. And yet she had taken not only the position with the paper but also at Bow Street, leading him to only one logical conclusion: Maria had additional expenses of which her family was unaware.

He would have time to inquire about those later; for the moment, he simply wished to see her reach her destination safely.

They walked for a long while, Maria moving at a swift pace and Jasper following behind. He listened for her booted footfalls and watched for every grey ruffle of her coat and flash of her brown hair. She turned down side streets and up thoroughfares until Jasper was well and truly lost. He marvelled at her sense of direction.

Rounding a corner onto a narrow side street, Jasper's senses were filled with the scent of sulphur and soot, in addition to smoke, urine, and the ungodly odour of rotted fish. Despite being unable to see his surroundings, Jasper could guess at their location by scent alone. They were just off the Strand. It was eerily silent but for the sound of their footfalls reverberating around them—no doubt alerting Maria to his presence. And—

Hell, there was a third set of footfalls. Alarm spread through his chest to prickle in his fingertips.

Keeping his ears trained behind him, he followed Maria through the whirling fog, his pace quickening to match hers... and their pursuer's.

In this part of town, footfalls could belong to anyone, and the magistrate had all but assured him that his cousin had fled London. But with a certainty deep in his soul, he knew who was in pursuit. *Francis*. Jasper could no longer waste time attempting to be stealthy. Maria must be made aware of the potential threat.

He sped his pace, but she matched him.

"*Maria*," he hissed.

She turned down another side street, and he briefly lost her.

Moving to a jog, he rounded the corner, and lost his breath altogether.

With swift, bewildering movements, Maria gripped his shoulders and spun him, slamming his back hard against an uneven brick wall. Air rushed from his lungs before she braced her forearm against his throat and held a dagger to his cheek.

Pain radiated over his neck, and he choked, gasping for air. *Fuck*, but it had all happened so quickly.

"Maria," he wheezed.

"Jasper!"

Her shocked features and the small, sharp dagger clutched in one of her gloved hands were scarcely visible through the tears that flooded his eyes.

"Oh, for heaven's sake, Jasper, I almost cut you! Why would you—"

He coughed. "Run!"

PULSE THUNDERING IN HER EARS, Maria gripped Jasper's hand and broke into a run. She did not need further explanation. The intense fog that blanketed London was the perfect opportunity for Francis to make his attack. It was likewise an ill environment in which to defend themselves.

Jasper's heavy, kerchief-muffled breathing and their hard treads echoed around them, before they turned once more into a thoroughfare. They could not run indefinitely. Maria's muscles burned and her lungs laboured—particularly with the barrier of her handkerchief—but the exhilaration of the chase kept her moving.

There. Her pulse jumped with anticipation as the fog drifted enough for her to make a swift decision, and she directed Jasper toward the alcove between two buildings. They hurried forward, and she silently urged him into the darkness to press his back against the cool, coal-darkened stone. The fog drifted closed once more, concealing their location.

Removing the kerchief from her face, she pressed her lips to Jasper's ear and breathed, "Take long, slow breaths. Try not to be overheard."

A shiver wracked his frame, but he nodded his understanding.

She aligned herself beside him, pressing back into the dark alcove and against the hard stone, and steadied her own breathing.

Staring into the obscurity, Maria trained her ears on their surroundings. Silence greeted her, and somehow that was worse than hearing their pursuer's footsteps. The anticipation, the not knowing where he was or what weaponry he might carry on his person...

The sudden shuffle of a boot caught her ear, and she turned in question to Jasper. He gave a swift shake of his head, and she knew. That sound had been Francis.

A chill prickled down her spine as they stood in wait.

"I know you're here, cousin." The voice floated through the fog toward them. "Your bergamot scent gives you away." He laughed, the sound low and menacing, and Maria's pulse sped in response.

Pressing her lips against Jasper's ear once more, she breathed, "We must attempt to seize him. I will approach from the left."

Another shiver shook his frame, but he nodded.

Then, Jasper was gone, entirely obscured by a swirl of fog as he crept to the right on silent feet. Her heart in her throat, Maria moved to her left.

"Come, now, *Duke*," Francis spat. "My siblings will not have perished for nothing."

Maria recalled that Francis and Miles' sister, Jean Sinclair, had perished fifteen years prior, but she did not know the nature of it.

The man continued to shout. "Come out and face—*oof!*"

Someone grunted, and the sound of boots scraping along cobblestone came from ahead of her. Maria gripped her dagger in one hand, and darted toward the sound of the scuffle. Breathing fast, she attempted to join the fray.

Out of the murk, she spotted the two men grappling for control of a pistol clutched tightly in Francis' hand, before the fog concealed them once more.

Maria's stomach sank, and she could feel the blood draining from her face. But she swiftly pushed through her fear and dashed toward the men, her dagger at the ready.

"I have you now!" Francis crowed in triumph, waving his pistol in the air as he disentangled himself from a slowly retreating Jasper.

Maria shifted her grip on the dagger and lunged, lifting her arm high. Francis' gaze darted to her, his eyes widening as he swung his weapon toward her. All at once, they collided. Her dagger-wielding arm was knocked off course by the blow, and it sliced into his upper arm.

Francis roared and reflexively pulled the trigger.

Crack!

Maria's ears rang, rendering them momentarily useless. Francis screamed something in her face, spun, and ran away into the fog, clutching his arm with one hand. But Maria could think only of Jasper.

She turned, her nose filled with the acrid scent of gunpowder and her ears ringing, and scanned the haze. Returning her dagger to the sheath hidden in her boot, she took a hesitant step.

"Jasper?" she said, a hint of panic in her trembling voice.

The high-pitched ringing was her only response.

Where had the ball gone? Had Jasper been hit? Where was he?

She rushed forward until she reached a wall. Her pulse sped faster.

"Jasper? Where are you?"

Dragging her fingertips along the stone surface, she walked on, scanning the fog and the ground for any sign of him.

"I can't hear you, Jasper," she whispered. "Where are you?"

A scream was wrenched from her lungs as a dark form reached for her. She put out a hand, bracing for attack—and lamenting the fact that she already sheathed her dagger. But then she saw his face.

"*Jasper*," she breathed.

He pulled her into an embrace, and she went willingly. His body was large, broad, warm, and wonderfully alive.

"You weren't harmed, were you?" She pulled back and traced her hands over his chest, arms, and shoulders.

"No." The word was only barely audible over the noise in her ears, but she felt the rumble against her palms, and the immediate relief that swept through her made her knees weak.

The danger has passed. The fearful tension that she'd held in her shoulders gave way, and she released a weary sigh. Francis would unquestionably make another attempt on their lives, but for the moment, they were safe.

"When I..." Jasper started, and then swallowed, his gaze pained. "When I saw you nearing Francis, I feared..." He grimaced in pain and slid his hands around her waist. "*Christ*, Maria."

His lips crashed down upon hers.

CHAPTER 9

Maria's eager kisses were like liniment to Jasper's soul. Damn, but he'd been frightened for her. He could have wept with relief when he'd heard her voice after the pistol had been fired.

Her tongue delved deeper into his mouth, sending sparks of heat directly into his rapidly-stiffening cock, and his arms tightened reflexively around her waist. He needed to touch her everywhere, over her back and down to her hips, and *bloody hell*, her arse in those breeches!

She moaned into his mouth and ground her pelvis against his erection, and his eyes nearly rolled into the back of his head.

"*Christ*, Maria," he moaned. "I want to—"

Unable to even *process* his desires, let alone voice them, Jasper cupped her painted jaw and brought his lips back down to hers.

"You want to what?" she whispered against his lips. "Tell me. Please?"

"I want to touch you," he blurted. Once the words were out, however, he couldn't seem to stop the flow, his voice low and unhurried "I want to tangle my fingers in your hair and have you with my mouth while I bring you to climax with my hands. I want to press you against this wall and kiss your intimate folds while I penetrate you with my fingers. *Hell*, Maria, I want to sink myself inside you and bring pleasure to us both."

Her pupils dilated, her cheeks flushed, and her breath came fast between parted, reddened lips. Damn, but he could scarcely wait to taste them again.

"Then do it," she breathed.

Jasper's cock twitched, but he internally rebuked the eager thing. "I cannot take you in the street, no matter how much I might desire it. You deserve better."

Her gaze was heavy-lidded and needy as she gripped him tighter about the shoulders. "The fog is too thick; no one can see. Please, Jasper."

She kissed him again, and he could feel his resolve slipping. He couldn't make love to her against a brick wall, but he could certainly satisfy some of their needs and give her pleasure—as long as the fog held. Indeed, in her men's breeches, access to her with hands or mouth needn't require removing any clothes at all. None of her skin would touch the brick façade, for with a gentle tug and a broader stance, she would be entirely bared for his delectation.

Quavering heat whirled in his belly and stiffened his cock to nigh-painful rigidity.

He broke off their kiss and clasped her gloved hand, leading her further into the darkened alcove, his pulse racing and breath coming hard. Next, his gloves; he tugged them off and swiftly stashed them in his coat pocket. Leaning his body gently against her, he let her feel the hard ridge of him pressing against her pelvis as he took her mouth in another searing kiss.

A sigh escaped her, her breath sweet and warm against his cheek, and his cock twitched once more.

His trembling fingers found the buttons of her falls, and

unfastened them. Brushing aside the loose fabric to hang between her legs, he reached inside, and—*holy hell*, she didn't wear small clothes. His pulse thrummed as his fingers hovered above her folds.

"Are you certain that you wish to do this?" he asked, unable to hide the needy desperation in his voice.

"Yes," she whispered back. "Oh, Jasper, yes!"

His heart leapt, and he nudged Maria's legs wider before he carefully delved one finger into her heat.

SOMEWHERE IN THE back of Maria's mind, the thought hovered that she ought to be concerned about her lack of modesty, but all she felt was the rush of anticipation and desire. She hadn't the faintest notion of what he would do with her, but she trusted him.

Then a finger brushed through her intimate curls to spread her open, and all thoughts of modesty fled.

"*My God, Maria,*" he breathed reverently, his breath brushing against her lips. "You're so wet for me."

Before she could think of a response, he brushed a fingertip over her cleft, pulling a gasp from her lungs and sending a jolt of pleasure through to her core.

"That's it," Jasper whispered.

The knowledge that Jasper—*Jasper, for pity's sake!*—was touching her so intimately was phantastic, indeed. But she wanted to touch him, too.

"Might I—" Her breath hitched as he dipped a finger inside her, gathering her wetness before returning his attention to her cleft. She moaned. "I want to touch you, if you'll let me."

His eyes slid closed on a groan and he nodded. "Yes. Please touch me, Maria. I need your hands on me."

Emboldened by his open need, she made quick work of his falls and small clothes, all while his fingers explored and teased. His erection sprang free, thick and long, jutting from a nest of dense black curls. The head was reddened and leaking a clear fluid that glistened in the dim light.

She hadn't the faintest notion of what to do. If that were to fit inside her, like his fingers—*oh!*—were doing at just that moment, she could presume that rubbing the exterior of his shaft would be akin to the sensation of being inside her. *I need your hands on me*, he'd said.

Assuaging her curiosity and acting on her assumption, she touched her fingers to his shaft. It bounced, and he grunted, his eyes dark.

His fingers moved, circling and whirling, tightening the coil of need inside her.

Feeling more confident, she wrapped her hand around his length. He was soft as silk yet hard like stone; an entirely intoxicating combination. "Is this what you want?" she asked breathlessly, somehow already knowing the answer.

"*Yes*," he hissed. "Stroke it. *Please*, Maria."

She began a smooth pumping motion, and he let out a deep groan, his lips returning to trail kisses along her painted jaw.

Tingling heat swelled in her core as his fingers circled her little pleasure centre. She tilted her hips toward him, seeking more. And he readily obliged.

Sensation rocketed through her, her body buzzing as a keening moan pushed its way up from her chest.

"*Fuck*, Maria!" he breathed in her ear. "What you do to me..."

"*Oh*," she gasped. "*Jasper*."

Her knees began to tremble, and she pressed her back harder against the stone wall in an effort to keep her knees from buckling.

"Yes, Jasper," she panted. "Like that." She rocked her hips in time with his movements, the coil of her impending climax winding tighter, all while she continued a steady rhythm of strokes on his cock.

Abandoning her clitoris, he curved his fingers deep inside her, pulling a sob from her throat. He didn't leave it untouched for long, however, for in addition to his fingers thrusting within her, his thumb resumed stroking her cleft.

She sighed. "*Yes...*"

He nipped at her jaw, his breath laboured and his gaze devouring.

Pleasure built, tingling through her limbs and speeding her pulse. It was almost too much, the sensations nearly overwhelming. Her panting breaths became hitched, nearly dizzy from his ministrations. Then abruptly, the coil broke. Pleasure burst through her, stiffening her limbs and causing lights to dance behind her eyelids. Her back arched as a cry of gratification ripped from her chest.

"*Oh fuck, Maria.*"

His erection throbbed in her hand and she tightened her hold, rubbing her thumb briefly over the clear liquid beading at the tip.

She blinked up at him. "I've never experienced the *little death* like that before."

His two-toned gaze bore into hers. "You've had one before?"

"Yes," she admitted. "By myself. I learned of them from a book."

His eyelids drooped, but his pupils grew larger, and he groaned. "*Hell*, that's... My God, I— Damnation, I need to see you do that." The veins in his neck bulged. "Maria, I'm going to— *Fuck*, I'm going to spend!"

Fingers fumbling, he unfastened his cravat and wrapped it around the head of his member. He bared his teeth in a silent snarl, and his body went rigid as he pulsed in her hand.

Maria watched in awe, her own pulse still racing, and the heat of desire thrumming through her. He was beautiful. And she most definitely needed to see him thusly again. Soon, preferably.

His forehead rested on hers before he took her lips in a passionate kiss. He flicked her tongue with his, and warmth settled through her.

The sound of footsteps and a cart rattling down the cobblestones had them springing apart. Maria glanced around, suddenly very aware of their public location. The fog was beginning to thin.

Jasper hurriedly wiped himself clean, tossed the cravat aside, and fastened his trousers as Maria hastily rebuttoned her falls and righted her queue. He gave her another quick buss and tugged at his coat sleeves.

"As much as I would love to remain in this alcove with you," she said, "the fog is dissipating, and our shelter will soon be gone."

He gave a sharp nod, his gaze penetrating. "Will you permit me to accompany you to my home? Your shift begins today, and..." He licked his bottom lip, his gaze raking her form. "I believe that we ought to have a discussion."

Twisting her mouth, Maria considered him. Her shift did not begin until that evening, and while in other circumstances it would be easy for her to accept, she could not allow him to take her home like *this*. First, she must return to her apartments to remove her men's attire. On the other hand, Jasper might grow suspicious if she sent him home with the promise to meet him there that evening. Perhaps he was already suspicious; he had, after all, just uncovered a rather large falsehood of hers. But could she trust him with the knowledge of her apartments...of *Thomas*?

Mayhap discovering her brother and his obvious twitches would turn him off of the idea of marrying her.

There was the possibility, no matter how unlikely, that he had already learned of Thomas but had kept silent through the years. At the very least, he ought to have heard the rumours that had followed her family since Thomas began to exhibit signs of twitching in their youth. Despite her parents' decision to leave their son anonymous in Bethlem Royal Hospital and to keep him secret, society was aware of his existence.

But was Jasper?

Despite society's—and their parents'—assertion, Thomas was *not* mad. He was bright, amusing, caring, intelligent... And Jasper might very well fail to see that. In which case, the question of marriage would rather not be an issue at all, for an intolerant man she could not abide.

The warmth that had flooded her after their encounter swiftly fled, and she knew what she must do.

"Follow me," she said.

CHAPTER 10

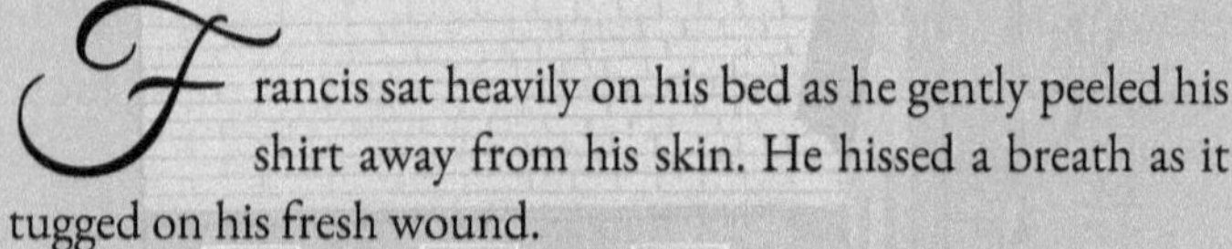

Francis sat heavily on his bed as he gently peeled his shirt away from his skin. He hissed a breath as it tugged on his fresh wound.

"What have they done to you?" Sarah moaned, fluttering around him while she gathered water and cloth for bandages.

"It's not so bad as all that," he assured her.

He glanced at his shoulder, and while there was a fair amount of blood, the cut did not appear to be deep. The wench, *Maria Roberts*, had only dealt him a glancing blow, thank Christ. And she would unquestionably pay for it.

He'd been following the woman for the past several days, learning her routine—and her secrets. The naughty bitch.

Sarah knelt at his side and washed the wound clean, all while muttering obscenities. "You ought to move your plan faster, Francis. They do not deserve to continue living in their luxury. The *duke*," she spat, "his loathsome family, and his whore ought to all be stopped. It should have been *them* hanging from the noose instead of Miles. When they and my husband are gone, and you've taken the title and made me your duchess, they'll all see..." She continued on her tirade, but Francis tuned her out.

He would, indeed, become duke once he'd dispatched his hateful relations and his agreement came to fruition. But Sarah would decidedly *not* be at his side. He appreciated her fiery hatred and need for revenge on his behalf, but she'd begun to consider this her own battle when it was so clearly his alone. The woman needed to calm herself.

And his cousins needed to suffer.

AFTER A QUARTER of an hour of walking, the fog had cleared enough that they were able to hail a hack. Jasper thought belatedly about his carriage that might very well still be awaiting him outside the newspaper offices. *The newspaper offices at which Maria works.*

Hell, but that was still a baffling thought.

He glanced at her from across the trundling equipage, and his heart leapt.

The woman was truly remarkable.

The hack turned into Cheapside, and Jasper's jaw clenched involuntarily. Soot-darkened buildings loomed over narrow streets while vendors drew out their dilapidated carts to resume selling their wares after the fog. Dogs and urchins roamed the filth-covered cobblestoned streets, stealthily searching for scraps of food.

Trepidation crashed through Jasper. Where was Maria taking him?

His curiosity was piqued, to be sure, but he had reservations about her safety in this part of town. Hell, this was very near to where he'd almost died at Francis' behest.

However—his inner voice reminded him—she had managed adequately while he'd been following her, and they were in a hack, not his carriage. She'd led him on a merry chase and attacked when left no other option. His throat still ached from that blow, in fact. She also had her little dagger, which she'd smartly used to frighten off Francis.

His gaze drifted down to her Hessians where, even now, said weapon was hidden. *Truly remarkable.*

He closed his eyes and allowed his mind to replay those blissful moments in the fog. Damn, but she'd been warm and wet and more than he could have hoped for. It had been a long bloody time since he'd taken himself to hand, let alone had a woman do so. There were too many young ladies vying for his attention who were willing to put themselves into a compromising position and force his hand. He'd sworn that the last time a woman—a widow, at that—had conveniently forgotten to lock the door before launching herself at him would be the last—thank Christ he'd had enough sense to leave before the acquaintance she'd arranged to catch them had arrived. He'd since eschewed intimacy altogether.

But *Maria*. He did not care a whit how public their interaction had been, because he knew that she did not wish to be with him solely for his money or title. She'd been aroused by him. *Oh God*, and she'd come so hard.

It made him want more touches, more kisses, more *Maria* with a ferocity that left him breathless. He wanted to learn everything about her. Mayhap he would take his time with their engagement, spend time conversing with her. And, damn it, he wanted to make her come again, to watch her grey eyes turn dark and heated and to hear her cries of pleasure...

Jasper blinked, twisting in his seat and clearing his throat. He'd come only a quarter of an hour before; he oughtn't become stiff again so easily.

"Here we are," Maria said, gazing out the window and breaking through his thoughts. She turned to him, her brows drawn together in puzzlement as the hack rolled to a stop. "Are you well, Jasper?"

"Yes, of course," he lied. He didn't know if he'd ever be fully well after what they'd done.

She nodded and descended the step before turning to face him. "I'll be but a few minutes."

"Just a moment." Jasper held out a hand to stay her. "We were just attacked by a man who the magistrate *and* Home Office assured me was no longer in London, and we're in bloody Cheapside. Francis could very well have followed us on our journey; I'll not sit in a damned hack while you go off alone."

Maria's lips thinned and her shoulders sagged slightly, her eyes dimming with resignation.

"Very well," she sighed. "Do follow me."

He flipped their driver a coin and followed Maria toward a set of old bachelor apartments above a cobbler. His eyebrows lifted and he glanced at Maria's profile in curiosity. Her jaw was set, her queued hair mussed beneath her hat, and there was a sort of determined acceptance in her gaze.

Bloody hell, what *was* this place, and who could possibly be there to call upon?

They strode through a narrow, begrimed foyer and up three flights of stairs before turning down a short hallway. She stopped before a door and turned to him.

"I..." Her lips thinned, and she straightened her shoulders before continuing. "I need just a moment, if you please. There is something that I must do."

With that enigmatic statement, she pressed the latch and squeezed herself through the narrow crack of the door—before she closed it in his face.

On quick feet, Maria darted from their small, open foyer and into the main corridor. "*Thomas!*" she hissed.

"Maria," Thomas returned from another room. "You've arrived in time." He paused to grunt several times before continuing, his voice growing louder as they drew closer. "Mrs. Fredrickson made mince pies this morning, and—*oh*. Whatever is the matter?"

Maria hurried toward him, her index finger extended over her lips in a gesture of silence. Guilt swam nauseatingly in her abdomen as she spoke softly, "You must hide."

His brows drew together and his eyes flared in alarm. "Why? What has happened?"

"The Duke of Derby is just beyond our door," she whispered. "We were attacked by Francis. He chased us through the London particular..." Maria quickly outlined the fracas with Francis, carefully omitting her tryst with Jasper. "Once we could summon a hack, we came directly here."

Worry filled his gaze as he looked her over. "Is the duke a danger to you?"

"No!" she lied, shaking her head. The man was most certainly a danger to her heart. She cleared her throat. "Not at all, I assure you. In fact, we are engaged."

"Engaged! But what of—"

"I simply cannot..." She hesitated, her mind racing.

In more than eight years, no one that had met *Mr. Robertson* had thought she was a woman. And it had felt... *good*. She'd built a life in which she could move as freely as possible, being who she was. Already, Jasper had learned part of the truth. She couldn't have him learning the rest, and unravelling her carefully built life.

"I cannot have him know about you," she concluded lamely.

Awareness dawned on Thomas' face, and he paled. Maria hid a grimace, guilt swelling in her chest.

"I apologize, Thomas. It is not for the reason that you might believe. I simply cannot ha—"

"Do not concern—*grunt*—yourself with me," he said, his voice gruff and a self-deprecating smile on his handsome face. "I will lock myself in my bedchamber. You will not hear—*grunt, click*—anything from me. I've a new coat to sew." He pressed a quick kiss to her cheek and walked stiffly down the corridor.

Drat. The guilt swirling through her increased to the point of nausea, but she swallowed it down. She must make amends with him later on, but for the moment, she would deal with Jasper.

As swiftly as she could, she raced to her writing desk, carefully tucked her current manuscript into a drawer, and locked it. She arranged the items casually on the desk's surface before slipping the small key into her pocket.

THE DOOR SWUNG INWARD, pulling with it a rush of air from around Jasper. The impatience that had filled him just moments before was swept away, replaced by fresh curiosity and admiration for Maria, whose hair was pulling from the once-neat queue and whose cheeks were flushed a delicious pink.

He wanted to taste her lips once more, but he resisted.

"Please come in." She stepped aside, allowing him to pass into the room.

Jasper was immediately hit with the scents of ink, parchment, leather, and a hint of mince pies on the air. He could smell Maria there.

"Is this yours?" he inquired.

She bit at her lips. "Yes, it's mine."

He followed her in and closed the door softly behind

himself as she removed her hat and placed it on a nearby hook. The room was spacious, an odd combination of foyer and sitting room in one.

There was comfortable-looking furniture situated before a low burning fire in the hearth, a writing desk, and bookshelves. A newspaper sat folded upon a table, and men's outerwear littered hooks near the entry. If he did not recognize the thought as entirely ludicrous, he would think that a man—other than *Mr. Duncan Robertson*—lived there.

"Please have a seat." Maria gestured toward the sitting area. "I must change my attire."

Their exchange was stilted, but he nodded and settled himself into the purple armchair by the hearth before Maria disappeared down a corridor.

She'd waited until he was seated before leaving him. Hell, but mayhap she had yet something else to hide.

Damn, he didn't know what to think any longer. In his youth, he'd thought he knew Maria, had found her entirely predictable and uninspiring, like most other young ladies of the *ton*. Over the years, however, she'd continuously proven him wrong. How ignorant he'd been! How unobservant! She was entirely the opposite. The more he learned of her passions and intelligence, the more he wished to know. He was utterly intoxicated by her exuberance. And intrigued by her mysteriousness.

He let his gaze travel around the room, taking as much of it in as he could from his seated position. It was sparse, but deliberately decorated. There were books on nearly every surface: some with folded bits of parchment inserted between pages, and others lying open. A little ornamental clock sat upon the fireplace mantel, ticking the seconds.

It appeared to be a space oft-enjoyed. *This* must be the reason for her two vocations; she was funding her housing.

But *why*? Surely this space was not used only as a means for storing her men's attire—which was utterly erotic.

Damn, but even now she was likely slipping free of her tight breeches and removing her waistcoat.

His cock twitched, and he shifted in his seat.

Sodding hell.

The woman was a veritable puzzle, and every piece left him more intrigued than before. She had him in entirely in knots.

PLACING the last pins in her hair, Maria gave herself a cursory glance in the mirror. Everything was in place. She'd donned the frock that she had worn when she'd left her home that morning. The grey striped muslin accentuated her eyes, and the purple ribbon beneath her breasts and decorating the half sleeves and hem was a lovely adornment in her favourite colour.

She clasped her travelling satchel—which carried her uniform for that evening—and a spare cravat, and hurried from the room.

Jasper stood at her entrance, rising from precisely where she'd left him, and a breath of relief left her so swiftly that it nearly made her dizzy.

Unable to help herself, her gaze darted between the corridor and her writing desk, irrationally concerned that Jasper had somehow discovered her secrets while she'd changed attire.

She gave him a bright smile and offered him the cravat. "Thank you for waiting. This is to replace the one you...er... lost."

His lips quirked in one corner as he accepted the cloth and tied it about his neck.

"Shall we leave?"

With a slow smile forming on his lips, he answered gruffly, "Certainly."

Undoubtedly he meant to question her about the journey and the apartments, but she knew not how to reply.

Her gaze drifted once more to the corridor. Would Thomas remain in his bedchamber long after they left? She wished that she could bid him farewell and, at the very least, apologize.

Jasper's gaze sharpened.

Drat. She must focus. She offered him another bright smile, and he gestured toward the front door.

"These are your apartments?" he asked again. "Alone?"

Avoiding his penetrating gaze, she opened the door and lied outright. "Yes."

They made their way silently down the stairs and out into the front lane. Her senses were on high alert, taking in the movements of the people around them and watching for any sign of danger. Francis could, even now, be lurking in preparation of attack.

Forced to walk a short way before Jasper deftly hailed another hack, Maria attempted to calm her nerves. She breathed deeply and slowly, filling her lungs with the tainted but comforting scents of Cheapside.

"We must retrieve Heather," she reminded him. "She is our chaperone, and you will want her to begin her shift once you've brought me home. I ought to nap if I am to remain alert this evening."

"Of course."

The hack was ill-sprung, the padding on the seats lumpy, and it smelled of meat that had gone off. But that wasn't what had Maria's stomach twisting as they jolted into motion.

Jasper ran a hand over his face and pinched the bridge of his nose. "I scarcely know where to begin, Maria. You've—"

He waved a hand through the air. "You've been living two lives. And now you wish to live a third?"

"Third?" She frowned in confusion.

He nodded. "As a runner. Another secret from your family, no doubt. How do you intend to maintain the ruse with so public a position? Your intended customers could very likely recognize you and collapse your scheme." He scratched at his furrowed brow. "In fact, I marvel at the fact that you've been able to keep your employer fooled for more than eight years. Think, Maria, about what could happen to you both should your secrets unravel."

She worried her bottom lip. That thought had occurred to her once before, but she'd concluded that people often saw what they wished to see, rather than what was in front of them. Additionally, Juliana had yet to encounter difficulty with her position in society and as a runner. So Maria had refused to consider it further.

The rules and social confines of society had never fit her. She had done a lot of things that others mightn't believe possible; this oughtn't be any different.

Now, however, Jasper knew part of her truth. Could she trust him to keep those secrets?

If her parents *did* learn the truth, they would be furious, particularly if Jasper justly called off their engagement and she was left a jilted spinster. Her stomach wobbled, and she internally rebuked herself. Mayhap if she was jilted, *Maria* could simply disappear—for surely her fate as companion to her aunt would come to fruition if she didn't. Indeed, she could truly become Duncan.

If she spent her days helping those in need by solving their mysteries, and spent her evenings writing while simultaneously providing for her brother, the approval of her family and society truly would not matter.

"I don't rightly care," she replied baldly. "I have a home and the means to provide for myself."

He inclined his head. "Is that why you chose to work for *The Morning Herald*?"

Pressing her lips together, she considered her answer. She couldn't tell him the full truth, but a part of it would suffice. "That is a large piece of it." She shrugged one shoulder. "I enjoy writing. It seemed a suitable option for me."

"And you've done this for eight-and-a-half years?"

"I have, yes." She clasped her hands tightly together in her lap. She didn't want to answer his questions, didn't want to put a strain on their already tenuous relationship. Instead, they ought to focus on the possibility that Francis had hired a hack of his own and was, at that moment, following them out of Cheapside.

The hack bounced and rattled along the cobblestones, drowning out any other noise from beyond the confining walls around them.

"We must discuss Francis," Maria said.

Jasper's back stiffened.

"He's been wounded, though I cannot be certain how badly. Have you any idea where he might stay in London?"

"No." He sighed, shaking his head. "As I said, I've had men search every brothel, gambling den, inn, and abandoned building in London, and I couldn't find him."

"Surely not *every* one—" She cut off her words at his sharp glance. "Very well, then. Perhaps he has rented rooms, or—"

"I've checked as many apartments as I could, Maria."

"What of acquaintances?" she offered. "Might he be staying with a friend?"

Jasper's face scrunched in a grimace. "My father's steward was acquainted with my uncle, but the man is in gaol. I paid him a visit weeks ago, and the man knew nothing of Francis' whereabouts. And, truthfully, I have never known Francis or

Miles to have a friend, so I wouldn't know to whom I should speak."

"Understood," Maria murmured. "I shall have Francis' likeness inserted into tomorrow's paper. Mayhap if the denizens of London see his face once more, we will garner not only renewed interest but also clues as to his whereabouts."

"Excellent." He turned to gaze out the window, and Maria allowed him time to think.

They were mere blocks from Heather's home, the hack's wheels jostling against the cobblestones and the hard seats doing nothing to cushion her bottom.

Looking out the opposite window, Maria watched as the streets of London rolled past. It was a vast city... Francis could be anywhere.

CHAPTER 11

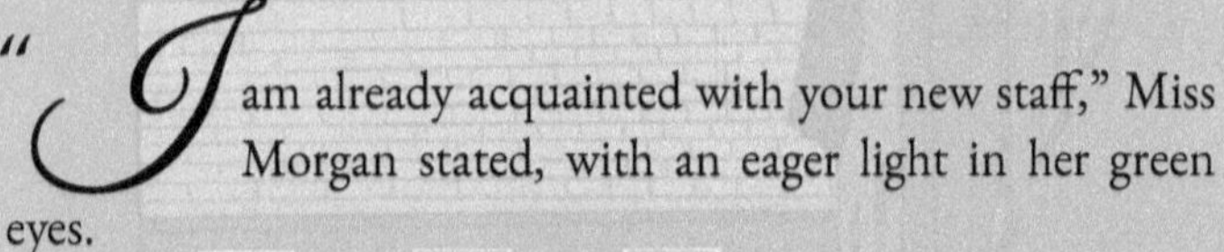

"$\mathcal{I}$ am already acquainted with your new staff," Miss Morgan stated, with an eager light in her green eyes.

The housekeeper's office was cramped, but welcoming. Sunlight shone through the small window behind the pale desk and brightened the springtime yellow of the walls. The brightness of the room seemed to lighten the red-blonde of Miss Morgan's hair, partially hidden beneath a lace mobcap.

"Of course," Jasper replied. "You and Maria shall have access to any room in the house that you require. You've been to most spaces in the home, I'm sure, but I daresay there are some you've missed. Come," he urged, leading the woman to the door, "I'll show you about."

Miss Morgan inclined her head and absently toyed with the skirts of her maid's uniform. "Thank you, Your Grace." The woman smiled, her cheeks puffing with the movement. "Harris and his men intend to patrol the grounds and observe for potential threats at a distance once the evening meal has concluded. Only a few men will remain indoors, ensuring all access points are secure while Maria and I carry out our duties."

Jasper's gut tightened as a bout of nerves caught him by surprise. *Maria.* Despite her terse answers to his inquiries earlier, he'd left her side feeling rather more curious than before. He wanted to know everything about her.

"Here we are. This is my study—" He stilled, his heart thundering and his eyes growing wide as he halted in the doorway.

A dagger stood erect on his desk, its blade dug deep through a folded piece of parchment and into the wood beneath. Jasper's heart stumbled in his chest. *Francis.*

Jasper sped to one of the large garden-facing windows beyond his desk and examined the latch and sash for tampering. *Locked and secure.*

"Blimey," Miss Morgan breathed. "Is that a new letter?"

Jasper's lips thinned as he inspected the other window. "I'm afraid so. *Damn.* This one is secure as well."

He returned to Miss Morgan's side before his desk and withdrew his handkerchief. "I was here this very morning, writing correspondence. Naught else appears to be out of place. How did the blackguard get past these alleged superior staff that are meant to prevent this very thing from happening?"

"I imagine we ought to ask them," she returned. "Your windows are easily accessible from the gardens but, as you say, the windows are secure. Mayhap Francis was given a key to your door and took advantage of a change in shift."

"*Hell*," Jasper said gutturally.

With a quick step forward, he wrapped his handkerchief around the knife's handle and wrenched it from his desk's surface. Alarm twisted distressingly in his gut.

"Damned inconvenient," Miss Morgan muttered. "You'll have to re-finish that, now."

He set the blade aside and carefully unfolded the parchment, protecting his hands with the kerchief.

*Fellow, I k**N**ow thee.*

...

[For] *a knave; a rascal; an eater of broken meats; a base, proud, shallow, beggarly, three-suited, hundred-pound, filthy, worsted-stocking knave; a lily-liver'd, action-taking, whoreson, glass-gazing, superserviceable, finical rogue; one-trunk-inheriting slave; one that wouldst be a bawd in way of good service, and art nothing but the composition of a knave, beggar, coward, pandar, and the son and heir of a mongrel bitch... Draw, you rogue: for, though it be night, yet the moon shines; I'll make a sop o'the moonshine of you: draw, you whoreson cullionly barbermonger, draw.*

Sodding hell. He would need to write again to the magistrate.

Miss Morgan leaned forward to sniff at the parchment. "Mmm," she hummed. "Yes, that is laurel water, for certain. Ought we to keep this as evidence?"

Jasper shook his head. "I shall pen a duplicate. I cannot risk anyone touching it by accident."

"Understood. I'll fetch Harris."

She darted from the room, and Jasper quickly copied then tossed the parchment into the fire.

"Miss?" A soft voice pulled Maria slowly from sleep. "Miss Roberts?"

Maria blinked the bleariness from her eyes, her sleep dissipating as awareness took its place. Bubbles of eagerness rippled through her abdomen, and a grin stole over her lips. Her assignment! Heather will soon require relief from her shift at Jasper's.

"Thank you, Louisa," she said to her maid. The woman was worth every ha'penny that Maria paid her to keep her secrets. "Would you be so good as to bring me a tea service, please?"

"Of course, miss." She curtseyed, and silently left the room.

Late afternoon sun shone in through her windows, lending a yellow hue to the deep purples and blues that filled her bedchamber.

Tossing the bedclothes aside, she rose and made her way to the wardrobe. She withdrew her costume from her travelling satchel and set it aside, then retrieved her ruby cloak.

By the time Louisa had returned with a tray of tea and a covered dish of food, Maria had dressed, stashed her sheathed dagger in the pocket of her skirts, and was pinning her hair in a severe knot at her crown. The maid closed the door swiftly.

"Your mother wishes to have a word, miss."

Maria spun around just as Louisa placed the tray on a table and gathered the cloak.

"If you please, miss." She held the material out toward Maria. "We must cover you up before your mother arrives."

Hurrying forward, Maria let the maid help her into her overlong cloak, then turned to face her mirror, ensuring that the entirety of her maid costume was covered. It was ludicrous, really, but she could not have her family see her wearing it—for they would certainly ask questions she couldn't answer —and she couldn't arrive at Jasper's *without* her costume, for gossip would undoubtedly spread that Miss Maria Roberts had spent hours ensconced in the duke's home.

It had occurred to her that she might change attire in the

carriage, but that would require greater preparation and more pennies to exchange hands. Indeed, the simplest option was for her to simply slip from her home with a cloak.

"You have my thanks again, Louisa."

She smirked at her reflection, her blue-specked grey eyes framed by dark lashes glittering back at her, and the fluttering in her stomach intensified. Not only was this her first foray into this sort of investigation, but it was also an opportunity to spend time in Jasper's space. *With Jasper.* Despite the grim circumstances, she could scarcely contain her excitement.

"*Maria!*"

The bedchamber door burst open and her mother swept in. Maria's stomach sank slightly in response.

"The maids said that you were sleeping," she drawled.

"I was." Maria retrieved her smallest reticule and strode toward her mother. "The duke is taking me to the opera this evening."

Her mother's eyes flashed with greed. "I understand that you were with him this morning, as well."

Maria inclined her head in confirmation. "We took a turn about Regent's Park, then found shelter at the confectionary during the fog."

"Mmm." Her mother's gaze snapped downward to take in her red cloak. "And what have you chosen to wear this evening? You are attending the opera with a duke, for pity's sake, you must dress the part." She stepped forward and reached for the seam of the cloak, and Maria's pulse tripped over.

"Beggin' your pardon, Miss Roberts," Louisa said urgently from the doorway. "But His Grace requested that you arrive directly."

Her mother whirled around to face the maid. "Did he not come himself to retrieve her?"

Louisa cast a harried glance at Maria.

"No," Maria said, stepping around her mother. "I must first fetch Heather, as she is our chaperone, and I'm afraid that I slept late."

"Very well," her mother capitulated. "Your father and I are to retire early, but I expect a full account of the evening on the morrow. Not that I expect particularly *good* news; Lord knows why the man chose *you*."

"Of course."

Maria gave a nod to her mother and sent a grateful glance to Louisa before she swept from the room.

Without pausing, she manoeuvred through the house and out the front door. Her familial carriage awaited. She withdrew some coins from her reticule and reached up to place them in the driver's awaiting hand. "Drive to the opera house. Ensure the carriage is seen, and await the opera's end. Have a drive about, then return home, if you will. I shall have another three shillings for you on the morrow."

"O' course, Miss Roberts." The reliable man doffed his hat with a grin. "Pleasure doin' business, as always."

The carriage trundled away, and Maria hurried along the street until she could discreetly hail a hack. Gooseflesh spread over her skin as a cool breeze wafted past her, and she pulled her cloak closer around her collar. Horses snuffed as an equipage drew up beside her, and she gave the driver the direction. Within, the air was chilled and smelled vaguely of stewed cabbage.

The wheels jolted into motion, and Maria settled back against the threadbare squabs. Anticipation fizzed in her stomach.

Francis was a very real and constant threat, and while she did not fool herself into believing that she would overtake him tonight, she hoped that she would glean some information. Learning how the man was finding his way into Jasper's home was essential. If someone among the duke's staff was being paid by Francis to permit him entrance or to provide aid, shelter, or food, they ought to face the repercussions of their actions.

Jasper really must have a care as well, for if his staff were indeed loyal and were *not* aiding Francis... Her throat grew dry, and she swallowed convulsively. If Francis had the ability to enter Jasper's home without anyone's knowledge and without aid, Jasper was in a great deal more danger than they'd initially believed.

Jasper. Her *affianced*, for pity's sake! It was possible that they would not see the engagement through to an actual marriage, but even the thought of his impromptu proposal sent tingles of joy down her spine.

Her tryst with Jasper had only added to her roiling emotions. She wanted more of his kisses, more of his touches, and *blimey*, but having him pulse in her hand had been—

Her body was betraying her at every turn. She shouldn't feel those things with regard to Jasper. While pleasure was lovely, she must remember that men were untrustworthy, adulterous cads, and she could not lose her heart or her head to one.

The hack rolled to a jarring stop at one corner of Grosvenor Square, putting a halt to Maria's dangerous ruminations. With a nod to herself, she exited the hack, paid the driver, and strode down the lamp-lit street. Her footsteps were sure and swift, and while she was in a lofty part of London, she still gripped her dagger tightly in the pocket of her skirts; Francis could strike at any time, and she *would* be prepared.

She turned down a close, hurrying between the buildings, the cool air and coal smoke whirling around her. Reaching the mews, Maria peered over the gardens' walls until she recognized Jasper's.

The back gardens were still and silent as she neared the kitchens' entrance. They'd chosen this point of entry rather than the front servants' entrance, for they preferred not to alert Francis to her arrival, should he be watching. Maria did not see that it would make much difference, but chose not to argue the point with Jasper.

Thunk-thunk. The sound of her gloved knocks broke the eerie silence of the gardens, and a shiver trailed down her spine. The hair on the back of her neck stood on end, and she spun to peer over her shoulder. A gentle wind blew the newly blooming trees, the unnerving shadows cast by the candles inside making the gardens seem sinister.

The door swung inward, and Maria jumped, despite herself.

"Maria," Jasper breathed, a breathtaking, crooked grin on his lips.

She gave him a relieved—if slightly embarrassed—smile. "Good evening, Duke."

"Do come in." He stepped aside, gesturing into the kitchens beyond.

Grateful to be out of the chilled air, she swept past him into the warmth. And her stomach swooped. She felt the barest brush of his hand against the small of her back, and her knees nearly buckled. *Dangerous*, she reminded herself.

"Why are *you* answering the door, and not a member of your new staff?" she inquired, removing her cloak to hang it on a nearby hook and attempting to garner control over her abruptly fluttering pulse.

"I daresay they're occupied elsewhere," Jasper returned. "Come, we'll inform them that you've begun your shift."

Maria nodded, withdrawing a mobcap from her apron pocket and placing it upon her head.

"Do you need that?" Jasper asked, gesturing to her attire with a mirthful gleam. "The costume?"

"Oh, indeed," Maria assured him. "It is best to keep up appearances, and a maid in your home—whether day or night

—is to be expected. A gentleman's daughter? I should say not."

They rounded the corner into the housekeeper's office, and stopped short.

"Have you caught any of them in the act?" Harris asked, his brow furrowed.

Mrs. Ross, Jasper's new cook, shook her head. "I didnae catch them, nae."

"Might we be of assistance?" Jasper inquired, stepping further into the room.

Both people spun to face him and bowed.

"It's nothing but a minor dispute, Your Grace," Harris assured him.

"Aye, 'tis a wee matter, Your Grace," the cook confirmed. "The other staff are pilfering food from the larder, and I daresay ye've pests in the gardens, tearin' leaves an' pullin' vegetables from their roots. I only thought t' let 'Arris know."

"Are you certain that it is the staff taking from the larder?" Maria queried. All gazes swung toward her.

"I 'ave my suspicions," Mrs. Ross returned. "But when on mission, all food and rations must be accounted fer."

"And we've ensured all ingredients are free from contamination?" Maria asked. "If Mr. Sinclair had access to the home, we must be vigilant."

Mrs. Ross nodded. "Aye. I inspected wha' was 'ere myself, and brought th' rest fresh from market."

"I will speak with the men, Mrs. Ross," Harris placated, and the woman left with a word of thanks.

"Is Heather here to give her report?" Maria inquired.

Harris shook his head. "She left just before you arrived, to report our dreadful oversight earlier to Grace."

"Oversight?" Maria asked, alarm lurching in her chest.

Jasper sighed. "I found another note from Francis in my study."

Her pulse sped. "*While* the new staff were in place?"

Harris' lips thinned. "At this time, we're unsure. Because His Grace was absent from the home, we cannot know for certain when it took place. I suspect, however, that it occurred during a shift change. It was an error on our part, and we've already implemented an alternating duty schedule to avoid such occurrences in the future."

Maria nodded. "Very well. Thank you." She turned to Jasper. "Was it another quote from *King Lear*? And the letters, was another—"

"Yes," Jasper interjected. "I've made a transcription; it's in my study."

Maria's heart leapt. "Might I see it?"

"Of course."

With well wishes for a pleasant night, Jasper led Maria calmly down the corridor, while the urge to run itched at Maria's legs.

"Jasper," she began. "The food thefts—"

"I've drawn the same conclusion," he interrupted.

She huffed. "Do you know of a place in which Francis could hide in your home? The attic, perhaps? The cellar?"

Jasper shook his head. "I haven't the faintest. We'd best look."

"Indeed. The letter first, if you please."

They traversed the corridor in silence, but nerves skittered just beneath her skin the entire time. Jasper was so close she could feel the heat of him through her uniform. It was a steady energy, as though the space between them hummed. Lord, but the man was too distracting by half.

What if Jasper did *not* jilt her? What if this home became hers?

Another swoop of nerves dipped her stomach and spread gooseflesh over her skin. It was dangerous to dream, and yet... she couldn't help herself. With every room they passed, thoughts of spending her time there with Jasper or managing a household tumbled through her mind. And she *wanted* it—*craved* it.

So dangerous, Maria. Have a care with your heart.

Soon, they turned into Jasper's spacious study. The room was warm and smelled like the man himself: bergamot and lemon. She inhaled deeply, relishing the erotic scent as she glanced around. It was much like any other man's study, full of large, dark furniture, walls of books, heavily stuffed armchairs by the hearth, and tall, dramatic windows. But this was Jasper's.

"This is it," Jasper said, extending a slip of parchment toward her. "Mind the writing; I was in a state."

Her heart fluttered at the small confession, absurdly pleased that he felt comfortable enough with her to admit a moment of weakness.

She accepted the note and scanned the words. "*N*," she mused. "The letters are *R*, *F*, *O*, and now *N*. I believe this might be a sort of *nomen deminutivum*. If, for example, we assume each letter is the first in a different word, a new message might appear." She cleared her throat. "We will discover the truth in time. For now, shall we begin our search?"

She folded the parchment and slid it in her apron pocket for further pursual later on, and followed Jasper from the room.

Despite the urgency of her assignment, the danger that was lurking within every shadow, Maria's body was all but entirely consumed with Jasper. Her skin prickled at his nearness, her insides flipped, and her heart whispered desires for not only his kisses and touches, but also a future with the man.

He was challenging and utterly infuriating, but...he was also caring. Since he'd happened across her at *The Morning*

Herald offices that morning, he'd been markedly undaunted by her unsettling revelations. Indeed, he hadn't even berated her for being Duncan—but had, in fact, reacted rather favourably in the end.

By the time they ascended the first staircase, Maria was veritably buzzing with unspent energy.

Jasper halted on the landing. "Allow me to fetch my pistol."

Without another word, he disappeared into his bedchamber down the corridor, and Maria heaved a deep breath. It was the one room in the home in which she had never been. She, Heather, and Juliana had explored every other corner of the building countless times and in countless ways through their childhood, while Jasper was off at Eton and Cambridge. She knew this home as well as her own, and yet... Since Jasper had become duke, it felt different.

Jasper re-emerged, a pistol clasped in one hand. They exchanged glances and, as though his heavy-lidded gaze was a caress, a current of desire washed over her.

Blimey.

As if by unspoken accord, they resumed their journey through the dim corridor.

"I meant to inquire," Jasper murmured, nudging her elbow with his. "How came you to be so proficient with a blade?"

Grateful for the dim light obscuring the flush that no doubt stained her neck, Maria hummed. "All runners in our offices must complete training before they accept their first client. We learn both societal rules and expectations of household staff, as well as fundamental skills in spy craft, basic fighting tactics, and weapons usage. My trainer, Mr. Greene, was superb, and I daresay we shall lament the loss of his instruction."

A *humph* of surprise escaped him as they passed a parlour

and music room and ascended the staircase to the next floor. "So many skills in so little time."

Maria shrugged one shoulder. "Yes. We learn merely the essentials at first, as we are meant to continue training and sparring to gain skill as time passes. Grace—that is, Miss Huntsbury—will oversee instruction until a permanent replacement is found."

"If Miss Huntsbury is experienced and knowledgeable in such things, why not continue teaching the women herself?"

The candle in a nearby sconce flickered as Jasper and Maria passed, rounding a corner beyond guest bedchambers and toward the last flight of stairs.

"Miss Huntsbury has many duties: supervising the women and our cases, managing finances, arranging resources, and supplying our required paraphernalia. Adding to her daily activities is ill-advised."

"Quite so. An admirably diligent and talented woman." Jasper was silent a moment before he whispered, "Much like yourself, I imagine."

Had Jasper just *complimented* her? Astonishment faltered Maria's footsteps and sped her pulse. The word *woman*—despite its accurate signifier of her sex—felt wrong, rather like an itchy coat that was too small, but the intent behind his words was flattering, indeed.

The attic's door loomed before them, and Maria forcibly redirected her thoughts. *Francis. I'm here for Francis.*

The fluttering of nerves that erupted in her stomach matched the racing of her pulse. She clutched her unsheathed dagger and stood poised to attack as Jasper reached for the door's latch.

Snick. The latch caught, and with a whirl of stale air and a swift *creak*, he pulled the door wide.

CHAPTER 12

While it had been some time since Jasper had ventured into his attic, and the lighting *was* dim, nothing seemed out of place. Old pieces of furniture draped with white material were piled before the wall that separated this storage space from the servants' quarters. Paintings were braced along the wall that connected his home to his neighbours—the baron and his wife—and musty rugs were rolled up in the middle of the space.

"Damn." Disappointment crashed through Jasper and sat like a stone in his stomach. For a moment, he'd been so certain.

The shaft of moonlight shining through the dormer window caught Maria's thoughtful gaze.

"While we weren't attacked upon entrance, Francis might still use this space," she murmured, striding past him into the room. "Come, let us investigate further."

His lips quirked and he did as he was bid. There was a reason this clever woman was in charge, after all.

Starting with the paintings, Jasper tilted first one and then another, noting nothing of interest—but for the damaged frame on the likeness of his great-uncle. He leaned them back in place and rubbed his fingertips together.

"The maid in charge of dusting up here is to be commended," he noted.

"Mmm," Maria hummed, the floor creaking as she bent to inspect the furniture under a cloth. "In that we agree."

Crossing through the shaft of moonlight, Jasper felt along the rolled rugs—*nothing*—then turned his attention to the dormer window. The latch was aged and stiff, but it was secure.

"I've found nothing out of place," Maria said, straightening from her examination of another bunch of furniture.

"Neither have I."

"Blast." She sheathed her dagger, striding toward him. "We had best check the cellar."

Reaching for his hand and rising on her toes, she pressed a soft, warm buss to his shortly-whiskered cheek. Hell, but his heart stumbled into a gallop at the light contact.

"Yes," he returned. "The cellar." He nodded, absently following the decidedly remarkable woman from his attic. *It will soon be* her *attic, too*, his inner voice whispered. Damn, but he wanted that. She was ambitious and wholly desirable. How had he not recognized it before?

Unable to keep away from her, he brushed the back of his hand against hers as he matched her pace in the third-floor corridor. And a jolt of—hell, he couldn't name the feeling, but it was entirely addictive—raced up his arm to settle somewhere in his chest.

Maria cast a sidelong glance at him, an erotic flush riding up her neck from beneath the fichu of her maid's costume. And his cods tightened.

Damn. He had to stop doing that. *Focus.* Maria was working, for fuck's sake, and his cousin might yet be hiding in his cellar.

They traversed the corridors and stairs with ease, greeting his staff—guards—with polite nods as they passed. And yet his body still felt...*stimulated* by Maria's nearness.

At last, they descended the final staircase into the servants' rooms. They passed the housekeeper's bedroom, butler's pantry, kitchens and scullery, and finally reached the cellar. A renewed sense of anticipation filled him, his pulse drumming and his breath coming quickly.

"I forgot that you had both a larder *and* a cellar," Maria noted.

Jasper nodded absently. "All of the larger homes in Grosvenor Square have both."

Despite his body's demands, his focus was entirely on the closed door to the cellar. Francis could be within, and Jasper must have his wits about him.

Lifting his pistol in preparation, Jasper reached for the door's latch and pressed, swinging it wide. Immediately, the scent of cured meats and fish filled his nose. Heart racing, he scanned the small space. Meats, fish, cheese, milk... No Francis.

He cursed and dropped his arm.

Maria brushed past him and into the room, bending low to peer beneath the bottom shelves, and his gaze narrowed unwaveringly on her arse. *Christ*, but the woman was endowed with a particularly spectacular bottom. Would that he'd given that part of her more attention during their tryst that morning. Would she be receptive to—

"There is no sign of someone bedding down in here," Maria said, cutting through his thoughts. "I daresay if he attempted to hide in a closet or cupboard, he would have been found out by your regular staff. I must have been wrong. Mayhap the new staff members *are* pilfering food."

"Mayhap," he said thoughtfully. Jasper carefully lowered the hammer on his pistol, feeling rather deflated that they hadn't found the blackguard. Whether he was willing to admit it or not, he was spoiling for a fight with Francis after their encounter earlier. He wanted this bloody nonsense done with.

The dagger she'd been holding disappeared among the folds of her skirts, and he marvelled at her fearlessness. She knew how dangerous his cousin was, and yet there she stood, prepared to face the man, to spend the night standing guard in Jasper's home, in the name of justice.

His body moved without conscious thought. Placing the pistol on one of the cellar's shelves, he stepped into her space, breathing in her scent of ink and parchment.

Maria's breath hitched, and the little sound tightened his cods.

He wanted to kiss her again, to press her up against the wall behind her and hear her cry out in pleasure as his cock rubbed against her sweet—

"Kiss me, Jasper," she breathed.

With a rough groan, he covered her lips with his. She opened on a sigh, her tongue reaching out to flick at his. She gripped the lapels of his coat before her hands found purchase in his hair, her nails gently abrading his scalp and sending gooseflesh over his skin. He pulled her closer, fisting her maid's costume in his hands as his body came alive with desire.

Christ, but she sparked a fire in him, the likes of which he'd never before felt. These new facets of her character that he was discovering had him scrambling for purchase on the edge of some precipice. He wanted to know more, to feel more, to *have* more of her.

Her sweet breaths came quickly, and she arched against him, tightening her fingers in his hair and creating a delicious sharp tug that went straight to his ballocks. He left her lips to trail kisses along her jaw, but she chased his mouth with a soft mewl of protest, and his eyes threatened to roll backward.

A floorboard creaked nearby, and they sprang apart, huffing for breath.

Jasper turned away, rubbing a hand over his face and discreetly adjusting himself in his trousers.

"No one is there," Maria breathed. "Seems the house was settling. But the timing was fortuitous, I'm afraid."

He turned a dry gaze on the woman, took in the sharp, determined set to her jaw and obdurate tightness to her lips, and internally deflated. There would be no more kisses tonight.

"I must see to my duties," she continued. "You had best get some sleep."

A frown tugged at the corners of his lips. "Would it not be prudent of me to aid you?"

She eyed him thoughtfully. "Help would be most welcome."

His chest swelled, and he grinned. "Capital. Where shall we begin?"

An endearing, snorted laugh escaped her. "On the top floor, Duke."

So, they did. With careful attention to detail, they began with the furthest guest bedchamber, examining every window and servants' corridor entrance for compromised locks or weakened seams. They peered in all wardrobes and cupboards in the rooms, and found nothing. Then, they moved down to the second floor.

They searched by light of the moon, foregoing candlelight, as it would make them more visible through the windows.

Multiple times through their search, Harris and his men found them and made reports to Maria, apprising her of their positions within the house. In every instance, Jasper was in awe of—and, he must admit, aroused by—Maria's role as supervisor in his case. And every time, he could not help but imagine Maria directing and organizing his—*their*—home and staff in such a way. He liked that thought very much indeed.

DARKNESS SURROUNDED Maria but for the fire still blazing in Jasper's study. It drew her into the room, the warmth and lingering scent of lemons and bergamot enveloping her. At some point during their examination of the second-floor rooms, they had agreed to separate and conduct their own searches. It was meant to save time, but it left Maria feeling lonely without his company. It also meant that she would not be able to explore Jasper's bedchamber.

Now, he was a door away in a parlour while she was alone in his study. A decidedly naughty part of her wanted very much to peruse his documents and personal effects, to learn more about him, to perhaps feel closer to him. She would, however, neither betray his trust nor disregard her duty as a runner.

Instead, this was her opportunity to search, unimpeded, for any proof that Jasper's father had nothing to do with Miss Jean Sinclair's death—in addition to searching for signs of Francis. Jasper had mentioned that he, Juliana, and their father had been in London, at an exhibit of wax sculptures, on the occasion of Miss Sinclair's death. Surely it was possible that evidence might have been left behind by the previous duke.

There was only one way in which to find out.

She scanned the room as low firelight flickered over every surface and threw shadows into stark relief.

A letter lying atop Jasper's desk caught her gaze, the scrawled *Mr. Sinclair* drawing her forward. She picked it up, tilting it toward the light, and scanned its contents.

YOUR GRACE,

. . .

I WOULD UNDERSTAND your concern if your accusations were accurate, but as previously stated, these letters are the work of Mr. Sinclair's hired ruffians. My men are working tirelessly to apprehend them.

SIR LUDLOW VAUGHAN

A FROWN CREASED Maria's brow, and she returned the letter to Jasper's desk. The magistrate was scarcely making any effort to capture Francis, and he was certainly not inspiring confidence in the abilities of the Home Office.

It was fortunate, then, that Maria and her team had taken the case.

She continued her pursual of the space.

If any evidence existed—and the old duke had chosen to hide it—it would no doubt be in a place that Jasper had yet to uncover. That would leave out strongboxes, false-bottomed drawers, or the like, for Jasper would undoubtedly have accessed them already.

It was possible that the old duke hadn't gotten the chance to inform Jasper of the information's location before his passing. But mayhap he would put it somewhere Jasper was inclined to look?

She tapped at her chin and turned in a circle, considering.

The wall of bookshelves called to her. If *she* were to hide something, she might choose a hidden alcove on her bookshelves, or a spot *within* a book itself. With the number of tomes she had amassed over the years, it was more likely that someone would give up in frustration before finding anything of use.

With a nod, she set to work.

Beginning with the oldest volumes of what she imagined

Jasper might read, she methodically removed books from the shelves and shook out the pages. Dust tickled her nose as she worked, but she persisted, stacking the checked book in neat piles upon the floor.

"Christ, but it's bright in here," Jasper whispered from the connecting doorway.

She glanced up, her pulse leaping at the sight of him. Heavens, but he'd removed his cravat. "Duke."

"Maria." A smile played over his features as he neared. "For what are you searching now? Surely you don't suppose Francis to be hiding in the books."

"Of course not." She clucked her tongue—decidedly *not* looking at his exposed throat and collar. "We discussed Francis' motivation for his determined incursion, and you had mentioned the death of his sister, Miss Jean Sinclair. While the chances are slim, I was hoping to find some clarification as to what happened, and perhaps evidence to prove that you and your father had naught to do with it."

"Ah. That is very shrewd of you. Allow me to help. What else have you yet to examine?"

Heat spread through her chest at his compliment, and she licked her suddenly dry lips. "The windows—again."

With a nod, he turned and strode toward the windows.

Maria's heart hiccoughed. He was so willing to accept her direction. But would it last?

She shook the thought away and resumed her task, selecting another book and searching it for hidden secrets. *Nothing.* She placed it on the most recent growing pile.

Twisting her lips to one side in an effort to stave off a sneeze, Maria lifted on the tips of her toes to reach an aged leather-bound book of English ballads. She flipped the pages open, and two folded pieces of parchment fell to the floor.

Something at last. Whether or not it was what she sought, she was pleased.

She retrieved the items and unfolded the first. Her heart leapt. It was a handbill for Marie Tussaud's exhibit!

Setting the book and handbill aside, she opened the other folded piece of parchment.

UNCLE,

AFTER CAREFUL THOUGHT, *I've come to the realization that my brothers' and my father's need for vengeance against you and yours is wrong. You are the legitimate heir to the dukedom...*

UNBIDDEN, a gasp escaped Maria. She scanned down to the bottom.

I FEAR *what my father or brothers would do to me should they discover my change of heart. For that reason, I must beg asylum with you and my cousins.*

WITH HOPE,
   Jean

A GASP CUT through the silence of the study, and Jasper's stomach dipped in alarm. He spun from the window to see Maria pouring over the contents of a letter.

Hurrying to her side and unable to keep himself from some sort of connection, he placed a hand to the small of her back.

"What is it?" he asked softly.

"I've found it," she said animatedly, her gaze slipping to his exposed throat and smattering of chest hair.

Her eyes widened, and a flush crept up her neck. Fuck, but that was arousing. His gut stirred, and pride swelled.

Hiding his smile, Jasper asked, "Found what, precisely?"

She held out two folded bits of parchment. "Proof of your father's innocence in Jean's death. Your father hid it, no doubt to exonerate him in the event that your cousins attempted to cause him difficulty."

Jasper blinked once more, taken aback. "And you found it, just like that?"

She nodded, a self-satisfied smile brightening her features. "It was between the pages of a book of English ballads."

"Damn." He squinted, scanning the documents and wishing he brought his reading spectacles to his study. His heart drummed faster as he read. "*Damn*! Maria, this is—"

"I know." Her gaze slid downward to his exposed skin, once more, and her flush deepened. "We will discuss it on the morrow, I'm sure."

"Mmm," he hummed.

She slipped the parchment in her apron pocket and turned her gaze toward the windows. "Did you conclude your inspection of—"

"No," he interrupted. "I'm afraid not."

On swift feet, she sped to the first window to complete the examination. Jasper, however, was rooted to the spot, his gaze eagerly soaking in her profile lit by the low-burning fire in the hearth.

His stomach was a whirling tumult of emotion. In this room, together, he could imagine their future: she, having designed the space to suit her purposes, would have a writing desk of her own at which she would compose newspaper articles, and he would work happily from his own desk—wherever she deemed it suitable to the space. And—*fuck*, would she don the attire of Mr. Duncan Robertson while she worked? Oh, indeed, he would very much enjoy that.

"There," she said, returning to his side. "Shall we continue? *Divide et impera?*"

"Divide and conquer?" He huffed a laugh. "Very well."

P ressing the hidden cupboard closed with a light *thunk*, Maria turned and searched the remainder of the small sitting room. In the past three quarters of an hour, she'd not crossed the path of another soul—not since Jasper had left with Harris to search the stables. Thirty minutes hence, she had heard two guards walk past the rooms on this floor and then descend into the service rooms belowstairs.

It was rather lonelier than she'd anticipated. She was, however, determined to complete her task.

She'd begun her search for evidence of either Francis' forays into Jasper's home or of Francis' possible collusion with an old member of Jasper's staff. But her mind endlessly wandered back to Jasper, and the view of his bared throat and collarbone. Despite the persistent eerie tingle down her spine, another flush crept up her throat and warmth swirled in her belly.

From what she'd seen of him in the study, the man, while lean, was soft and in possession of a thin layer of curling hair on his upper chest. It was decidedly arousing. She'd wanted to press her lips to his skin right then.

She scanned the dim room, ensuring that she'd searched the space entirely, when her attention caught on a partially opened book atop a little round table. It was a copy of Mr. Mystery's latest adventure novel, and a pair of spectacles was trapped between the pages.

A small grin quirked the side of her lips. She'd been in this room on countless occasions, the cheerful pale-green wallpaper and cream wainscotting matching the cushions on the comfortable furniture. She had even seen Jasper wear his reading spectacles. But she'd never been given a hint of his preferred reading material. Of all readers, she'd have never guessed the duke—

Creak. Maria spun around, following the sound with her gaze.

Nothing. Blimey, but Jasper's home seemed in constant movement.

With every room she'd traversed, a part of her wanted to imagine her life as the lady of the house—the duchess!—or how she and Jasper might use each room. But, as tempting as those thoughts were, her body was too...*alert.*

With a shake of her head, she strode out of the sitting room and into the adjoining parlour. It was ordinarily a comfortable room of middling size with yellow-striped wallpaper and purple accents. Now, moonlight shone in through the large windows, lending the space a faint milky blue hue. Dark shadows crept around the room, every piece of furniture creating long, ghostly reaching figures that only added to Maria's unease.

Creak. A shiver raced up her spine, and she turned toward the sound, the handle of her dagger digging deeply into her palm.

Something felt *off.* Her focus was diverted by the gooseflesh spreading in repeating waves over her skin, and the eerie settling of the house.

Her hand tightened reflexively around her blade's hilt.

With quick steps, she rounded the furniture and reached for the parlour's main door. She wrenched it open, flooding the space with the faint glow of the hall's sconces.

She left the parlour and strode down the corridor toward

the next room, peering deeply into each shadow as she passed. She'd not encountered a single opened or unlatched window, nor any breeze. And yet she couldn't dispel the feeling that she was being observed...*taunted*.

Thump-thump.

She spun around, her gaze locked on the opened doorway to the parlour she'd just left. The sound had unquestionably come from within.

Gooseflesh spread over her skin, and her stomach swooped unhappily. Swallowing down her disquiet, she retraced her steps toward the parlour. She walked slow, careful to keep each footfall silent on the hall's runner, and steadied her breathing.

Coming to a stop before the parlour's opened doorway, Maria paused to prepare herself.

Her pulse raced, and a wave of exhilaration rushed through her as she whirled around the corner to face...an empty room. At least it *appeared* to be an empty room. She strode further inside, nearly bumping her leg on a low table. The moonlight and dim light from the corridor offered little relief to the nerves dancing along her spine.

"Blast," she said into the silence.

A slow, hoarse chuckle filled the room, and Maria felt the rancour within it through to her soul. *Francis*. She hadn't been a surprise to him, after all.

She darted her gaze about the room, searching for any sign of him, still clutching her dagger. She was determined to have answers.

"This house is protected, Francis," she said.

Another low chuckle surrounded her, and awareness tingled at the back of her neck.

A breeze ruffled the curtains, and Maria realized that one of the windows sat open. A chill raced through her. She had *just* been there...

"Where are you?" she asked. "How—"

Thunk.

A trinket from atop a low table rolled along the floor and came to a gradual stop. Had he bumped the table? Her gaze swung around the room wildly, searching for any sign of the man but coming up short.

Shink. Darkness engulfed the room as the curtains were pulled closed. Her heart hiccoughed alarmingly and set her pulse to throbbing loudly in her ears.

"Jasper!" she called.

The low laugh came again. "He's still in the stables, pet."

Maria shifted her stance, adjusting her hold on her dagger as she prepared for an attack. She was abruptly grateful for the training, however basic, that she'd received from Mr. Greene.

Fabric shifted across the room, and her gaze sharpened. She could see almost nothing through the obscurity, but she knew he was there, watching her. The back of her neck prickled, and a shiver wracked her frame.

"How did you get in, Francis?" she asked, marvelling at the calmness of her own voice.

"I'll not fail where Miles did," he replied, ignoring her inquiry. His voice was low and steady, with a slight gruffness to it.

She wanted to tell him that he had it all wrong, but she'd only just found the letter and wasn't certain that she was entirely correct regarding his intentions, so she remained silent.

There was another shift in fabric, and Maria was certain that he'd stepped nearer.

"Surely there is an amicable solution for you and His Grace."

A hiss came from the darkness. "No." The word was barked, Francis' voice low and biting. "There is no *amicable* path for us. I will end this as I ought to have from the start: with death."

The cruelty in his voice took on a verve that sent cold dread through Maria. The man's longing for the dukedom and his need for revenge was not borne out of a sense of duty or obligation; he *wanted* to do this.

"Why have you been quoting *King Lear*?" she asked, in an attempt to get him talking.

"Everyone Jasper cares for will face me," he replied, again ignoring her inquiry.

He stepped closer, slowly revealing himself in the dim light from the doorway.

His brown hair appeared freshly washed, his face clean-shaven, and his blue eyes dark as pitch in the dim lighting. She eyed him carefully, watching the play of his coat for any sign of a hidden weapon, but he didn't appear to be armed. Still, she held her dagger at the ready.

The man's lips curled malevolently, and another shiver skittered down Maria's spine.

"And," he continued, his voice dropping ever lower, "I do so like to play with my toys."

CHAPTER 13

His toys, Maria thought, her stomach wobbling. Francis wanted to *play* with—

Before her thought could be completed, the man lunged, his lips pulled back in a gleeful snarl. Pulse jumping, she braced for his attack.

She held one arm up in defence and drew her dagger-wielding arm back, preparing to strike. His sudden blow glanced off her elbow while his other hand struck her fist, knocking the dagger from her grip.

His eyes flared with triumph, and he wrapped one hand around her neck. "Not so brave when you're unarmed, are you?"

A beat of fear pulsed through her, but she squelched it.

His sharp, rum-and-cake–scented breath wafted over her cheek as he leaned in to watch her eyes.

"How shall I play with you?" he asked slowly. "What would cause more pain to our dear Jasper?"

Maria glared at him. She could not concede defeat, yet.

With as much strength as she could muster, she lifted her knee into his cods.

Francis howled and released her with a string of curses.

She stepped back in retreat but caught her heel on the leg of the low table and toppled backward onto her arse. Pain lanced up her spine and rattled her teeth. With a groan, she scrambled to her knees and reached for her fallen dagger.

Pinpricks of pain shot through her scalp and neck as Francis wrenched her head backward, her mobcap and hair caught in the cur's fist. Fear clawed its way back into the forefront of her heart, briefly squashing her steely determination.

The man clutched wildly at her hair and frock, dragging her backward along the carpet. A hoarse cry tore from her lips before the man settled his weight against her back, his panting breaths sounding increasingly like *enjoyment*.

The breath rushed from her lungs on a wheeze, and terror fluttered in her heart. *No fear*, she reminded herself. *Not now. Remember your training.*

The muscles of her arm burned and strained as she reached, her fingertips just brushing her dagger's handle. *There!* She slid it toward her with the tips of her nails and clutched it tightly, prepared to stab wildly over her shoulder. Then searing pain lanced through the flesh connecting her neck and shoulder.

Maria screamed, bucking again and finally throwing off his weight. They both clambered to their knees, a thundering noise in her ears drowning out the heaving of her own breaths. With one hand pointing the dagger at the bastard and her other holding her neck, she cursed.

"Did you bloody *bite* me?" She staggered to her feet. The man was like an animal, for Christ's sake!

"*Maria!*" Her heart flipped over at the sound of Jasper's voice.

"In the parlour, Jasper!" she called over her shoulder. "Francis is—" Her words died as she turned her gaze back to where the man had been, and saw nothing. "Gone."

"ARE YOU WELL, Maria? Where is he?" Jasper asked breathlessly as he rushed into the parlour, Harris and two other men at his back.

With a racing pulse and a twist in his gut, Jasper took her in. She had her blade at the ready and was clutching at her neck. Alarm sparked in his chest. Was she hurt? *Christ, please don't let her be hurt.*

Eyes wide, Maria shook her head then hissed a breath. His gaze narrowed on her.

"I am well enough," she said. "Francis left the same way in which he arrived: shrouded in darkness and all but entirely silent."

Jasper's spine stiffened and his stomach churned once more. "Is he armed?" His feet moved, carrying him into obscurity.

Harris and the others spread out through the room, looking for traces of Francis.

"Not that I could ascertain," Maria said with a wince.

Cool air blew about his ankles and sent gooseflesh skittering along his skin, tightening his nipples into little nubs.

Movement caught his attention from the edge of his vision, and he swung toward it. Air billowed the heavy green curtains, and he silently cursed.

"The window is open." Tugging the fabric wide, Harris exposed the opened window, which led out to the shadowy, moonlit gardens. "Had this room been inspected?

"No," Maria returned. "I entered through the sitting room's adjoining door and heard a noise. I opened the door and ventured briefly into the corridor, and when I returned, the window had been opened and Francis was inside."

Jasper turned toward Harris. "Do you suppose he was waiting for us to leave Maria alone in the home?"

Harris' jaw bunched. "I imagine so. No doubt he knew you and I had ventured into the stables and the others had begun their rounds out of doors." He sighed self-deprecatingly. "My apologies, Maria, Your Grace. He slipped past us somehow."

"Acknowledged." Maria sheathed her dagger. "What I would like to know is *how* he was aware of our movements, and how it was so easy for him to slip past. From now on, we ought to have at least two of your men keeping guard *within* the house, as well as those without, regardless of shift change or rounds."

Despite the circumstance, warmth rushed through Jasper at once again seeing Maria take charge. And yet, she continued to hold her neck...

Harris nodded. "Of course."

"Are you certain you are well, Maria?" Jasper asked.

She waved her free hand insouciantly through the air. "Of course."

Another gust of cool wind brushed past him, and with another lingering glance at Maria, Jasper strode to the window. He slid down the sash with a *thunk* and turned the lock. But it kept turning. "Bloody hell, the lock's broken."

"The staff checked the locks in the windows belowstairs, and I tested the others on this floor, but found none with a broken lock. This must have been his only access point," Maria offered from behind him.

"Who among my staff broke the lock from the first?"

Maria returned his frown with one of her own. "When Francis is apprehended and your guard relieved of duty, I daresay we ought to conduct interviews of your staff to ensure your safety. Come to it, we must uncover Francis' method of escaping the noose—for, once caught, he could very well do so again."

Jasper hummed in agreement. "In the meantime, we

require a wedge to keep this window shut until the lock can be repaired."

"I'll see to it," Harris offered. "None of my men have reported any unusual activity. However Francis is gaining access through your gardens, we have yet to discover it. I apologize again for the oversight. We'll seek to rectify this at once."

Jasper returned to Maria's side and nodded at Harris. "Thank you."

Harris turned to the men behind him. "Fetch some wood to bar the window in this room, and search the grounds beyond this parlour. There must be evidence of Mr. Sinclair's escape and his means of reaching the sash. I expect a report in three quarters of an hour." He turned back to Jasper and Maria. "I apologize once more for the incident this evening."

The three men uttered their assurances and swiftly departed, leaving silence in their wake.

Maria rubbed at the back of her head, catching Jasper's eye.

"You're hurt," Jasper noted, his chest constricting. He stepped closer to her side and peered at her neck, and the redness rapidly staining her fichu.

"It doesn't pain me greatly," she muttered.

His gut clenched as the gentle moonlight revealed the bleeding crescents on her skin. "He *bit* you?"

She nodded once. "Yes. The women on Bow Street require further aid in learning combat. I was taught a number of actions meant to surprise or disarm potential attackers, but Francis was able to block and overpower me rather easily. I'd managed to gain some footing only due to training with my dagger and sure aim with my knee. Grace is often occupied elsewhere, however, and there are newer recruits with far less instruction than me."

Fury burned behind his chest. How this woman could countenance educating herself and facing off with his cad of a cousin again was beyond him. And hell, but she'd just fought the bastard off—been sodding *injured*—and was calm and in command. Would that he had her steadiness, for at the moment, he was veritably buzzing with anger and trepidation.

"Come along," he urged. "My chambers are warm and private, and your wound requires cleaning and bandaging. I've also the implements you will need to write your superior."

She nodded with a grimace, and the stone in Jasper's stomach dropped further as they quit the room.

Her injury was *his* fault, damn it. If he'd but remained at her side that evening, Francis would not have... He internally sighed. There was no way of knowing what Francis might have done had Jasper been there. And, hell, if Jasper had failed to show up at all, mayhap Maria would have gutted the bastard, and they would be done with this nonsense altogether.

Indeed, there was no sense in considering the things that might or might not have occurred had he behaved differently. He ought simply to accept things as they came, and move forward with his support of this...remarkable woman.

He didn't have to *like* that she put herself in danger— particularly on his behalf—and his guilt would undoubtedly remain, but she had managed to live a life independent from her family for nearly a decade—having apparently begun her independent pursuits at age sixteen—and was clearly capable. He'd learned his lesson in attempting to protect women from the difficulties of life when he'd arranged for Juliana to be wed and she'd absconded into the arms of Lord Livingston. And hell, Maria hadn't been too fond of him at the time, either.

This, now, was Maria's life. If he intended to be a part of it —which he most decidedly *did*—then he ought not only to resume his old practice of pugilism, but also to learn more about administering to wounds. The woman was worthy of so much more than he could currently offer...so he must *make* himself worthy.

Jasper led her through the house and into his bedchamber. He guided her to the armchair nearest his writing table and then set about lighting the candles around the room with a taper. The knot in his stomach twisted tighter as he caught sight of her in the flickering light. There was far too much blood for his liking.

Hurrying to the washbasin, he poured in fresh water and dipped a clean cloth, wringing it out before returning to Maria's side.

"Will you permit me to..." He gestured lamely at her wound.

"Oh," Maria breathed, tugging her fichu free and setting it on the nearby table. "Yes, thank you."

Jasper dragged the other chair toward her, sat with his knees straddling hers, and—decidedly *not* looking at her distinctly immodest bodice—bent to his task. She hissed a breath at the first swipe of the cool, wet cloth, and he murmured an apology.

"There's rather a lot of blood," he said. "Though most of it appears to have soaked into your fichu."

"Mmm," Maria hummed, another grimace contorting her features.

"I can't believe the fucker bit you," Jasper said gutturally, his guilt gnawing at him.

It was only once she'd turned her wide grey gaze on him that he realized he'd said the thought aloud.

"Bugger it, I'm sorry. I wanted to be there, I oughtn't have gone with Harris to—"

"You've nothing to apologize for. *This*"—she indicated the angry red bite mark that slowly seeped blood—"is not your fault."

She touched her fingertips to his hand, and heat spread up his arm.

"You are not responsible for the actions of your cousin. You are a good man, Jasper."

Several emotions passed across Jasper's features, his blue-and-brown eyes glittering with something impossible to name. It was the gratitude in his smile, however, that made her heart twist.

The words had tumbled from her lips, but did she truly mean them? When it came to his sense of duty and his desire to protect his family and acquaintances, certainly he was a good man. But—though it was years past—Maria had seen the side of Jasper that was willing to make a wager over a woman's heart and virtue. He was still a gentleman who believed them to have agreed upon a marriage of convenience, and she had best remember that.

With a self-deprecating smile, she rose and strode to his mirror, a huff of agitation escaping her as she examined her maid's uniform. The costume was all but entirely ruined: blood-soiled and marred by small tears on her bodice, waist, hem, and... "Drat." Some hooks had been torn off entirely, leaving the back of the uniform to gape in places.

She detested the thought of having to request a new commission from Grace. Mayhap she ought simply to have Thomas repair it.

Her gaze slipped past her reflection and into Jasper's bedchamber. She was *in his bedchamber*, for pity's sake! It smelled of him. She inhaled deeply, taking it in.

Another pair of reading spectacles sat upon the table at his bedside, which also sported a short stack of books—one of which she recognized on sight: another by Mr. Mystery. Her heart fluttered and she hid a grin.

The space was decorated to match his eyes: dark brown

furniture and blue fabric. She wondered if it was designed so apurpose.

Soft footfalls approached, and fluttering erupted in her abdomen. *Blimey*, but she felt as though she'd been caught spying on him—which, of course, she hadn't.

Dipping the cloth back into the washbasin and wringing it out, Jasper appeared at her side and continued cleaning and examining her wound. It bled quite a lot for what it was, and while the skin was swollen and already bruising around the bite, she believed that it would heal adequately—so long as infection did not set in.

"How is it?" Jasper asked, appearing at her elbow, his eyes clouded with concern.

Maria set aside the cloth and turned toward him. "It will be well; I shall simply have to don a fichu for a sennight or two to hide the marks from my family."

He nodded, catching her gaze. His eyes were earnest, yet troubled. The air around them was warm and filled with his fragrance of bergamot and lemon. She breathed deeply of the scent, and his eyes flared with heat.

The man was so close, so warm and inviting, and memories of their encounter that morning caused desire to bubble beneath her skin.

Would he renege on their agreement? If she gave in to her desires and made love to him, would he then leave her unwed and deflowered? If the duke spurned her, it was unlikely that any other man would have her. Then, no doubt, her parents would force her to become a companion to her aunt...unless she eschewed all *feminine* aspects to her personality and *became* Duncan. She could then pursue her life as a runner while concurrently providing a home for Thomas and writing as much as her heart desired. It was not ideal—as Duncan was just a much a part of her as Maria was—but it was better than losing the life she'd built, and losing Thomas.

Indeed, if she gave her virginity to Jasper, there would be no angry future husband to feel deceived.

Her lips quirked, and his gaze dropped to follow the movement. His chest rose and fell with a quick breath and, all at once, she became abundantly aware that they were standing alone in his candlelit bedchamber.

She ought to speak, to break the spell by reminding him that they needed to arrange a plausible story for her parents and the newspaper's gossip column about their attendance at the opera. But the words wouldn't come; she didn't want them to.

The air between them grew thick with need, and Maria grew dizzy with the smell of him. She caught his gaze once more. It was heavy-lidded and sparking with desire, and her instincts took over.

Surging upward on her toes, she kissed him full on the mouth. There was nary a heartbeat of surprise before a deep growl emanated from his chest, and he wrapped his arms around her.

CHAPTER 14

Lust surged through Jasper's veins, his heart racing and his cock throbbing. Maria nipped at his lips, and he moaned. *Christ*, but the woman's kisses drove him nigh mad with desire.

His tongue tangled with hers once more, the warmth and sweet flavour of her sending a jolt of heat to his groin.

"My God, Maria," he groaned, sliding his hands down her back to cup her arse.

Without him having to urge her, she ground her pelvis against his hard length, and his knees very nearly buckled. He'd come off that morning in the fog with her, and yet his body was reacting as though he hadn't been touched in months.

Maria pressed her lips to his neck then flicked his earlobe with her tongue before giving it a nip. He growled. *Growled*, for fuck's sake.

With his right hand, he lifted her leg by the knee and hooked it over his hip, thrusting his hips gently into her soft flesh. She cried out, her head dropping back and exposing the length of her neck—and the angry-looking wound there.

"I need you inside me, Jasper," she said on a moan.

The urge to toss her over his shoulder, deposit her onto his bed, and rut into her like an animal was incredibly tempting. But he was not an animal, and she deserved a damned sight more than that.

"I would be delighted to bring you pleasure," he said, his breathing rough and his voice far deeper than he recalled hearing it before. "If you wish for your maidenhead to remain intact—"

She shook her head brusquely. "The postulation of virginity was created by men to ensure that brides were untouched by another man before him. *My* only concern is for my happiness."

A rush of possessiveness and lust crashed through his veins, and his grip tightened on her. The woman veritably embodied radicalism, but knowing now what he did about her, it didn't surprise him. She also posed an excellent argument, one he had no intention of disputing. "Then I shall endeavour to make you happy."

ALL AT ONCE, their lips connected, their breath mingled, and Maria's pulse buzzed with anticipation and desire. She clung to him, wrapping her arms around his impossibly sturdy shoulders and lifting one leg about his hip for better friction as she rubbed herself against the erection straining his falls.

She gasped at the contact, and yet she still burned for more.

Maria's stomach swooped with uncertainty, but determination took the fore. She knew what she wanted, and he wanted her, too.

Without thought, she traced an explorative touch along the hard ridge of him.

He hissed a breath, his head thrown back and the muscles in his neck bulging. "*Christ*, Maria."

Her body heated further at the sight of him. *She* was causing this reaction in him, and it was entirely empowering.

With a heated glance, Maria slowly unfastened the undamaged hooks of her costume. Jasper's breath came quick as he followed the movement with his gaze. She let the costume drop to the floor and she nudged it aside with one foot. Next, she reached for her front-lacing stays.

"Allow me," Jasper said gruffly.

Despite the slight tremble to his fingers, Jasper made quick work of her stays, and those, too, dropped to the floor. Her stomach fluttered and her core swelled with heat as Jasper worked. Each brush of his fingers and molten flicker of his gaze had her pulse speeding and her breath coming faster. Soon, he'd slipped down her petticoats and Maria had toed off her slippers, until she stood only in her chemise and stockings.

His gaze was hot and hungry, and her body responded in kind. Now it was her turn.

With determined movements, Maria unfastened the buttons of Jasper's waistcoat, relishing the feel of his body against the backs of her fingers. A low groan vibrated through his chest as she slid the heavy, warm material from his shoulders and left him in only his gaping shirt.

Impatience tore at her. She'd felt *parts* of him before, but she was nigh desperate to get at his chest. The teasing glimpses that she'd had that evening were not nearly enough to assuage her curiosity. Her desire.

In one swift motion, she pulled his shirt over his head and dropped it to the floor with his coat and waistcoat. And her heart all but flew out of her chest.

His hair was endearingly mussed, his shoulders broad, and his body...

Tracing her fingertips along the expanse of his pale

torso, through the thick, dark, downy curls that spread across his chest, she followed the narrowing line that encircled his navel and disappeared beneath the waist of his breeches.

He was entirely breathtaking.

Jasper grunted and reached for her, pulling her tightly against his chest and taking her lips in a passionate kiss. Starting at her thighs, he slid his palms up her sides, slowly gathering the material of her chemise.

She smiled against his lips, and her belly gave another little flutter.

"Lift," he whispered, raising the bunched cotton yet higher.

Maria obeyed, raising her arms over her head as he removed her chemise altogether.

Finally free of her restrictive skirts, Maria clutched Jasper's shoulders and, with a short jump, wrapped her legs around his waist. He gave a muffled grunt of shock against her mouth before clutching her close, one hand on her thigh and another on her bottom.

The heat of his soft yet hair-roughened skin warmed her everywhere they touched, and it sent tingles of awareness through her abdomen. He shifted his grip on her, and the bulge of the erection trapped behind his trousers rubbed into her sex, pulling a cry of pleasure from deep within her.

All at once, she lay upon his bed with Jasper hovering over her, his body half in shadow from the golden rays of the flickering firelight.

Maria's uncertainty came roaring back, clouding her thoughts with reminders of the softness of her belly, the width of her hips, the freckles that sprinkled her body, and the jagged scar that ran along her hip and waist from when she'd fallen from a tree as a child. That feeling, however, was short-lived in the face of Jasper's scrutiny.

His heated gaze travelled the length of her body and back, slowly taking her in.

"*My God*," he breathed. "I need to taste you."

"Taste me?"

His lips quirked in a devilish grin before he positioned himself lower on the bed and spread her legs wide.

"Jasper!" she whispered, sudden embarrassment heating her chest and neck. "What are you—"

His grin widened and he leaned forward to flick his tongue over her cleft. Maria hissed in a breath as shock and pleasure jolted through her.

Settling in, Jasper lowered to his elbows and gripped her arse in both hands, deepening his attentions. *Swirl, lick, flick.*

She tilted her hips toward him, seeking more of his touch. And he readily obliged.

Sensation rocketed through her as he combined intimate licks with flicks of his tongue. Her body buzzed, her pulse raced, and a keening moan pushed its way up from her chest.

Jasper growled, the heat from his breath adding to her pleasure.

Her hands found purchase in his hair, gently stroking through the silken strands as he devoured her. *Swirl, lick, flick.*

He shifted and let out another growl before she felt a gentle probing. His finger slid in easily, drawing out a sigh of satisfaction from Maria.

"So *wet*, Maria," he murmured against her. "So good."

His words barely registered in her mind because his finger began to thrust and curve in tandem with his mouth.

"*Oh*," she gasped. "*Jasper.*"

He licked in earnest, swirling and flicking his tongue around her sensitive clitoris while he fucked her with his fingers. Maria rocked her hips in time with Jasper's movements. Pleasure rose, tingling through her limbs and speeding her pulse. Her paroxysm built, the coil tightening.

Starting in her stockinged toes, tingles raced up her legs to gather in her core.

"*More*, Jasper," she breathed. "I'm so close."

He let out a low groan.

She was panting, nearly dizzy from his ministrations, when abruptly, the coil broke. Pleasure burst through her, stiffening her limbs and causing lights to dance behind her eyelids. Her head pressed back against the pillow, her back arching off the bed as a cry of gratification itself tore from her chest.

She heard a low curse and the sound of fabric shifting. She blinked as he rose up the bed to cover her once again.

"Maria, you..." He trailed off, but his gaze was blazing before he took her lips in another searing kiss.

The flavours of tea and her musk lingered on his tongue, and she returned his kisses fervently, somehow relishing the taste of herself on him.

The tip of his bared erection pressed insistently against her hip, and a thrill raced through her body. Not only was he still *very* eager for her, but he had removed his trousers! Her inner core throbbed with want.

His eyes were molten in the firelight, his gaze intense as it traced the lines of her body. "Maria, you're..." he said gruffly, before swallowing, his throat bobbing.

"As are you," she noted on a whisper, her own gaze travelling over his form. He was soft from a life of leisure, but also muscled from pugilism and fencing. His muscular body was much like Greek statues that she had seen: toned and sleek, but also soft, and entirely arousing.

The muscles in his arms and shoulders bulged as he dipped to take one of her nipples into his mouth.

Pleasure rocked her, and she instinctively arched into him.

With a hum of satisfaction, he began an exploration. Every curve, dip, and ripple of her body was explored by his lips, his tongue, all while he teased her with delicious languid touches to her throbbing cleft. Needing the contact, she touched him as well, tracing the skin of his shoulders and running her fingers through his hair. She watched his body while he moved, his heavy erection hanging stiffly between his legs and his ballocks drawn up tightly.

"*More*," she moaned. "Take me, Jasper. I need you inside me."

His lips took hers on a groan as he positioned himself at her opening.

Breathless, Maria spread her legs wider, eager for what was coming.

"Wait," he muttered.

Maria's heart plummeted as he scrambled sideways to reach in his bedside table's drawer.

"Aha!" He grinned, holding aloft a strange sort of sausage casing with ribbon on one end. "A condom."

Relief washed over her. She knew of condoms, had heard them discussed, but had never before seen one.

He gestured vaguely with the thing dangling from his pinched fingers. "It's meant to protect against—"

"I know, Jasper," she said, a laugh bubbling through her words.

He blinked. "You do?"

"Of course. I read books..."

One of his eyebrows lifted as he returned her grin, slid the casing over his erection, and fastened the bow at the bottom. He then retrieved a jar with trembling fingers and opened it to reveal a fruity-smelling substance.

"Allow me?" she asked softly, nerves and desire weaving through every rapid beat of her heart.

His cock bounced and his throat bobbed, but he nodded, extending the jar to her.

Maria dipped her fingertips inside and took her time in

spreading it over his length, earning a hissed breath from him when she gave him a hard stroke.

JASPER'S CODS drew up and he moaned as pleasure shook him. "*Fuck*, Maria. I'll spend if you continue that."

She released him with a smirk. "Take me, Jasper."

His gut tightened in anticipation as he positioned himself at her entrance. He wanted this, wanted *her* so desperately, but...

He gave a swift shake of his head, and in one fluid movement, rolled them over so that Maria straddled his hips. *Damn*, but seeing her in this position was erotic.

She eyed him questioningly, her palms bracing on his chest, and his heart hiccoughed.

"Like this," he ground out. "I've no wish to hurt you. This way, you will set the pace."

Guiding her with his hands, he urged her to lift onto her knees and take him inside while he positioned his cock with one hand. She nodded her understanding and slowly sank down onto him.

"*Fuck*," he growled.

Her dampness smoothed the way along her passage, letting him slip in. A thrill raced up his spine at the intimate knowledge that he was *inside Maria*.

"Are you well?" he panted.

She nodded. "Yes. It's just so...*full*."

Fuck, yes.

A low moan escaped her as she slowly sank down, digging her fingertips into his chest—and no doubt leaving marks that he would relish for days to come. At last, she was fully seated.

Heat surrounded him—even through the condom, the slick wetness of her hot cunny had him nearly coming off.

"Christ, Maria, you're so hot," Jasper groaned. "So tight."

Her breathing slowed until he slipped his thumb over her clitoris and swirled lazy circles. She arched in pleasure, chasing his touch and riding his cock inside her. Sparks of pleasure rushed through Jasper, but he kept himself still, waiting until Maria was ready.

"*Oh*," she breathed wonderingly.

"Yes," Jasper grunted.

He gripped her hip in one hand while his other teased her.

Then she started to move. At first with hesitation, and then with growing need, her hips first rocking, and then pumping and grinding against him. A small part of him wanted to take over, to thrust into her until they both found completion, but watching her take her pleasure on him was far headier than anything he could do.

Fingers twitching and tangling with the springy hairs on his chest and digging deeply into his muscles, Maria chased her own desire. She canted her hips and sank down on him over and over again, and Jasper's heart soared.

The room was filled with the sound of their slapping flesh, panting breaths, and cries of delight as she rode him. His release was close to the fore, waiting to be set free. But he wouldn't come until she'd had her pleasure a second time that evening.

He worked his thumb in earnest, circling her delicious little nub as she sought her release. Her chest and neck were flushed, her eyes half-lidded as she kept her gaze locked on his. *Holy sodding hell.*

"Jasper," she said breathlessly. "I'm going to—" Her words broke off on a cry, her head thrown back as her cunny squeezed around him.

"*Fuck*," Jasper said gutturally.

He thrust up into her once, twice, and then stilled as sparks ignited in his blood, his cock throbbing and pulsing within her as he came apart. Panting, he urged her down into the circle of one arm at his side, and she rested her head upon his sweat-slicked shoulder.

"My God," he breathed. "That was..." *More than I've ever felt before.*

Maria huffed a breath, then lifted her head to rest her chin against his chest. "You're speechless, then?"

"Utterly."

CHAPTER 15

rancis fixed his gaze on the wooden slats of his ceiling and half-listened to Sarah's incessant carping. She twirled her fingertips in his chest hair while her head rested on his shoulder; it ought to have been a restful moment after a tupping, but the woman wouldn't bloody well stop talking, and anger at the trouncing he'd gotten from his cousin's whore still vibrated through him.

"You really just ought to kill them next time. Get this over with. Forget your blade and bring your pistol. March right into his home and shoot the man dead. Then do the same to everyone he loves."

She didn't understand. He could explain his methods to her—again—but she sodding refused to listen. The woman was growing increasingly tiresome, and decreasingly useful. The sex was adequate, but any additional time spent in her presence was not to be borne. In fact, he'd spent far too much time being distracted by her wiles already. It was rather past the time for him to focus.

Irritation and fury bubbled up through his abdomen and settled heavily in his chest.

What he required was another level of torment for his cousin. Jasper's whore had bested him that night, but he would best her in the end. Francis needed them to be off balance, unsure of themselves and their abilities. He wanted them squirming with fear and discomfort, begging him for relief. *That* was how he would prevail.

His connection, Ludlow, had assured him that he'd been successful in diverting the attention of the Home Office, which ought to have afforded Francis more freedom. But that *bitch* and her interfering friends had brought in additional guards and limited his movements.

A scowl marred his brow.

Ludlow had *also* assured him that no one would realize he'd not attended his hanging alongside Miles, as he'd ensured the man hung in his place had been given his name. But people fucking noticed. Hell, but the man had better make good his other promises... Regardless, he was going to die once Francis was duke.

"Are you listening to me, Francis?" Sarah's voice grew shrill, and he winced. "You must kill them and be done with this swiftly. Once you've inherited the title and become duke, we shall dispense with my dreadful husband, you will marry me, and we shall put to rights—"

He stopped listening to her rant, the urge to shove her off his bed nearly overwhelming. However...the woman might very well prove useful in his plans, after all.

THE CARRIAGE ROLLED TO A STOP, and Maria glanced up into Jasper's watchful gaze. He sat with his side pressed to hers, warming her even through the thick layer of her cloak.

"Will your parents believe our tale?" he asked softly.

She shrugged one shoulder. "They will have no reason to dispute what appears in the paper."

"And you'll speak to Grace directly after the newspaper on the morrow?" His eyebrows knit in concern.

"I will. She must be kept abreast of my encounter with Francis."

He nodded, his gaze intense. "Have you any regrets?"

The colours of his eyes were difficult to see in the dim light of the carriage, but she felt as though she'd begun to know them like her own. *Do not become enamoured with him, Maria*, her inner voice warned. Indeed, she was very well aware of what societal men believed of marriage. But would Jasper *truly* behave the same?

"No." Her lips quirked upward in one corner. "I do not regret our time together."

Leaning forward, she captured his mouth with hers. He responded instantly, tangling his tongue with hers in languid strokes that had her body thrumming once more.

He pulled back with a groan. "Good," he breathed. "Neither do I."

She gave him a smile then reached for the carriage door's handle.

"Wait," he whispered urgently. His eyes clouded. "Please be careful. Francis will return, and he is known to carry a grudge."

A mirthless laugh escaped her. "Indeed." She squeezed his hand in hers.

Jasper nodded, and with one last glance, Maria exited. The oil lamps that lit the street for her familial home scarcely permeated the mid-night opaqueness. A shiver travelled up her spine, and her breath escaped in visible puffs. For a night in spring, it was rather cold.

Marching up the steps to her home, she gave a parting glance to Jasper's waiting carriage before she enclosed herself within the familiar warmth. The servants and her family were to bed, leaving the building silent and still.

She made her way into her bedchamber and stashed her costume in her travelling satchel before she settled in at her writing desk to pen the article for *The Morning Herald*.

DIM LIGHT CREPT past the curtains in Jasper's bedchamber as he was slowly pulled from sleep. Memories of the past evening filtered through his mind, making his morning erection throb with eagerness. Bedding Maria had been impetuous, but he could not bring himself to regret it. The woman did sensational things to his body and mind, and he was eager for more.

Breathing deeply, he caught the scent of their sex and smiled. He hoped Maria's scent lingered on his bed for days— though Lord knows one of his new 'maids' would likely wash it before then.

A faint screech echoed through the corridors, and Jasper sat bolt upright in bed, his pulse abruptly racing and his chest tightening with alarm. A second scream joined the first, followed by some lower voices. *What the devil—?*

Jasper tossed aside the bedclothes and bound from the bed, hastily donning stockings, a pair of trousers, a shirt, and a waistcoat before a knock sounded at the door.

"Yes," he called, fastening the buttons on his waistcoat.

The door crept open, and a red-faced footman stepped forward. "My apologies for the interruption, Your Grace," he said, bowing. "But there's been a...disturbance belowstairs. Harris sent me to fetch you."

Jasper nodded with a jerk of his head. "I've heard the commotion. Please lead the way."

The air in the corridors was sweet with the scent of Mrs.

Ross' morning baking and the gentle fragrance of fresh garden flowers. Jasper breathed deeply of the aroma, bolstering himself for whatever it was that had occurred.

They descended the stairs into the foyer and followed the high notes of weeping and the low voices of Harris' men. A group of them turned their worried gazes on him as he neared his library. A maid he didn't recognize sat upon the floor, weeping into her arms while two footmen crouched helplessly at her side and attempted to offer comfort.

Christ. What had happened? Taking the last few footsteps at a run, Jasper darted through the doorway. In an instant, the comforting fragrance of home was replaced by the cold scent of whisky...and death.

There, standing in the centre of the library was Harris, his eyes dark with concern and anger. And at his feet was the form of a woman, pale and still.

Jasper cursed soundly and rushed forward. "Is she...?" But he already knew the answer.

"I'm afraid so," Harris murmured.

He nodded. *Fuck*.

"Ought we to summon a doctor?" Jasper stepped closer, and his heart all but stopped. "Holy hell. I know this woman."

"Do you?" Harris asked, his eyebrows lifted. "That poor maid found the lady in the mews. Having just concluded our shift change, the men were exchanging information when we heard her scream. It began to rain, and in order to preserve any evidence on her person we thought it best to bring them both inside. Haven't been able to get a word from the maid since."

"This is my neighbour, Lady Cartwright. Damn. I thought her to be out of town with her husband," Jasper said on a breath. He knelt next to her but was unwilling to touch her lest he disturb something.

He scanned the scene. Poor Lady Cartwright. Her lips

were blue and surrounded by a dried white crust, her eyes wide and entirely devoid of life. Fear dipped her eyebrows and puckered her forehead, and a responding swoop of sympathy dipped his stomach. *Poisoned*, his inner voice whispered.

"You don't suppose..." Jasper began, unable to complete the thought.

"Indeed, I do," Harris responded, clearly having reached the same conclusion. "I'll leave the suppositions as to *why* to you and your runners, but the lady was on your property, Your Grace. From my perspective—and I have some years of experience—I would take this as a message. The lady was your neighbour, she was seen as close to you, and that made her a target."

A grimace pulled at Jasper's lips. Regardless of the means or reasons, the poor woman was deceased, and he must now answer for it. Hell, as much as the thought grated, there was another person that must be a part of this.

Jasper glanced up toward Harris. "Have you sent a summons to—?"

"Not yet," Harris interjected, shaking his head. "Best send one, now."

Standing, Jasper strode to the writing desk across the room, wrote a swift note, folded it, and jotted the direction on the front in swift, slanting strokes.

"Bernard," Harris called to a footman who lingered near the doorway. "See that that note is delivered in person. Take whatever conveyance you require."

"Yes, sir." The man nodded, accepted the parchment from Jasper, and left on silent feet.

"What of the magistrate?" Jasper asked, gesturing toward another bit of parchment.

Harris shook his head. "Best let Grace see to this personally."

With a weary sigh, Jasper rubbed at his eyes and pinched

the bridge of his nose. It would seem that Francis' attempt to incite fear and panic had come to an end, and he was now attacking in earnest. When would the next come? Who would be the target?

Christ, he must warn Maria and Juliana. They were all in danger.

CHAPTER 16

"Thank you all for agreeing to aid our runners," Grace said, smiling broadly at a group of maids, modistes, shopkeepers, and...one prostitute. "If you have questions or concerns, please call upon me at any time." She gestured toward a stack of calling cards on her desk behind her. "My information is just there."

There was a general murmur in response.

"For those of you who wish to remain anonymous, we have ways of communicating in a public setting to ensure that you are undiscovered. Additionally, our runners will be made aware of your places of business and, should it be required—or permitted—might solicit your services as a means to engage contact."

Another of her runners entered the front rooms, catching Grace's eye and gesturing with a note in her hand. Grace nodded in response, then turned her attention back to the new recruits for her *galère* of women.

"Payment will be provided on the first of each month unless you require it every fortnight, in which case please seek me out for further discussion on the morrow."

She closed out her meeting, sharing smiles and polite—if short—discussions, before the women took their leave.

"Apologies," Grace murmured as she accepted the proffered note from her runner.

She opened the note, tilting the parchment toward the morning light coming in through the large windows.

"*Ballocks.*"

"THOMAS!" Maria called as she entered her apartments for the second time that morning.

She hung her hat on one of the hooks near the door and removed her gloves, satisfied with the delivery of her article and the likeness of Francis. She and Jasper had been *officially* in attendance at the opera the previous evening, and the denizens of London would once more be reminded of Francis. It had taken some clever manoeuvring to insert her addition to the genuine article once she had arrived at *The Morning Herald* offices, but she'd managed it.

"Thomas!" Was the man still abed, for heaven's sake?

He appeared from the short corridor's entrance, a half smile on his face as he tied his cravat. "Good—*grunt, click*—morning to you as well, dear sister." He gestured toward her writing desk. "A parcel arrived for you this morning."

A parcel! Her heart skipped happily. Could it be from Jasper?

She hurried to her desk, but with one glance at the harsh, slanted writing, she knew that it was not from someone she knew. Her sigh rushed from her lungs, and her shoulders sagged slightly. It was silly to be hopeful.

"I—" She cleared her throat, and turned to her brother as nervousness tripped her tongue. "I've something to discuss with you."

His eyebrows puckered, and the mirth fled from his gaze as he nodded mutely and took to his favoured chair by the low-burning fire.

Kneeling at his side, she clasped one of his hands between hers. "Firstly, dearest, I must apologize for my abysmal treatment of you yesterday."

Thomas shook his head. "Oh, but you—"

"No," she asserted. "I most certainly *must* make amends. I ought never to have hidden you from Jasper—regardless of the reason. Even should our marriage not come to pass, he deserves the truth. And you deserve to be treated with respect. I am so sorry, Thomas, that I dishonoured you in such a way."

Thomas leaned forward and pressed a quick kiss to her forehead. "All is for—*grunt*—given, Maria."

She smiled up at him and stood, her stomach fluttering with nerves. "Thank you. Now, there is another matter..."

"Another?" His eyebrows lifted in curiosity and concern.

Maria began a slow pace on the brocade rug. "Last night, I began my post at Jasper's home..." Pulse racing, Maria detailed the events of the previous evening.

Thomas' light brown gaze grew darker as she spoke, his jaw clenching and his shoulders tensing with ire as his twitches and grunts grew more frequent. A low growl escaped him as she described her struggle with Francis. And then she hesitated.

She and Thomas had always been forthright with each other, and despite the sensitivity of the topic, she would not shy away from the truth with him. Mayhap she ought simply to be blunt. Thomas was an understanding sort of man; he would likely be shocked but accepting.

And yet, the words wouldn't come. A part of her thought that despite her intention to be honest with Thomas, she ought to keep her intimacies with Jasper private.

"What happened after—*grunt*—Francis escaped?" Thomas asked, his voice low and steely.

Maria was silent for a long moment while she considered her response.

All at once, Thomas surged to his feet, his mien thunderous. "I'll shoot the—*grunt, grunt, grunt, grunt, click*—bastard!" He gasped a breath. "Where's my pistol?"

"You'll do no such thing," Maria scolded. "Sit down and have a cup of tea," she urged. "You'll impel yourself into an attack of spasms." And heaven knew she could not use that guilt on her conscience; the last time, Thomas had very nearly stopped breathing.

"Jasper—*grunt, click, click, click*—assaulted your virtue, Maria!" Thomas' face squeezed tightly for several long moments before returning to normal, the motion leaving a slight flush on his cheeks.

Maria's stomach twisted, and a damp sweat started beneath her breast binding. Nerves tingled along her spine and thickened her throat, forcing her to tug at her suddenly too-tight cravat. "You know very well that I do not conform to the *haut ton*'s expectations, and I never shall. But Jasper did *not* assault my virtue, for pity's sake. Besides, how could you even—"

"It's—*click, click, grunt*—written all over—*grunt*—your f-face. Tell me it isn't t-true."

Despite her best efforts, she was unable to prevent the heat that crept up her neck and stole into her cheeks.

"*Ugh!*" Thomas' features crumpled in a cringe.

At least they'd taken precautions. While their Mama hadn't detailed encounters with men during her discussions with Maria and her sisters, taking on the alternate identity of Mr. Duncan Robertson had afforded her access to rather enlightening reading materials and information.

"Enough of—*click*—this. I c-cannot th—*grunt, grunt*—

think on it any longer." He cleared his throat. "Now, what are —*grunt*—we to do about the bastard, Mr. Francis Sinclair?"

"I shall visit Grace this morning to report in after the events of last evening. I should also like to confer with Heather to discover if she learned anything of import during her shift yesterday. Would you be so good as to examine my maid's uniform and see if it might be repaired? I could not determine the severity of the damage in the darkness of night, but I know for certain that there were tears."

Thomas nodded. "Of course—*click, grunt*. I'd intended to walk to the haberdashery this morning anyway; I'll fetch the necessary items."

"Thank you, Thomas." Maria pulled him into a familial hug, and his arms wrapped around her tightly. She was surrounded by his comforting scent of jasmine and vanilla before he strode for the door and retrieved his gloves and hat. The man was kind beyond words and she loved him dearly; how could anyone not see past a few sounds and uncontrolled body movements to the wonderful person within?

The door closed behind him, and she heaved a sigh. The frock that she'd donned before leaving her home that morning was waiting, and Grace certainly required an update on events. On the way to her bedchamber, she spotted the parcel sitting upon her desk.

It was curious indeed.

She sat at the desk and cut the twine with the dagger hidden in her boot. The parcel was soft, though slightly lumpy, and it had been wrapped several times. Nimbly, she peeled away the wrapping one layer at a time. An odd wave of trepidation stole over her, and the closer she came to revealing the contents, the worse she felt.

Dark moisture seeped through the packaging, and a growing sense of dread quavered deep inside her. Fingers trembling, Maria pulled back the last layer to find...

"*Holy hell!*"

She stood so swiftly that her chair toppled backward with a loud *crack*. Heart in her throat, she closed her eyes, clutching at her chest. *It isn't... It couldn't be.*

But it was.

Willing her speeding pulse to slow, she stepped closer to peer at the parcel's contents. Fur, bones...and blood. A gag caught her unaware, and she swallowed against it. This was the work of Francis Sinclair. The monster had killed a...well, an animal, to be sure, the poor beastie. And he knew her home address.

The dread that had settled in her bones spread throughout her body, making her fingers tingle with the force of it. Francis knew of her apartments! She and Thomas were in danger here. She must see Grace immediately.

"SHE WAS POISONED, YOUR GRACE," the doctor said gravely, confirming Jasper's suspicion. "And this was found on her person."

Jasper gave a sharp nod, his gut churning with guilt, and accepted the bit of parchment. "Thank you, Doctor."

"I can prepare her body for transport. Might I have the help of three of your footmen?"

"Of course," Jasper said, gesturing to the footman who was lingering in the doorway. The man bowed and disappeared into the corridor.

The doctor knelt to his task, and Jasper joined Miss Grace Huntsbury by the hearth. She leaned her back against the wall, her grey-green eyes dark with concern.

He sniffed carefully at the parchment—no laurel water—before opening it.

. . .

Expose thyself to feel what wretches feel,
*   That thou may'st shake the superflux to them*
*   And show the heavens more Just.*

Fuck.

"It is as we suspected," Jasper confirmed, offering the parchment to the woman.

Her lips tightened, dimpling her gently rounded cheeks as she accepted the proffered note. "I imagine he reserved the laurel water for Lady Cartwright." She hummed. "We must inform Heather and Maria. This is their assignment, after all."

"Of course." Jasper nodded. "I've sent a missive to the baron, and I've spoken with the neighbouring staff. Harris mentioned an inquiry, but I daresay that will take time, and it will come to naught, for we already know the perpetrator."

Miss Huntsbury sighed. "Indeed. It would seem that Mr. Sinclair is no longer content with minor threats and near misses; the man is in earnest."

"I should say so," Jasper confirmed, his gut knotting with remorse once more. "Mayhap this wouldn't have happened to Lady Cartwright if Maria had remained a short while longer, or if I'd been awake."

"I'll have Maria's report later." The woman gave him a sad smile and shook her head, her brown curls wobbling with the motion. "You oughtn't blame yourself, Your Grace. These acts are the design of someone driven only by greed and revenge, with no regard for the lives of anyone but himself."

The tension in his neck eased slightly, but his heart remained troubled. "Thank you."

MARIA'S EARS echoed with the thud of her pulse, the pounding of horses' hooves, and the rattle of the hack's wheels along the cobblestoned streets of London. Nausea tossed her stomach and, though she hated to admit it, *fear* stiffened her spine and caused the hair upon her nape to stand on end.

She'd raced down her apartments' stairs in time to reach Thomas and warn him of the danger, but with their home no longer safe, where would he go? He'd assured her that he would be well, and she ought to put her faith in that.

They hit a rut, and Maria jostled against the tattered squabs. The hack carried the odour of unwashed bodies and, undoubtedly, the contents of the parcel, which she had resealed and brought with her. She ought to have buried the poor thing, but it was possible there was another message within the carcass. And she simply didn't have the stomach to search on her own. Indeed, the moment she'd finished tying the last knot on the parcel, she packed her frock into a travelling satchel and carried both items out the door.

Even now, it is possible that Francis is following me, her thoughts whispered. He'd left the parcel at her door. Surely there ought to be a way for her to ascertain if the man was in pursuit.

"*Whoa!*" the driver hollered.

Someone cursed and horses whinnied as the hack jolted sideways.

With a gasp, Maria dropped her satchel to the floor with the parcel and braced herself against the hack's wall, her entire body wracked with trembling.

Crunch! Crack! As though a great battle had been waged and lost, the hack slumped at a perilously sharp angle, tossing her to one side with a hard *thwump.*

Pain radiated through her temple, but she only gave it a passing notice as ice chilled her veins.

Francis.

CHAPTER 17

The gentle patter of hastening footsteps and the low murmur of voices followed Jasper back into the parlour, where Miss Huntsbury awaited him. Guilt thickened his throat, and he tugged at the fabric of his curst tight collar.

Miss Huntsbury stood as he neared. "Has your business concluded?"

He nodded. "Lady Cartwright's body has been removed, and the temporary staff are preparing for the inevitable fracas with Francis."

"Good. We haven't a moment to lose; we must return to Bow Street and summon the others. Lord knows what mischief in which Mr. Sinclair might find himself if we do not hurry."

"Your Grace," a footman—Sebastian—said from the door, his cheeks flushed and his gaze concerned. "I beg your pardon for the interruption, but Harris thought you would want to see this."

Jasper accepted the proffered slip of vellum and scanned it. A low curse fell from his lips.

"There were more just like it among Lady Cartwright's

things, according to her staff, Your Grace," the young man continued.

"That's fine, Sebastian. Thank you for this."

The lad bowed deeply and left on quiet feet as Jasper handed Miss Huntsbury the note.

She gasped softly. "This is a letter from—"

"From Francis, yes." Jasper turned around, his hands fisted on his hips and his pulse roaring in his ears. "He had instructed her to burn the missive after reading, but clearly she held some sort of attachment to the bastard." He paced to the window. "But why kill her?"

Miss Huntsbury shook her head and pursed her lips. "Perhaps she had served her purpose and was no longer useful. And what better way to be rid of someone with whom he'd shared secrets than to create a problem for *you*, Your Grace?"

Despite the awful circumstances, a small amount of relief loosened the knot in his chest. His shoulders fell, and the stiffness in his back eased. Her death was not directly his fault, then; she had formed an attachment to—and had likely been aiding—his cousin, and the hateful man had murdered her because he was done with her.

That knowledge, while immensely freeing, did not ease his responsibility. Francis remained a very real threat.

"Come." Jasper offered Miss Huntsbury his arm. "To Bow Street."

FOR THE BRIEFEST OF MOMENTS, shock, fear, and an aching pain froze Maria in place. Somewhere, a horse whinnied and snorted, breaking her from the moment.

Damnation.

She hadn't the time to dither about whether or not the man had caused the accident; she must leave. Quickly. Voices rose up without, men shouting and cursing. Pulse racing, Maria pressed the latch of the door and shoved it open with a *creak*. The voices grew louder, and cold dread spread to her limbs.

Francis would not get her; she wouldn't let him.

She grimaced, and cursed the tremble in her fingers as she stowed the parcel in her satchel. With stiff movements and her heart all but entirely in her throat, Maria hefted herself out of the equipage, straightening her coat and cravat.

The sky was filled with rolling clouds that seemed to darken with the repeated threat of rain, and she hastily retrieved her fallen hat from within the inoperative hack. A shiver travelled down her spine.

With one scan of her gaze, it was clear what had happened to the hack: one of the wheels had broken in half, leaving the entire thing nearly on its side. She knew better than to assume that Francis would have been able to impair her hack, but he could certainly have run them off the road.

Her stomach squeezed and her breath caught as she eyed the milling crowd. The driver and several other men were shouting at each other and gesturing wildly, but she saw no sign of Francis. Maria hadn't the time to waste solving the small mystery or attempting to engage in discussion with her driver; she must make haste.

One of the carriage horses snuffed as she neared, and she muttered soft nonsense to it in an attempt to calm it. The poor things had been through a small trauma and were not trained to run with a rider on their back, but Maria was desperate.

With sure—if slightly trembling—movements, she unfastened one hesitant horse from its moorings. "Sorry, dearest," she cooed. Her voice, while soothing for the animal, was heavy with trepidation. "I'm going to ride you today. I promise to give you as many apples as you desire once we're through."

Reaching inside her inner coat pocket, she withdrew several pound notes and put the outrageous sum on the driver's seat.

More shouts rose up around her, and she chanced a glance over her shoulder. Then, she spotted him. Walking a mount through the growing crowd of spectators was Francis, his eyes narrowed menacingly and a smirk of satisfaction on his lips.

Her heart hiccoughed.

"That man is Francis Sinclair!" Maria shouted, pointing. "The man who escaped his hanging!"

Alarm spread briefly over Francis' features as the crowd around them attempted to reach his horse's reins.

Without another moment's hesitation, Maria put a boot upon the edge of the broken hack, and hefted herself upon the horse, awkwardly juggling her satchel and the overly-long reins. The beast sidestepped and shook its head, rejecting her presence on its bared back. But she held firm, absurdly grateful that she still wore her men's suit of clothes.

The cacophony grew ever louder, and her mount's eyes grew wide before she nudged it with her legs. They burst into a run, with the driver shouting behind them, and she narrowly secured her satchel upon her lap before it slid off.

Crack! Something whizzed past her ear, and with tumult in her chest, she realized that someone had shot at her. She was in the Strand, for heaven's sake! Anyone could be injured by a wide shot.

Pressing her hat more firmly on her head, she manoeuvred the struggling mare down the thoroughfare, around carts, carriages, horses, and people, and into Covent Garden. They were close to Bow Street, but not anywhere she could easily lose a pursuer.

With her pulse speeding and her breath coming fast between numb lips, she hooked her satchel's handle over her wrist and flicked the reins, urging the mare faster. The mare's eyes were wild, the beast clearly unused to having someone on her back—most particularly bared. Maria, however, would do what she must.

She desperately attempted to avoid passers-by while guiding her horse over the slippery cobblestones, her ears filled with the sounds of people shouting, her panting breaths, and the *clip-clop* of the horse's hooves. She rounded a corner onto a narrow street, less populated than the one she'd left, and pushed her mount faster.

Crack!

A small section of the stonework on a nearby building exploded with the force of the ball hitting it, dust falling to the ground.

"Shit," she breathed.

Sweat beaded beneath the brim of her hat, dampened the fabric along her spine, and between her breasts.

Crack!

Dust flew at her from the other side of the narrow street, and a woman screamed in fear as Maria rode past.

How many pistols did the man have? He could not possibly be loading them while on horseback.

The street let out onto another thoroughfare, and she turned toward Bow Street. She couldn't lead him to the offices, but perhaps she could lose him along the way. She gave the mare a nudge and glanced over her shoulder just as Francis burst from the narrow street and spotted her.

He was not far, but it was possible to lose him; she would simply have to take the risk of dismounting. It was a matter of timing, of awaiting the perfect moment when he was out of sight. She couldn't hide from him forever. If she but had time to gather any weaponry aside from her small dagger, she would be grateful.

Her wrist burned with the bouncing weight of her satchel, and she shifted it awkwardly on her lap.

Crack!

That was four pistols. Clearly the man was well armed.

More screams rent the air, and Maria made a quick decision. She tightened her legs' aching grip around the mare's girth and led her down a side street. The buildings blocked the dim light shining through the clouds, and there were several vendors with carts selling their wares. *Perfect.*

With awkward, painful movements, Maria drew to a stop and slid from the mare's back, landing on the uneven cobbles with a hard *clunk* of her booted heels. She clapped the horse on the flank, sending it darting between the vendors down the street, while Maria crouched behind a barrel and a vendor's cart. The man whose space she'd invaded was fortunately too distracted by Francis' entrance onto the street to give notice to her.

Hoof-beats drew nearer, and Maria withdrew the dagger from her boot, her heart clambering wildly in her chest. Would Francis notice that her horse had no rider? Would he see her? The cold fingers of dread prickled over her skin, creating an icy film of sweat between her palm and the handle of her dagger. She clutched it tighter.

Clop-clop, clop-clop, clop-clop.

"Hyaa!" Francis' growled demand came from just steps away, before he pushed his horse into a run.

Soon, the sound of his galloping had faded away, and she sheathed her dagger once more.

"Wot ye be doin' be'ind my cart, lad?" the vendor asked indignantly.

Maria cleared her throat and affected a lower voice. "I beg your pardon, sir." She withdrew some coins from deep within her inner pocket and handed them to the man as she stood. "I had a need to not be seen just then. I'll be on my way."

The man's eyes lit up at the sight of the coins, and he doffed his hat. "Thank'e kindly, sirrah."

Biting back a groan, she hefted her satchel and started the short walk toward Bow Street.

GONE. The bitch had disappeared, and Francis was furious. He gripped the handle of his tankard tighter, careful not to slosh any of his ale, while the whore on his lap licked at the rim of his ear.

He'd been a fool to come here, but it was the first place that he'd thought of in which to fuck through his anger. These women cared naught about his rough handling of them, and he was in need of it. Once he had his desires sated, he would return for *her*.

The woman was far too easy to ruin, if he so chose. He merely had to reveal her secrets to the wagging tongues of the *haut ton*, and they would destroy her. But Francis didn't want her merely destroyed. No, he wanted so much more than that.

The wench on his lap nipped at his neck, and he silently cursed her for distracting him from his tumultuous thoughts. She'd have her turn, damn it.

While he was pleased that Maria sodding Roberts—dressed as a man, for Christ's sake—had been frightened enough to flee him in the street, she hadn't been nearly fearful enough. He wanted more. *Needed* more.

CHAPTER 18

oft voices swirled around Jasper as he paced the cream-and-green drawing room in the Bow Street building, which also seemed to serve as the women's offices. Juliana, her new husband, and Mr. Percy Baxter sipped tea around a small table while Miss Huntsbury served, and Miss Heather Morgan stood gazing out one window.

"The summons came some time ago," Juliana said to the room. "What do you suppose is keeping her?"

Jasper glanced at her while he paced. "She was to bring a gossip article to *The Morning Herald* offices this morning as a means to secure our excuses for the evening with her family and society. I imagine that she will receive the summons once she has returned to her apartments from the offices."

Juliana shook her head and swallowed a sip of tea. "Knowing Maria, she would become distracted by the pile of work assigned to her. If it was urgent, Thomas would undoubtedly have delivered it to Maria at the offices—"

"*Hsst!*" Heather spun from the window to pin Juliana with a wide-eyed stare.

Jasper's heart skipped a beat, and he realized belatedly that he'd stopped his pacing. Thomas was Maria's brother's name, was it not?

Both women turned to glance at him with a mixture of guilt and trepidation. What in the bloody hell was going on?

The front door slammed open and shut, and within a heartbeat, Maria was framed in the doorway. Exclamations of shock and disbelief rose up around the room at the sight of her. Damn, but she was a right fine mess: dirt streaked her cheeks and coated her suit of clothes, her bottom half was almost entirely caked in mud and muck, and her queue was all but wholly matted.

"*Maria!*" Juliana breathed, hurrying forward.

A snort escaped Miss Morgan before she attempted to cover it with a cough. "Whatever happened to you?"

Maria reached inside her dirt-smudged satchel, withdrew a poorly-wrapped parcel, paced forward, and tossed it onto the surface of one of the low tables in the seating area.

"*That* happened to me," she said emphatically.

Miss Huntsbury and Miss Morgan bent to open the parcel as Maria continued. "I returned to my apartments from *The Morning Herald* offices, and that parcel awaited me. I didn't recognize the writing, but I opened it anyway. I knew at once that I must come here."

"*Holy Christ, Maria!*" Miss Morgan reared back from the parcel's contents, her cheeks pallid.

"This is clearly the work of Francis," Juliana said grimly, and clucked her tongue. "Poor thing."

The contents of Jasper's stomach roiled uneasily at the sight of the bloody mess. Livingston and Mr. Baxter peered over Juliana's shoulders to get a look.

"It's a message," Mr. Baxter noted.

Maria grunted. "I should say it was. The bastard gave me a demonstration of what he wished to do to me before he ran my hack off the road and sent me fleeing through the streets of London!"

"He *what*?" Red-hot fire burned across Jasper's chest as fury and fear flared to life inside him.

His rage scorched ever hotter the longer Maria spoke, detailing the harrowing events of her morning.

"I believe that I lost him on the way here," she continued, "but we must accept that he already knows our location and could pursue us at any time." She shook her head and curled a dislodged lock of brown hair behind one ear.

"We've news, as well," Jasper put in, the muscle in his jaw bunching as his gaze caught hers. "Lady Cartwright was found deceased in the mews behind my home this morning..." He swiftly outlined the events, and with every word, Maria's mien grew increasingly grim.

"*R, F, O, N,* and *J*," Maria mused. "I daresay the man intends to spell *for Jean*, though that is hardly a secret. He said as much when he and Miles attempted to take Juliana's life."

"Mayhap it was a ruse meant to distract us from our search," Miss Huntsbury put in.

"I imagine you're correct. Of course, our current plan has failed," Maria stated baldly. "Despite our efforts, Francis not only continues to have access to Jasper's home, but has redoubled his efforts. We need to formulate a new course of action."

"In that we agree. What of your assignment last evening?" Miss Huntsbury asked. "I learned of the most recent note, but naught else."

With quick, succinct words, Maria detailed the events of their evening and her encounter with Francis. "If it had not been for the duke's interruption, Francis would have overpowered me," she continued. "I've come to the conclusion that we as runners require more weaponry and further training in combat as we advance."

"Again, we are in full agreement," Miss Huntsbury replied. "I am still in search of possible candidates—"

"I beg your pardon, Miss Huntsbury." Mr. Percy Baxter stepped forward and exchanged a long glance with Lord Livingston, which ended in them both nodding in some sort of accord, before Baxter returned his attention to Miss Huntsbury. "I would be honoured to offer my services."

Miss Huntsbury's eyebrows rose and the dimples on her cheeks deepened as she considered him. "Have you much experience with close combat and weaponry?"

A faint flush rose up the man's cheeks, but he maintained eye contact with the woman. "I do, yes."

Curious, Jasper mused. The man was inscrutable, yet Jasper didn't doubt his ability to wield a weapon.

"I can attest to his skill," Livingston offered.

Miss Huntsbury eyed Baxter curiously for several long moments before breaking into a smile. "Thank you for your kind offer, Mr. Baxter. We would be glad to have you among our ranks."

"Like so," Mr. Percy Baxter concluded, replacing the newly loaded pistol on the dining table with a *thunk*. "Despite the additional step, it has been proven the swifter and more efficient method of reloading your flintlock—and it is easier to accomplish in battle. Now, this would be different for a double-barrelled flintlock, but you will learn that later."

The wave of relief that had spread through Maria when the man offered to help continued to ripple through her as he spoke. He had only begun his instruction an hour hence, and Maria already felt so much more prepared than before.

They'd begun their instruction by retrieving all their weaponry, laying them out on the dining table, and engaging in a review of what she, Heather, Juliana, and Grace already knew about each piece—which had been a rather great deal. But Baxter knew more.

"I wish I'd known that months ago," Juliana grumbled.

"There is, of course, much more to learn," Mr. Baxter continued, "particularly with regards to aiming and shooting—"

"Do we not merely point and pull the trigger?" Heather inquired.

He tilted his head sideways and shrugged one shoulder. "One could shoot that way—and many do—but you would be likely to incur an injury in your hand or wrist. You would also have little hope of hitting your target with any accuracy."

"Mr. Greene mentioned that in his instruction," Juliana began, "but before he left, we'd not had many opportunities to learn."

"Or practise," Heather offered.

There was a heavy knock from the front door, and the group of them glanced at each other. The women and Mr. Baxter stood around the dining table, while Leonard—Lord Livingston—and Jasper sat in chairs and conversed at the other side of the room.

"It could be a client," Grace said, as though reading the path of Maria's thoughts.

The knock sounded again before there was a deafening *bang* and a cry of pain.

As one, they rushed for the foyer as their only footman, James, opened the door, and Thomas tumbled through it to the floor.

"*Thomas*!" Maria hurried forward to kneel at his side.

And then she saw it: seeping through his coat and onto the floor was dark, glistening blood. Horror froze her throat, and she instantly pressed her hands to the tear in the side of his coat, hoping to stem the blood's flow.

"Thomas?"

The fear that had taken hold of her tightened as though a fist clutched her heart, the icy sensation spreading through her to the tips of her fingers. Thomas was unconscious.

"He's been shot!" she said to the group behind her.

Grace cursed under her breath. "Bring him to one of the bedchambers inside. We cannot stand here while we offer ourselves as further target practice for Francis."

"But why Thomas? He was meant to find a safe place in which to sequester himself!" Maria said through gritted teeth, keeping pressure on her brother's wound while the men surrounded and carried him inside, up the stairs, and into one of the bedchambers.

"Francis wanted to hurt you," Jasper replied grimly, his gaze shifting between her and Thomas, who lay bleeding on the bed's counterpane. Curiosity, guilt, and concern mingled on his features.

Anger, hot and swift, took hold of her. She could not let the bastard win. Could not let him believe that he'd bested her yet again—even though he had.

With a firm set to her lips, she nodded at Heather. "Could you please put pressure on this wound?"

"Of course." She hurried forward and placed her hands just where Maria's had been.

Maria considered the water in the washbasin at one side of the small room, wishing that she could clean her hands, but they would require that water for Thomas, and at the moment, he was far more important. Instead, she wiped her blood-covered hands down the front of her coat—the thing was already half-covered in Thomas' blood anyway—and left the room.

Her objective was clear, and there would not be any dissuading her. She reached the dining room, retrieved the newly loaded pistol, then stormed out the front door.

Several women walking nearby gasped in surprise, and one appeared to faint, but Maria's attention was set on the shadows surrounding the buildings. There were no hunched or human-like shapes, and nothing moved in any of the places she looked. And there were no shots directed at *her*.

Blast. He could have ridden his horse far from there by now. And Thomas needed her.

With a curse, she turned, and spotted the old satchel in which she'd placed her maid's costume the previous night near the door. Thomas must have brought it with him, but dropped it when he'd been shot. She flattened her lips into a grim line, and brought the thing inside and up to the bedchamber where Thomas had been carried.

The room was humming with tense energy while Grace, Heather, and Juliana prepared bandages, cloths, water, and a poultice. Thomas' torso had been exposed, and Livingston, Jasper, and Baxter worked together to assess the damage done.

"He's losing a fair amount of blood," Baxter said. "But it appears to be only a flesh wound alongside his ribs; there is no ball to remove. I will stem the flow and set him to rights swiftly."

Maria's stomach clenched as she rounded the bed to sit at Thomas' side. He was pale, his eyebrows twitching even in his unconscious state.

Livingston accepted the washbasin and cloths from Grace, and he and Jasper began wiping away the crimson streaks from Thomas' narrow frame.

"You know how to do that?" Heather asked bemusedly, tearing another strip of linen.

"Percy had to take on the role of physician on our ship for nearly two years after ours perished in battle," Livingston offered as he washed the wound entirely clean. "He is fully capable."

Thomas moaned, drawing everyone's attention away from

the fascinating history of Livingston's and Baxter's previous lives as pirates.

"Thomas?" she whispered. "I'm here, Thomas. You've been shot, but the very capable Mr. Baxter is taking care of you."

Mr. Baxter leaned forward and gently touched Thomas' shoulder. "My name is Percy Baxter. I need to sew up your wound."

Thomas groaned, and his eyes fluttered before he returned to unconsciousness, and Mr. Baxter bent to his task. Maria's stomach knotted with worry. She'd never before seen a man lose so much blood as to be rendered unconscious, and for that man to be her brother... A shiver travelled up her spine and gooseflesh spread over her skin. She hated to think what could happen.

Clutching Thomas' hand, she waited while Mr. Baxter finished the sutures, then cleaned and bandaged him. As a group, they changed the bloodied counterpane. And then they waited.

A full quarter of an hour passed, and with every second, Maria felt increasingly ill at ease. Her focus was on Thomas, but she could not help the awareness of attention upon her. Jasper's gaze veritably burned into her back. He was, no doubt, desirous to learn more about the brother to whom he'd not been introduced.

A swell of protectiveness rushed through her, and she tightened her hold on Thomas' hand.

Then, at last, he stirred.

"Thomas?" she whispered, her voice garnering the attention of the others, who sat at a table across the small bedchamber.

Groaning, he blinked his bleary eyes before focusing his light-brown gaze on her face. "Maria," he mumbled.

He reached up to palm his forehead, then winced in pain. "*Bl-bl-ast!*"

"You were shot," Maria said, sitting closer on the edge of the bed. "Do you recall what happened?"

Thomas nodded, then groaned. "I felt—*grunt, grunt*—fire lance through my—*click*—side, then hit my—*grunt*—head on the s-s-s—*click*—sodding door."

Thomas grunted and clicked several more times, but nodded, his eyes wide and chin wobbling. His hand scrambled along the counterpane for hers, and she clasped it tight. She hadn't seen him this frightened since she had rescued him from Bethlem Royal Hospital, and it put a deep ache in her chest.

The room had grown silent. While her friends knew of Thomas and his spasms and twitches, the others had likely only heard rumours about the man. In that moment, however, Maria couldn't bring herself to care. She hadn't intended for Jasper to learn of her brother's place in her life this way, but either the man accepted Thomas for who he was, or he could go to the devil. As painful as severing ties with him would be...

Swallowing past the thickness in her throat, she bent to press a soft kiss to Thomas' forehead. "I'll be right here." *Always.*

Thomas' throat bobbed. "I came here bec—*grunt, grunt, click, grunt*—I came because—*click, click.*" His face scrunched in spasmodic twitches, and Maria smoothed back the hair on his forehead. The poor man's spasms grew worse when his emotions were high, making it difficult for him to speak.

"Shh, shh," she hushed. "Take a slow breath in, and a slow breath out. Breathe through it, Thomas. I'm here."

His light eyes grew dark and tempestuous as he breathed slowly.

With a slight wince, Thomas tried again. "I came—*grunt,*

grunt—because when I'd returned—*grunt, click-click, grunt*—from my walk to the haber—*grunt*—dashery, our door was ajar."

A bewildering combination of emotions rushed through Jasper as he observed the interaction between Maria and Thomas. With every kiss, every stroke to the man's skin and soothing word from her lips, Jasper's body grew increasingly turbulent.

He'd come to the conclusion that the man was Maria's brother—the very one that their parents had disavowed and refused to even speak of. Evidently, he and Maria had remained close.

And yet, even that assumed knowledge didn't assuage the...*Christ*, the *jealousy* and abhorrent, boorish possessiveness that had taken hold of him. The familial affection that she shared with her brother didn't impact how she might feel about Jasper, and yet... And yet, he selfishly wanted to keep her all to himself.

He ran a hand over his face and pinched the bridge of his nose before returning his attention to the events unfolding in the cheerful yellow-and-white bedchamber from his position against the wall.

"I came—*grunt, grunt*—because when I'd returned—

grunt, click-click, grunt—from my walk to the haber—*grunt*—dashery, our door was ajar."

A small gasp escaped Maria. "I told you of the danger, Thomas! My costume was not so important as all that."

His throat bobbed once more, and he licked his lips. "I bolted the door when I left."

Her horrified gaze met Jasper's, then swung around to Miss Huntsbury. "Francis."

A tremor of cold dread travelled down his spine just as the realization dawned that Mr. Roberts' grunts were not due to pain. Had he a speech impediment? Or, perhaps he hit his head a great deal harder than... *No.* That couldn't be it, at all. If it was something new, surely Maria would have shown concern. Indeed, the man must always have difficulty with speech.

"But why would he taunt Thomas before following him here and then shooting him?" Maria asked. "If Francis had wanted to kill him, would he not have done so at the apartments?"

"He didn't want to kill him," Jasper realized aloud, pushing off against the wall. "He wanted to frighten Mr. Roberts into leading him here."

The emotions playing over Maria's features tugged at something deep inside Jasper. He wanted to wrap her in his arms and offer comfort, to spread kisses along her puckered brow and tight lips, to ease her disquiet. It was distinctly unnerving, and he was at sixes and sevens over how to react.

FEAR, anger, and confusion crashed through Maria's chest. "Surely he would already know of these offices. He seems to follow us often; I do not see how it would be possible for him not to have seen it before."

Jasper shrugged one shoulder. "Perhaps it was a message to you, then, letting you know that he knows where you are and how to hurt you."

It seemed devious enough for the bastard.

"I'm—*grunt*—sorry, Maria," Thomas said softly, shifting his prostrate position on the bed.

She leaned forward and gripped his hand tighter. "Please, do not—"

"I ought to—*click, grunt*—have been more cautious—*grunt*—when I left." He gestured wildly with his other hand. "I hate the—*grunt, grunt*—thought of putting you in danger. I brought your—*click, click-click*—costume and the—*grunt*—items from the haberdashery, but—*grunt, grunt*—I haven't repaired it yet. If you—*click, grunt*—give me the items, I sh-sh-sh—*grunt, grunt*—shall begin now."

Concern rippled through her abdomen. "You must rest, dearest."

A guttural groan, followed by Jasper's mumbled apology, came from behind her, but she ignored it.

Thomas shook his head vehemently against his pillow. "If—*click*—Francis remains a—*grunt*—threat, then I will make sure that your—*grunt, grunt*—costume is prepared for the—*click*—assignment."

Maria sighed as a mixture of familial affection and worry filled her. "Very well. I shall arrange for a room at an inn—"

"There is no need for that," Grace cut in. "Mr. Roberts is welcome to stay here while Mr. Sinclair poses a threat. In fact, I insist on it."

"Thank you, Miss Huntsbury," Thomas breathed. "I am—*grunt, click*—very grateful."

Grace smiled at him, then turned her gaze on Maria. "You oughtn't return to your apartments, either. Lord knows what the madman will do if he finds you alone once more."

Maria nodded, pulling her lips between her teeth and

clamping down. She *wouldn't* protest, but surely, if she knew Maria's reasoning, Grace would understand her need to return home. Her writing notes and current manuscript were there, as well as her entire wardrobe for Mr. Duncan Robertson. The suit of clothes that she currently wore was all but entirely ruined, soaked in filth from the streets of London and stained with her brother's blood; there was no hope for it.

If she could but retrieve a mere satchel full of items, Maria could accept Grace's orders without protest and not return to her apartments until after Francis was gone. It wouldn't be difficult to do.

"How do you feel about returning to the duke's home this evening, Maria?" Grace asked. "As long as His Grace is amenable?"

Jasper blinked, then turned his heated gaze on Maria. "Of course. I am at your disposal."

"I shall find a suitable excuse, I'm sure," Maria added.

"Excellent. Might I count on you, as well, Heather? Juliana?" At their nods, Grace continued, "Maria is correct: we cannot remain idle while Francis continues his assault. You will, therefore, all be armed and prepared for his inevitable arrival. We will utilize Harris and his men as decoys belowstairs and through the stables and gardens. If you are able, incapacitate him, bind his wrists behind his back, and then summon me. I shall be stationed with Harris and his men—though out of sight. After what occurred last night, we cannot take any risks."

"It would be wise to question Lady Cartwright's staff," Maria mused. "See if anyone could account for her activities in the past weeks. Mayhap she visited Francis in his hidden location."

Grace nodded. "A sound supposition, Maria. I spoke with Harris, and he intends to arrange inquiries with the staff. Though I daresay the baron will put a halt to the questioning once he reaches town—no doubt under the belief that his wife's indiscretion will be kept from the papers."

"It shan't," Maria assured them. "If the staff have no inducement to remain silent, the news will spread swiftly.

"I've been corresponding with the magistrate's secretary," she continued, "with the intention to investigate *how* Francis escaped the noose. There must be someone among the guard who was capable of making the switch, and unless we find a remedy, he will repeat his flight."

"An excellent point, Maria," Grace put in. "Have you established a solid footing with the woman?"

Maria grimaced. "We are building trust, and it is taking longer than I'd hoped. I have yet to receive a response to my most recent missive, but I daresay I ought to request she redirect it here, for I shan't be at my apartments." She sighed. "Let us hope she will have answers to my queries."

As the others rose to quit the room, so did Jasper, lingering behind so that he might offer Maria a ride home.

Maria bent to press a kiss to her brother's cheek. "Our plan is in place, and as much as I detest the thought of leaving your side, dear brother, I must take my leave of you now."

"Not to worry. I—*grunt*—have much to occupy me." The man smiled, gesturing to the maid's costume and sewing implements clutched in his hands. "And be sure to burn those ghastly, soiled clothes now that you've changed back into your frock."

Maria laughed. "I shall."

With a glance toward Jasper, she led the way from the room. Jasper nodded at the man in the bed before following.

"Might I—*click*—have a word with—*grunt, grunt*—you before you leave, Your Grace?"

Jasper watched Maria's retreating form disappear around the far corner of the corridor, then turned toward Mr. Roberts.

Mr. Roberts sat with his back braced with pillows against the bed's headboard, his hands moving swiftly with each stitch he made.

Jasper cleared his throat. "You wished to speak with me, Mr. Roberts?"

The man winced. "Thomas, please. *Grunt.* I do not answer to my pater's name. C-c-c—*click*—close the door, if you—*grunt*—would, please."

With apprehension crawling over his skin, Jasper closed the bedchamber door and sat hesitantly at Thomas' bedside.

Countless questions ran through his mind. Why had Maria lied about her brother's place in her apartments in Cheapside? Her adoration for the man was plain to see, and yet she'd mentioned naught to Jasper in the many years of their acquaintance—even after their engagement. Was his speech impediment the reason for his withdrawal from society, the reason for his estrangement from his parents?

In observing Thomas' discussion with Maria, it was obvious he was in full possession of his faculties, and yet there was so much secrecy.

"My sister has—*grunt*—explained your agreement—*grunt, click*—to me: you've both decided on a f-f—*grunt*—false engagement as an excuse to spend time—*click, click*—finding your cousin. But," he continued, before Jasper could correct him, "I would like to know your—*grunt, click, grunt*—true intentions with her."

The man paused in his stitching to level Jasper with a meaningful stare, his soft grunts and clicks the only sound in the room, aside from the rush of blood in Jasper's ears.

Nervous anger began to bloom just behind his sternum. He'd *intended* to marry Maria. Could he have misunderstood?

A quiver of unease danced along his spine. It bothered him that Maria believed him capable of jilting her after all that they had endured together. But...mayhap a marriage was not what she truly desired.

His thoughts raced, attempting to replay his offer of marriage—and her acceptance—in his mind's eye. Had she been enthusiastic, or did she feel obliged to accept? And—*hell*—they'd been intimate! Had he trapped her in an engagement against her wishes?

He cleared his throat, and opened his mouth to reply with Lord knew what, when Thomas cut in.

"What would you—*grunt*—do, for example, if a child should result from—*click, click, grunt*—your intimacies last night? Would you make g-g—*click*—good on your proposal, and save her from ruination?"

The words "of course" hovered on his tongue, but his brain and heart had all but entirely stopped. *A child.* Hope began to bloom in his chest, but the memory of Thomas' previous words squashed it. *False engagement...* Jasper had wanted a marriage, and a child wouldn't change that. But what of Maria? If she didn't believe them to be truly *affianced*, a child mightn't alter her opinion. He would have to convince her of his sincerity—regardless of whether their tryst resulted in pregnancy.

His pulse rushed in his ears, and he was vaguely aware of Thomas speaking, but it didn't reach him.

A child.

His heart tripped, then began a steady staccato beat against his ribs.

She was trapped. He'd trapped her in an untenable situation, just as surely as he had trapped Juliana in her engagement to the viscount before she'd fled. *Christ,* what if *Maria* fled?

Of course she would. She was better than he could ever

hope to be. Indeed, he was entirely unworthy of her admiration...which was why he'd vowed to *make* himself worthy.

Jasper took a steadying breath and attempted to slow his pulse. He couldn't allow Maria to flee without first knowing his true intentions. If flight was her intent, he could not stop her, but at least he could provide her with the truth. *His* truth.

"... I can understand why Maria—*click*—has such conflicting feelings—*grunt, grunt*—about you," Thomas said thoughtfully, returning to his sewing, one eyebrow raised in challenge.

Jasper blinked. "Maria said that?"

Thomas eyed him with a tilt to his head, his gaze assessing. "She did."

"Is that why she—" *Is that why she wants me to jilt her?* Jasper leaned closer, placing his elbows upon his knees. "What do you mean by conflicting feelings?"

The man grimaced and waggled his shoulder before returning his attention to Jasper. "Well, because you—*grunt*—made that wager and broke her h-h—*click*—heart ten years hence, I very much—*grunt, grunt, click*—doubt that she will ever fully trust any—*grunt*—man. Most particularly you. I can—"

"Just a moment," Jasper interjected, his pulse tripping once more. "*What* wager ten years ago? And her h-heart?" he rubbed a hand over his face, then pinched the bridge of his nose. "I'm so confused."

"Of course—*grunt*—you are." Thomas dropped his sewing to his lap and sighed, a reproachful frown pinching his brows. "Your wager with Billingsly at—"

"*Christ*," Jasper cursed with feeling. "That is, I... Goddamn it, I turned the bastard down! He wanted me to break a woman's heart, and I couldn't do it. The man then attempted to offer the wager to another of our acquaintances nearby, and I wouldn't stand for it. I called the man a cad, and approached the nearest... *Hell*." A nervous, cold sweat began between his shoulder blades, and he could feel the colour drain from his cheeks. "Maria was the nearest woman. She heard Billingsly's wager."

"Maria!"

Maria paused at the sound of Jasper's voice. She turned away from the Bow Street offices' front door to eye him trotting down the main staircase.

"Maria," he breathed as he reached the bottom. "Might I have a word before you take your leave?"

Her stomach gave a swoop, and she nodded.

They strode into the corridor and toward their room reserved for storing records. It was sparse at the moment, with only two tall tables—meant for use while standing—and the shelves that lined each wall.

Cognizant of their lack of privacy, Maria entered and turned to face him.

"I..." He cleared his throat. "I just spoke with your brother, and knew that I could not wait until this evening to clarify something important."

Another wobble rippled in her abdomen, and her heart gave a hard thump.

"Indeed?" she croaked.

His gaze caught hers, regret lining his features. "The wager with Billingsly..."

"Oh," she breathed, waving a hand through the air in dismissal, despite the sharp pang of hurt in her chest. "It's quite all right. It was ten years ago."

"It's not all right," Jasper asserted. "I cannot countenance your not knowing the truth, Maria. I admit that I joined in the laughter at the man's crude jokes, which only served to encourage his behaviour. But Billingsly was a cad for proposing the wager from the first, and I told him so that night. I sought your hand in a waltz not to satisfy the wager, but because I wished to dance—*and* to prove to the blighter that not all wallflowers are undesirable."

Hope swelled in Maria's chest as Jasper spoke, but her fear smothered it. Jasper mightn't have behaved the scoundrel years ago, but that did not assuage her trepidation for their current arrangement. While ten years was far too long to hold resentment or pain over his behaviour at that ball, hearing the truth was akin to the relief of a balm on a very old wound. It wasn't, however, what she'd hoped to hear in that moment.

Jasper was still a duke who would not only benefit from, but also likely desire, a *fashionable* marriage to a more ordinary woman. And her heart—*if* she gave it to him—could not withstand that pain.

"We ought never to have deigned such a discussion at all, never mind in the presence of others," he continued. "I am profoundly regretful for the hurt it caused you."

"Thank you, Jasper," she whispered.

"Additionally, I—"

"Oh!" One of their new runner recruits stilled in the doorway, her eyes wide as her gaze flicked between them. "My apologies."

"It's quite all right," Maria assured her, even as disappointment thudded in her chest. "We've concluded our discussion; you may have the room."

This was decidedly not the time to discuss such matters. Indeed, they had a devil to capture and must remain focused.

THE BRAISED PIGEON pie sat like a stone in Maria's stomach as her family stared at her from their seats around the dining table. The air was thick and warm, heated by both the fire in the hearth and the afternoon sun shining in through the large wall of windows. It carried the rich, savoury scent of the meat pie and was heavy with expectations that she could not fulfil.

She swallowed the suddenly flavourless food. "I cannot be certain when His Grace will wish to begin preparations, Mother. We've only just announced our engagement, as you saw in the paper this morning. Surely we have some time. He has not yet posted the banns. And I do not wish for so much pageantry."

Her father's face disappeared once more behind his newspaper.

"I'll not have our name slandered, Maria." The woman's face blotched with outrage, her scowl a familiar one. "You will marry the Duke of Derby expediently and with the great fanfare due to your future station. I've arranged all of our appointments, beginning tomorrow afternoon, when we shall visit the modiste to have you fitted for your wedding dress."

"Shall *I* get a new dress for the wedding, Mama?" Caroline bounced in her seat, her dark blonde ringlets jiggling in her excitement.

"But of course," Mrs. Roberts purred.

Augusta toyed with the sleeve of her day dress and offered a pretty pout. "And me, Mama? Shall *I* get a new dress, as well?"

Their mother smiled indulgently at her second eldest. "We all shall. Your sister is to marry a duke, after all!"

"What of stays, petticoats, and chemise?" Caroline asked hopefully.

"Oh! Gloves and bonnet?" Augusta added.

Mrs. Roberts clasped her hands together at her flushed chest. "Of course! We cannot appear to be paupers. I'm certain that Maria will repay us generously from her stipend."

Why had Maria not seen that coming? Naturally, her mother would assume that Maria's advantageous marriage would mean additional funds for her family. But that didn't normally come from the daughter in question.

Her mother's eyes gleamed with avarice, and Maria's gut twisted. This would be a regular occurrence, no doubt, her family expecting funds—she could see it clearly in their smirking lips and flushed cheeks.

"I remain astonished that a *duke* would pay any mind to Maria. She's entirely too plain." Caroline adjusted her bodice.

"Indeed," Augusta replied. "There are many handsome ladies among the *ton*, and even more with superior breeding. I cannot fathom his reasoning."

Maria suppressed a sigh, an ache building in her chest. Not only was her appetite gone, but the food that she'd consumed was threatening to resurface.

"Please excuse me," she muttered.

Her sisters watched her with narrowed eyes.

"Where do you think you're going, Maria?" her mother asked. "We have far too much to accomplish—"

"His Grace is taking me for a drive—with Heather as chaperone—before we attend the theatre again this evening. I must rest."

CHAPTER 20

"Your Grace."

Jasper nodded at the footman stationed in his foyer as he strode toward the door. Anticipation buzzed beneath his skin. He was eager to retrieve Maria and resume their search.

"The post arrived, Your Grace." The footman held out a silver tray with a folded missive atop it.

"Again?" Jasper frowned, accepting the note. "Thank you."

He recognized the slanted handwriting of the direction, and his pulse tripped. *The magistrate.* Had he news, at last? He tore the missive open and read.

Your Grace,

I saw Mr. Sinclair's likeness in the newspaper this morning, and I confess I'm disappointed. I have already told you that we have evidence that the man is bound for the Americas aboard a merchant ship. Your interference in our search for Mr. Sinclair's hired ruffians is unacceptable. I must insist that you publish a retraction in tomorrow's paper, and halt your obstruction to justice immediately.

Sir Ludlow Vaughan
   Magistrate

DESPITE THE WOBBLE in Maria's stomach, she strode with affected confidence toward the parlour's window. The still-fresh wound between her neck and shoulder gave a twinge as she reached to inspect the temporary locking fixture. *Secure.*

She sighed. The last time she had been in this room, she had been set upon by Francis. No doubt he was too intelligent to repeat his attack of the previous night, but whatever his method, she would be ready.

Muffled footsteps echoed down the corridor, and she wondered who it was. Harris and his men were already stationed belowstairs and in the gardens, many keeping out of sight. And it wasn't Jasper, for his tread was familiar.

Jasper. Memories of their last moment of privacy filtered through her mind, and her heart hiccoughed. She wanted a *true* engagement with him. But how could she tell him, when her words had already failed her? She'd not even introduced him to her brother, for pity's sake. To tell the man that she desired a devoted love match was too much to be borne.

Indeed, Jasper would likely jilt her once his cousin had been apprehended and hanged. And her heart would break.

Oh no. Her steps faltered as she strode through the dimly lit corridors of Jasper's home. *No, no, no!* She could not have allowed herself to lower the walls she'd erected around her heart, and permitted him entrance.

And yet, there he was, secure in her heart with every beat. *Jas-per, Jas-per*.

"How are you faring?" Grace appeared at Maria's side, drawing her into the empty dining room.

Maria's heart gave a little *thwump*, but she offered her friend and superior a tremulous smile. "I'm well, Grace. Thank you."

"A great deal has transpired in a short amount of time," Grace noted. "I imagine it to be quite overwhelming."

Maria's chest squeezed, but she brushed the feeling aside. "Busy, yes. Though I imagine it is naught when compared to your previous life as a spy."

"Oh *pish*." Grace frowned. "I was veritably raised in that life, trained for years in a school designed specifically for Crown spies. You were trained for scarcely a month before you were plunged into a level of danger for which you were ill prepared. Despite the obvious challenges, you are doing an exemplary job."

Warmth spread through Maria's middle at the compliment. "Thank you."

"I see the struggle in your eyes, dear." Grace gave her a sad half-smile. "I would understand if you felt this position no longer suited you and chose to leave."

Maria's heart gave another *thwump* as she eyed Grace closely.

"I've no intention of leaving my position as a runner," Maria assured her.

Grace's smile broadened, turning genuine. "I thought not, but I needed you to know that you have my support regardless of what you choose to do. Not all assignments will be so all-consuming as this.

"Now," she continued, giving Maria a swift wink and a pat on the arm. "Best get back to work."

The woman swept from the room, leaving Maria to continue her task. She brushed a hand over her newly repaired maid's costume, straightened her mobcap, then strode toward the external wall.

Snick. She secured the lock on the dining room window and moved on to the next.

"The morning room is secured," Heather said from the doorway, before drawing close and linking their arms. "Are you well, Maria?"

A snorted laugh escaped her. "You are the second person to ask that question in the past quarter of an hour. Do I truly look so miserable?"

"Oh! Dearest, no—"

"It is well, Heather." Taking a deep breath, she rested her head upon her friend's shoulder. "I've been better."

"The others are securing rooms as well; we have some time. Talk to me."

Maria sighed, and her heart gave a twinge. "I'm afraid."

"You are worried that Jasper will not understand your devotion to Thomas, and that Thomas will not approve of the man that you love?"

"That is part of it, yes," Maria whispered, nodding against Heather's shoulder before stiffening her spine and turning to look at her friend.

"You've been half in love with Jasper for years, and now that you've had relations, it's blossomed into—"

"Hush!" Maria hissed, darting a glance toward the opened door before returning her stare to Heather. "How could you possibly know that we had..." She gestured wildly, hoping that she would not have to say it aloud.

"It was in the way that you looked at each other today. I

must say, it's about bloody time. The two of you have been dancing around it for some while."

Maria put her hands to her suddenly hot cheeks, the nerves in her stomach taking flight. "Do you think that *everyone* noticed?"

Heather shook her head and opened her mouth to speak, but a voice from the doorway halted her.

"The rooms on this floor are secure," Jasper said, his gaze warm on Maria. "I've spoken to Harris as well; two of his men are on patrol belowstairs, and he and the remainder of the staff are in the gardens and mews."

She cleared her throat, heat spreading across her chest. "Thank you."

His look, while warm, didn't appease her worries. *What does he think of Thomas?* He might even regret their connection. Her chest squeezed painfully. Would he jilt her after all? *Damn, but that thought hurt far more than it ought.*

HOURS PASSED with excruciating sluggishness as they awaited any sign of Jasper's infernal cousin. The bastard was taunting them with his sudden silence, no doubt deliberately wishing for them to grow increasingly discomfited by his absence.

Jasper and the Bow Street women had withdrawn to the drawing room, their weaponry close at hand as they waited. But hours had passed, and Jasper's hope of apprehending his cousin that night was waning.

Despite occupying the same space, he'd not had the opportunity to draw Maria aside for another discussion.

His chest squeezed, and the knot in his stomach twisted deeper.

The notion that Maria thought their engagement to be

anything but genuine was painful. And the probability that he had *forced* her... His heart fluttered with fear. It was not to be borne.

He flipped the page of the book in his hand, though he'd scarcely registered the previous one. Juliana had recommended the works of "Mr. Mystery" to him and, despite himself, he found the adventurous stories rather engaging.

The women's whispered conversation drew his attention, and he glanced at them from overtop his spectacles. Maria sat between his sister and Miss Morgan, her features forbidding, and her grey eyes darkened as she spoke. She wore the maid's costume that her brother had remarkably mended in time for the women's "assignment" to begin.

Damn, but he needed to speak with her.

She must be worried for her brother. Jasper certainly would be, were their roles reversed. He—

Thump-thunk. The sound from overhead echoed through the silent building, and Jasper surged to his feet, dropping the book to his seat.

As though in unspoken agreement, they darted through the corridors and up the two flights of stairs, searching through the rooms for the source of the sound. His pulse thrummed in his ears, his spine tingled with anticipation. And yet...there was nothing.

"Have you servants' corridors or any hidden passages?" Miss Morgan asked hopefully.

Jasper shook his head, then adjusted the spectacles sitting on the bridge of his nose, as they made their way back to the drawing room. "I'm afraid not. I searched after the first letter that Francis had left for me."

With his body still buzzing with unspent energy, he retrieved his book and resumed his seat in the drawing room. A part of Jasper wondered if he would ever face Francis in his home again, since they'd secured the one unlocked window.

That could, truly, have been his cousin's only entry point, and without his personal staff—and, presumably, the person aiding Francis—in residence, the man mightn't have another chance.

He should have been pleased, and yet...he'd hoped they would capture the man that night.

Sometime later, Miss Huntsbury appeared at the rear servants' entrance. "It is nearing dawn."

Jasper nodded, having ushered the women to the servants' hall, where they donned their capes, gloves, and bonnets at the agreed-upon time.

"The air is chilled out of doors," he hedged. "Why do I not give you all a ride home in my carriage?"

Miss Huntsbury curtseyed. "I thank you, Your Grace, but I must refuse. I drove my phaeton."

Miss Morgan gripped Juliana's arm and smiled knowingly at him. "We shall ride with Grace, but if you would be so kind as to drive Maria, I'm certain that she would be ever so grateful."

The friends exchanged glances that bewildered Jasper before they said their farewells, and the three women were gone.

He turned to Maria, the narrow space between them suddenly feeling infinitely smaller, and the air around them growing thick with meaning.

Her gaze caught his, and held.

"I'm sorry that the evening was uneventful," she said softly. "I know that you must be hoping for Francis' swift capture."

"I imagine we all are. I cannot be sorry for the company, however."

"Nor I." She stepped closer. "But...I need to forget everything for a moment. Will you help me with that, Jasper?"

His pulse sped, and he whispered, "I will."

The breath was sucked from his lungs as she dropped her satchel and outerwear to the floor and swept forward to capture his lips. Heat rushed through him in a wave of untamed lust, and he wrapped his arms around her, clutching at the fabric of her costume.

He'd wanted to speak with her about...*what*? Hell, the arousing flicks of her tongue against his and the thrust of her mons against his straining cock had his entire body aching with the desire for her. *The discussion will keep.*

Maria threaded her fingers into his hair, rasping her nails gently against his scalp, and he groaned. Pulling back, she put just enough distance between them to work at unfastening the buttons of his waistcoat.

"The bedchamber," he murmured against her lips, walking them backward through the diminutive foyer of the servants' entrance.

With a light laugh, Maria palmed Jasper's erection through his trousers and darted from the room. Jasper groaned as his cock throbbed. He raced after her.

Following her breathy pants and light laughter through the corridors and up the sets of stairs, they at last reached his bedchamber. Maria spun to face him, her chest heaving and a wicked grin on her lips.

Christ, but the woman was amazing.

With a *snick* of the lock, Jasper gave a predatory growl, and reached for her.

He caught her laugh with his mouth and she latched on to him, her fingers making swift work of his cravat and remaining waistcoat buttons. He, likewise, reached for the fastenings of her maid's uniform and loosened them one by one with trembling fingers.

The room was deeply shadowed; the only light was that of the low-burning fire from the hearth that offered a scant orange hue. And yet even with the meagre light, Jasper saw every inch of skin revealed.

With another growl, he took her lips once more.

She moaned in return. "Take me, Jasper."

"Yes," he ground out.

Raw need thrummed through his veins, and he lifted her bodily and deposited her on the edge of his writing table. Her legs widened to accommodate him as he stepped between them. The head of his cock rubbed between her delicate folds, and Maria gasped, clutching at his shoulders.

"Now," she breathed. "Please, Jasper."

He leaned in to nuzzle and tongue the soft skin of her neck as he slid two fingers inside her.

"You're ready for me, love," he groaned.

Sliding out, he coated his impossibly hard cock with her essence to ease the way, and then he pressed into her.

Her lips sought his, and he greedily took them, tangling his tongue with hers as he thrust. He cupped and squeezed her arse, before guiding her legs higher on his hips to allow for deeper penetration.

She gasped into his mouth. The musky scent of their coupling hung in the air, driving his need higher. His climax was building fast, so he slid his hand between them, found the little cleft among her folds that he knew would give her the greatest pleasure, and circled it with his thumb.

Her breath stuttered, and a keening cry came from deep inside her as she clutched at his back and shoulders, urging him faster with the heels of her feet.

"Oh Jasper," she moaned. "*Jasper!*"

The sounds of their slapping flesh, heavy breathing, and passionate grunts echoed through his bedchamber, driving him even further toward the edge.

"Come for me, love," he urged.

He continued to swirl his thumb, then arched her over his

arm and bent to take one of her pert nipples into his mouth in a hard suckle. And with that, her head fell back on a silent cry, her body tensing beneath his as her sweet flesh pulsed around him.

"*Fuck*," he said gutturally.

With three more thrusts, he withdrew and spilled his seed in hot jets over her belly and inner thigh.

"My God, Maria," he breathed into her neck.

He nuzzled her soft, warm skin and breathed in her fragrance of books and ink mixed with the musk of their sex. A shudder ran through him, spreading gooseflesh over his skin.

Being married to Maria would surely be the same, but better: having long discussions over the dining table, breakfasting together in his bright morning room, satisfying their every desire at all hours, kissing at their leisure, lying abed in each other's arms, finishing inside her enveloping heat—

The thought stilled him, and his discussion with Thomas came rushing back through his mind. He *wanted* that image of his future, but he was unsure if Maria felt the same. His heart gave a pang, and the realization hit him full in the chest: he was in love with Maria.

CHAPTER 21

Jasper's arms tightened around her, and Maria smiled into his shoulder, her body replete.

"Are you well?" she asked softly, stroking the hard muscles of his back.

He pressed a kiss beneath her ear, and then helped her to her feet. "Of course."

His blue-and-brown gaze bore into her before slipping down toward the ropey lines of his seed that were slowly sliding down her skin. With a muttered apology and a flare of heat in his gaze, Jasper strode to the washbasin across the room to dip and wring out a wash cloth.

Maria marvelled at the way his naked body moved, his muscles and tendons bunching and stretching beneath his skin, his now-flaccid member and testicles swaying and bouncing, and delectable dimples forming in each cheek of his rear end. Those dimples reminded her markedly of the ones on his face. He was utterly distracting, and entirely beautiful.

Returning to her side, he tenderly wiped her clean.

"Thank you," she murmured, her chest swelling with warmth.

"Of course." He offered her a half-smile that didn't quite reach his eyes. "I think we ought to have a discussion."

Maria's stomach wobbled. "Ought we?" *Will he take this moment to plan his jilting of me?*

Jasper nodded solemnly. "Would you care for something to eat? I'm certain that there are more than adequate provisions in the larder."

"Provisions that Francis has not touched, I hope?" she hedged with a small smile.

He huffed a breath and shook his head. "The food as of this morning was all fresh, and it is now behind lock and key."

"Mmm."

Nerves tingled disconcertingly over her limbs as he donned a pair of trousers and she his discarded shirt. Silence filled the space between them. Mere hours ago Maria had likewise desired a discussion with Jasper, but... Mayhap it was his wording or his mien that had her on edge.

Dressed, if slightly mussed, Jasper left.

By the time he returned with a tray laden with foodstuffs, Maria had concluded her ablutions and fixed her hair.

She joined him at the table—upon which they'd just made love—her stomach rumbling at the scent of cheese, cured meat, fruits, and freshly baked bread. She broke a piece off with her fingers and popped it into her mouth with a slice of meat and cheese. The salty, savoury flavours filled a need that she hadn't even recognized, but they did nothing to ease her nerves.

"Mmm," she hummed. "This is delicious."

Jasper nodded, chewing, his hot gaze roving over her to settle on the gaping neck of his shirt.

"I'd like to apologize for not introducing you properly to Thomas," Maria whispered in a rush. "I confess, I was afraid that you wouldn't like him."

Reaching across the table, he clasped one of her hands in

his and gave it a gentle squeeze. "You have naught to worry about on that score. Will you tell me about him?" His gaze was warm and imploring.

Maria's stomach gave another nervous wobble, and she cleared her throat. "We knew that Thomas was different at a young age. He and I were so close, he being only one year my elder. We played in the nursery together and got along famously. He began to make repetitive noises and gestures as a child, and our parents sought help from a doctor. They didn't know what to do with him, as his movements and twitches would change frequently." Rubbing a hand against her chest in an attempt to relieve some of the pressure building there, she sighed. "It did not take them long to call him mad and lock him away in Bethlem Royal Hospital.

"Thomas was there for years, and it was as though our parents suddenly had no son. They moved on with their lives and never spoke of him again. I would sneak away to visit him, and I swore that as soon as I was able, I would free him from that awful place."

Her hands turned to fists on the table and her voice strengthened with conviction. "He does *not* belong there. In fact, for the past several years, he has been producing costumes for the performers in Covent Garden and the Drury Lane theatre."

"Commendable, indeed. I look forward to furthering our acquaintance." Jasper hummed, his two-toned eyes glittering with affection and understanding. "And that is why you became Mr. Duncan Robertson? To provide for Thomas?"

"I... Y-yes." Maria nodded, unease creeping back into her heart. "I became Duncan in order to garner a position at the newspaper and acquire our apartments." *And becoming him felt* so *right.*

Jasper pursed his lips in thought. "Do you intend to *keep* your alternate identity, now that we are engaged?"

Maria's ire rose, even while a fluttering of nerves erupted in her abdomen. She lifted an eyebrow in challenge. "What if I do?"

"Despite the financial struggles instigated by my father's gambling and perpetuated by his thieving steward, my estate is gradually recovering. In fact, this autumn our crop yields are set to significantly increase the coffers." Jasper shook his head. "What I mean to say, Maria, is that soon, I will be able to aid Thomas on your behalf—should you wish it."

She put another piece of cheese in her mouth and chewed, scarcely registering its flavour. They were being honest with each other, and she wanted him to know this essential part of herself. And yet... She was terrified.

"If, however," Jasper continued in a rush, "you desire independence for yourself or for Thomas, then I would encourage you to continue donning the role of Duncan to support him."

"What if..." Her fingers began to tingle, and she shook them out at her sides. His shirt slipped from one of her shoulders, and she tugged it back up. "What if I wish to keep Duncan in my life, but it has naught to do with independence, or with Thomas?"

JASPER'S HEART was lodged firmly in his throat. The notion that Maria wore his shirt, carried *his* scent was...*stirring*. She watched him expectantly, and he knew that his reply meant a great deal to her. He was, however...confused.

"I'm afraid I don't understand," he admitted. "I've read your articles in the paper, and I admire your work. If you wish to continue on there, I encourage you to do so—"

"That's not what I meant." She licked her lips and shifted her seat. "Have you ever felt uncomfortable?"

Jasper blinked, thrown by the change in topic. "Yes."

"Has there been a moment in which you felt *so* uncomfortable that your very skin felt wrong?"

He raced through scenarios in his mind, recalling being thrown from a horse as a lad and being entirely covered in manure—then retching on himself. He shook away the memory. "I daresay I've felt something like that."

"Well..." Her hopeful—and trepidatious—gaze held his as she wrung her hands. "I feel that often. I always have."

"That's dreadful," Jasper murmured.

"When I donned my first ill-fitting, second-hand suit of men's clothes and called myself Duncan, I felt...*right*. And while there are days in which dressing in a gown and wearing fashionable hair is lovely and brings me empowerment and satisfaction, there are likewise days in which being Duncan is liberating."

It didn't precisely make sense to his mind, but neither had there been a revelation with Maria that had ever felt out of place to him. He'd been surprised at each discovery, yet in the end, every new thing about her had only increased his admiration and regard. When he'd learned about the women's position as runners, he'd been worried for their safety, but he'd also been impressed with Maria's capabilities. And as Duncan working for *The Morning Herald*... Hell, but he'd found that attractive. And utterly remarkable.

A slow smile pulled at his lips and his heart gave a hard *thump*. "If you're informing me that you intend to *be* Duncan at home with me after we're wed then, I confess, I mightn't be able to keep myself from touching you."

Her brows lifted, and a hopeful smile curved one corner of her lips. "Truly?"

"Truly."

"If I were to feel more masculine and dress as Duncan for days at a time, you would still find me appealing?"

Heat crept up Jasper's chest and flared hot in his ears, despite his efforts to suppress it. Maria as Duncan was not just appealing, but mouth-watering. He wanted desperately to drop to his knees for her again and taste her sweet flesh while gripping her arse in those breeches.

"Yes," he croaked, then cleared his throat. "Most certainly. I'd never before considered trousers alluring, but the feelings you inspire in me when you're wearing them are undeniable." Memories flashed through his mind's eye, and he quirked a grin. "In fact, I was also rather taken with your strength and ability to command a team and engage in combat. You're remarkable, Maria."

Her grin broadened as she leaned her elbows on the table. "And if I suggested that you allow me—as Duncan—to take full control of our lovemaking, would you permit me to engage in any act of my choosing?"

Blood rushed directly to his cock, filling it almost painfully to hardness. He coughed, blinking away his sudden dizziness. "I would be receptive to that, yes."

With a glint in her eyes and one arched eyebrow, Maria reached back to remove pins from her chignon.

"Disrobe," she demanded.

His prick gave a hard throb and he stood to do as he was told. His pulse thundered, and his stomach erupted with erratic fluttering.

Maria's gaze was intent, her movements deliberate as she tied her hair back in a queue. Jasper heated everywhere her gaze touched as she watched him slowly slide his trousers off his hips and down his legs.

She approached him in silence. He knew not what she was about to do, but his body was veritably vibrating with the anticipation.

With the tip of one finger, she traced the line of hair that bisected his soft abdomen. His muscles quivered as she rounded his belly button, then delved lower.

The pads of her fingers traced the underside of his prick, and he hissed a breath. Then, with a playful quirk of her lips, she gripped him hard. His hips thrust into her palm of their own accord.

He groaned. "Touch me, Maria."

"Duncan," she—he?—corrected, gliding her hand over his prick.

"Duncan," Jasper repeated. "*God, yes, just like that—*" His thoughts trailed off as Mar—*Duncan*—tightened her grip.

"Mmm," Duncan hummed. "I am both Maria *and* Duncan; is that agreeable to you?"

"*Christ*, yes." He wrapped an arm around her shoulders, bringing their bodies closer, then lowered his forehead to hers. "You are agreeable to me. In every way."

With kisses to his jaw, his neck, and across his chest, Jasper felt Duncan move lower.

"What are you—?" he began, but choked as Maria—Duncan—drew Jasper's cock into their mouth. "*Jesus fuck*! What are you—"

Slick heat enveloped his cock as Duncan slowly took him deeper into their mouth, and Jasper gritted his teeth in an effort to keep from spending immediately. Their tongue gave tentative flicks to the underside of his prick, shooting jolts of pleasure through him.

"*How* do you— *Fuck, yes!*"

The soft glow of firelight wavered over their skin, their hair, and lent a transparency to his shirt that they'd donned. Unable to keep his hands from them a moment longer, Jasper placed his palms to their head.

Their gaze flicked upward to meet his, and he cursed long and low at the sight. Red lips pulled tight around his girth, eyes glazed with arousal.

Fuck...

Duncan pulled off with a damp *pop*. "You must instruct me. What do I do?"

"What you're doing is amazing," Jasper gasped. "But a little suction would— *Fuck, yes*. Just like that."

Duncan's hand traced a path down the inside of Jasper's thigh then disappeared below the hem of his shirt. The other wrapped around his waist, pulling him closer and going deeper into that luscious mouth with every thrust.

"My God," Jasper panted. "D-Duncan, are you...? Are you touching yourself?"

They gave a hum that vibrated through Jasper's cock, and his ballocks drew up tight. As they combined the flicking of their tongue with deep suction, he was overwhelmed.

"I'm close. *Fuck*, I'm so close." His hips thrust forward, chasing the pleasure.

Gasping for control, Jasper realized he should pull away. This was their first time, he couldn't...

"Oh fuck, Jasper, don't stop!" Duncan pulled back to beg.

He blinked. Shock and arousal rippled through his chest. "Pardon?" Surely they didn't mean to continue. There were other ways...

With a heavy-lidded smirk, Duncan placed their hands over Jasper's. The dampness from their arousal coated their fingers and threw Jasper's pulse out of rhythm.

"Find release with my mouth," they enunciated, "and spend down my throat."

His prick throbbed again, and Jasper released Duncan to give its base a hard pinch.

He gently lifted their hand and sucked their wet fingers into his mouth. "It would be my pleasure," he growled.

Tightening his grip on their head, he guided them forward, and they opened eagerly, once more reaching down to pleasure themselves.

Beginning slow, Jasper drew his hips back and thrust, earning a surprised gasp and a moan from Duncan. Again and again he moved, gradually increasing his speed, until their moans and muffled cries of pleasure echoed through the room.

Their gaze held his as they sucked, and lifted a hand to cup his tight ballocks.

"Oh fuck," Jasper gasped, thrusting faster. "*Oh fuck!*"

With another long moan, Duncan shuttered, their eyes drawing closed as they came.

"*Fuck!*"

Jasper stilled, spilling ropes of his seed down their throat.

Somewhere deep in the house, a clock chimed six, signalling the end of their time.

A FROWN RODE Jasper's brow during his departure from the magistrate's office and his ride home. He fisted his hands in his lap, his back lightly bouncing against the squabs of his equipage as they rumbled over the cobblestoned streets of London.

"These occurrences are naught but hired ruffians paid to carry out your cousin's demands," the magistrate—Ludlow Vaughn—had grumbled. "We followed his trail to the docks, where we were advised that he boarded a frigate bound for the Americas."

"I assure you," Jasper had pleaded, "I saw him in town not—"

"I've told you before, Your Grace, that it is merely a hired ruffian who *shares a resemblance* to Mr. Sinclair," the magistrate had rebutted. "We've closed out the case on your cousin, but the dockworkers will keep an eye out for a man matching his description. And, of course, we'll do our best to capture those hired men."

"Sir, I implore you to—"

"Good day, Your Grace."

With a growl, Jasper punched the side of his carriage.

He sighed. After meeting with the magistrate his positive feelings of that morning had dissipated. No matter how satisfying the evening had been.

Despite not having apprehended his cousin the previous night—and the decided lack of sleep—he'd awoken feeling significantly lighter than he'd thought possible. That, of course, was due to Maria—Duncan.

He hadn't, however, continued his discussion with Maria to disabuse her of the notion of his interest in a *false* engagement. He needed to tell her how he felt.

His emotions continued to war within him, but irritation took the fore once more. Bloody Vaughn and his curst optimism.

The carriage rolled to a stop in front of his town house. He leapt down before the step could be lowered and jogged up the front steps.

He nodded to the footman who had just taken his morning post into the foyer. "Good morning. Would you be so good as to have a half bath brought to my chambers, please?"

"At once, Your Grace." He bowed deeply and hurried from the foyer.

Jasper trotted up the stairs and strode to his chambers. He'd only wiped himself off after making love to Maria earlier, and he needed to get in a proper cleaning before going back to sleep.

A swift grin stole over his lips as memories flashed through his mind.

He reached his bedchamber, but froze in the act of shucking his coat, his gaze riveted on the knife protruding from his opened door.

"*Harris*!" he bellowed, hoping that the man was still in residence.

His harshly uttered curse echoed in the room as he searched the room for a pair of gloves. His heart thundered in his chest. Francis had been here! But how? They had searched every room and locked every entrance!

At last he found two used neckcloths. He freed and unfolded the letter.

Come not bEtween the dragon and his wrath...

"Sodding hell," Jasper muttered, his stomach all but entirely in knots. "*Harris*!"

Christ, but his skin was slick with icy perspiration, and yet his home felt too warm.

A pleasurable hum tingled just beneath the surface of Maria's skin as she donned her cloak, grabbed a newspaper, and dashed out of doors.

She'd scarcely gotten any sleep for replaying her night with Jasper through her mind; the warm flicker of firelight that wavered over Jasper's skin, the way he looked as she gave him pleasure... A smile spread across her lips. He'd been markedly encouraging of her feelings, almost entirely liberating her from any concern she had regarding their engagement.

Does he wish for a fashionable *marriage?*

A pang shot through her belly.

Her friends frequently teased her about having amorous feelings toward Jasper, but while there had always been some spark of truth to their words, she'd never truly believed them.

Love.

Her heart skipped, and she placed a hand over her chest.

Blimey.

A quavering huff of breath escaped her, which betrayed her nerves. It was time to stop thinking about Jasper.

"To the apartments, Jonah," Maria whispered to her favoured coachman as she entered her familial carriage.

"Right away, Miss Roberts."

She shut the door quickly and leaned back, her stomach buzzing with nerves as the carriage jolted into motion.

Focus, Maria. You're about to defy Grace's orders.

She peered out the window into the light of morning. The sky was clear of clouds; only the faint haze of London obscured the sun.

It was early enough that Maria could be certain that her family remained abed, but after a night of no sleep, she was exhausted. It was important, however, that she retrieve her suits of clothes, her manuscripts, and the bank notes that she had hidden around the space. Without her things, she would she not be able to work. Worse yet, she would no longer be able to provide for Thomas, and that simply was not an option—no matter Jasper's pretty assertions.

She toyed with the ties of her bonnet and tugged at the sleeves of her pelisse, her stomach fluttering riotously.

With a sigh, she unfolded the newspaper and scanned the columns, coming to a stop when she sighted news of Lady Cartwright's death.

"Mmm. The baron won't like this," Maria muttered as she began reading.

Baroness Sarah Bantry, Lady Cartwright, was found poisoned on the property of none other than a certain duke. A lover's quarrel?…

Lover's quarrel, indeed.

The carriage rumbled over the cobblestoned streets of

London, steadily getting closer to Cheapside. Ordinarily, when she journeyed to her apartments there were so few people about, that the journey was swift. That morning, however, the carriage slowed far before the turn into the close.

"*Fire*," Jonah called from his driver's perch.

Maria scrambled to the opposite window and looked at the chaos surrounding them. Men and women worked together to pump water into buckets and toss it onto the burning building. *Her* building.

Her heart jumped to her throat and her stomach dipped ominously. *No, no, no!*

"*Stop!*" she hollered to the coachman, scrambling for the door's latch.

The door swung open, admitting a cacophony of shouts from people attempting to douse the fire. Her half-boots hit the uneven cobbles and she ran to join them.

"*Return home!*" she called to Jonah over her shoulder.

She caught a flash of the worry in the man's gaze, but he doffed his hat and did as he was told.

She wheezed, and a cough caught her by surprise. She blinked back the sting to her eyes. The air was thick with smoke, and each choking breath made her heart ache further.

"Water!" a man shouted before handing a bucket off to another man.

Maria recognized them as residents—*neighbours*—and her stomach twisted painfully.

Seeing an opening in the line of hands, she hurried forward to pass a bucket of water.

The intensity of the blaze heated her through her clothes, causing perspiration to bead at her hairline and between her breasts. Her heart beat a tattoo against her ribs, but she couldn't think past her efforts with the water. Mustn't think of what she might have lost. There was no way for her to ascertain the damage to her apartments from the street, while the light of the fire still flickered angrily in the windows. She wouldn't yet give up hope that her home would survive.

As time passed, Maria's arms began to weaken and her back began to ache, but she continued to pass the buckets. Coughs racked her frame, and soot covered her from head to foot.

Eventually the crowd dispersed, and the fire was reduced to smouldering embers. Her neighbours entered the building, everyone hoping to recover items, while the cobbler stood, forlorn, at the smoking entrance of his shop.

Midday sun glinted off broken shards of glass, catching Maria's eye as she passed through the crooked front entry and into the small foyer. The overwhelming stench of smoke and wet wood permeated the air. Her stomach lurched and her eyes stung with tears as she picked up her filthy skirts and ran up the creaky staircase toward her apartments.

A sharp gasp stung her oesophagus, and her cough turned into a sob.

The door hung askew, and inside...

Another sob caught in her throat, the weight on her chest nigh-suffocating. The walls were now fire-blackened brick, her furniture naught but piles of ash and jagged bits of metal. There was nothing left. Neither a pen, a pound note, nor a stitch of fabric. Every piece of her independence had been instantaneously reduced to nothing.

The floor creaked behind her and, despite her desire to continue her fruitless search for *something*, she knew she ought to vacate before the floor collapsed.

She was taking one last glance around her charred bedchamber when a blinding pain crashed through her temple and the room went dark.

CHAPTER 22

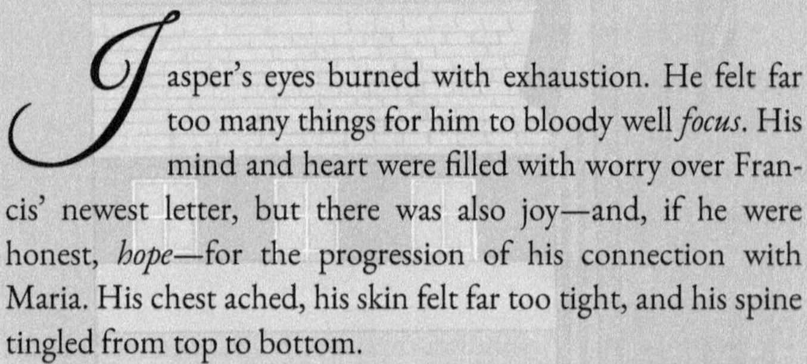

Jasper's eyes burned with exhaustion. He felt far too many things for him to bloody well *focus*. His mind and heart were filled with worry over Francis' newest letter, but there was also joy—and, if he were honest, *hope*—for the progression of his connection with Maria. His chest ached, his skin felt far too tight, and his spine tingled from top to bottom.

Climbing the steps of the Bow Street building, he rapped his knuckles against the door, and stood back. Despite himself, he glanced over his shoulder into the bustling street. He scanned the patrons, but didn't see anyone that resembled Francis.

The door swung open, and he breathed a sigh of relief.

"Good day, James," Jasper said. "Are Miss Huntsbury and Miss Roberts in?"

The young footman nodded and opened the door wider, bowing deeply. "She's in the—"

"Your Grace!" Miss Huntsbury stood in the doorway to their offices. "Whatever is the matter?"

He marched across the foyer. "I received another letter from Francis, and I'm..." His voice trailed off. *I'm worried.*

She hummed. "Do you recall the quote?"

"I do, yes."

With a swift gesture, she turned and ushered him inside. To Jasper's surprise, Thomas sat upon a settee, his pale features appearing warmer in the golden sunlight through one of the large windows.

"Good day to you, Thomas." He nodded at the man.

Thomas grimaced, but replied with an affable "Good day, Your—*grunt*—Grace."

"Please be seated, Your Grace." Miss Huntsbury took the armchair to Thomas' right, and Jasper sat opposite. She adjusted a portable writing desk on her knees and dipped a pen in ink. "The quote?"

Jasper recalled the note—and the bolded letter—while their footman delivered tea.

Miss Huntsbury hummed. "I do not see any obvious way to interpret the quotes as hints at a location. They're certainly visual and visceral, but they seem more to me like threats. I daresay Maria was correct: *R, F, O, N, J,* and now *E* are a form of *nomen deminutivum* intended to spell *for Jean*. I imagine Maria will have some more insight, but for the moment, we oughtn't waste more time attempting to decode something undoubtedly meant to distract us."

Jasper's heart gave a squeeze, and he sipped at his rapidly cooling cup of tea. The tepid liquid, while suddenly flavourless, would aid in keeping him awake for the next several hours.

The silence was broken only by Thomas' soft grunts, clicks, and the rustle of fabric when his body twitched.

"My apologies for interrupting," the footman—James—said from the doorway, "but an urgent missive just arrived for Miss Roberts."

Miss Huntsbury surged to her feet and accepted the proffered letter with a murmur of thanks. Her eyes widened with hope as she noted the direction. "This is from Maria's correspondent in the magistrate's office." With a swift motion, she broke the seal and read aloud.

Miss Roberts,

I'm so grateful for your friendship...

"*Et cetera, et cetera,*" Miss Huntsbury hummed as she scanned ahead.

I confess I've suspected Sir Vaughan's involvement for some time, but I had not known to whom I should speak. When I broached the subject of Mr. Sinclair's suspicious escape from the noose with Sir Vaughan, he made threats against my dear papa —who is already quite ill, you see. He then informed me that as I now knew and am employed by him, I would be implicated and hung alongside him should he be caught. I've been so frightened to speak to anyone, and I do so worry over my papa's health should he learn the truth...

"S-s-sodding hell," Thomas breathed, his left eye giving a hard blink.

"Too damned right," Miss Huntsbury agreed, scanning further and flipping the parchment over.

. . .

ONCE HE KNEW I was too fearful to speak out, Sir Vaughan began to confide in me. He outlined his and Mr. Sinclair's plans to use forged documents to prove his legitimacy while simultaneously discrediting the Duke of Derby—posthumously. In return for Sir Vaughan's aid, Mr. Sinclair, as the new duke, would support Sir Vaughan's attempt to remove Lord Liverpool as Prime Minister...

MISS HUNTSBURY STOPPED READING, letting her hands fall to her sides as she stared in shock at Jasper.

Heart drumming against his chest and breath coming fast, Jasper cursed soundly. "This is worse than we thought. Sir Vaughan needs to be stopped, and I... *Hell*, I've been updating him on our sodding actions!"

"You couldn't have known, Your Grace," Miss Huntsbury replied soothingly. "But you're correct: this is, indeed, worse than we'd thought. I must seek out the aid and advice of my previous employer. Leave the magistrate to me."

"Might I inquire as to what tasks you assigned to Maria this morning?" Jasper asked. "She must be made aware of this news, and I'd hoped that we would discuss our next steps after our failure to capture Francis last night."

The frown on Miss Huntsbury's brow was swift. "I have not yet heard from her."

It was Jasper's turn to frown. "Might she still be abed? She would have written her article as soon as I brought her home, but she was to send it in with a messenger..." A bead of icy perspiration travelled down his spine, spreading gooseflesh over his skin in its wake. He turned to Thomas. "You don't suppose," he gritted out, "she would have attempted to return to your apartments for a change of attire and deliver the article by hand, do you?"

Thomas' face turned ashen. "Grace told her n-n-n—*click* —not to. Surely she wouldn't be—*grunt*—so rash."

The worry in the man's eyes, however, told Jasper that she *would* be that rash.

Jasper surged to his feet, spilling some of his cold tea on the tip of his Hessians. "Thomas, have you your key? I'm going in search of her."

M ARIA WAS SWIRLING, floating around an echoing room that was filled with the voice of—*Francis*? *Oh no*. The knowledge was alarming, and yet she couldn't seem to muster the concern...couldn't seem to *focus*. Where was she? What was Francis doing?

She lay on her side, her eyelids too heavy to open, and could scarcely feel where her body connected to a hard, flat surface.

"... will be so very worried after he sees the remains of the fire."

What fire? Oh yes. The one at her apartments. Had Francis started that? Perhaps he had. And who would be worried?

Damn, but she couldn't shake this mental fog. She was heartbroken about the fire, she knew, but at the moment, her heart remained unmoved. In fact, she was rather unconcerned about her current circumstance in its entirety.

"We'll send him a little gift," Francis was saying, his voice growing nearer.

She felt his warmth as he knelt on the ground beside her. *Am I on the ground?* A part of her thought that she ought to pull away from him, should fight back, but she felt neither the ability nor the inducement to move.

One by one, her hairpins were removed from her chignon,

the tightness against her scalp gradually easing. A hand slipped beneath her head, gathering her hair at the back of her head.

"No need to take it all just yet."

Snick.

"There," Francis purred. "This will be a nice gift for your paramour."

The shifting of fabric sounded loud in the quiet space as he moved away and returned. Something cold pressed to her lips—a spoon, she realized—and poured liquid into her mouth.

"We cannot have you awakening and causing yet more trouble for me."

Maria didn't care, truly, but there was a small part of her mind that made her hold the liquid in her cheek and feign a swallow. Mayhap, then, she could finally think beyond the dratted fog.

Francis rose and turned away, and Maria slowly let the liquid dribble from the corner of her mouth.

"*Stop!*" Jasper hollered to his coachman as they neared Maria's apartments in Cheapside.

"My God," Thomas breathed.

The carriage rolled to a stop on the narrow, crowded street, the scents of urine, bitter ale, and smoke hitting Jasper as he stepped from the carriage. His gaze was riveted on Maria's building.

"When did this—*grunt*—fire—*grunt*—happen?" Thomas asked a vendor selling questionable-looking vegetables.

"Just this mornin'," the man replied with a soft Scottish burr.

Jasper's feet hit the cobblestones hard as he ran toward the building's entrance. Thomas was slow to follow, his pale features contorted in a grimace as he retrieved a key from his borrowed coat. But the door was already open, hanging from its hinges. Beads of perspiration formed on Jasper's upper lip, and he swiped angrily at them.

The stairs were charred in places, and creaked under his weight as he stormed to the next floor. Her door hung open at an unnatural angle, and Jasper's heart hiccoughed. Palms beginning to sweat and fingers trembling, he walked into the scorched room.

Thomas let out a throaty sob, his hands covering his mouth as he took in the damage. "Maria must be—*grunt, grunt*—devastated. Her *everything* was—*click, grunt*—in this apartment." He gasped and turned his wide eyes on Jasper. "You d-d—*click*—don't suppose she—*grunt*—was *here*, do you?"

Jasper scanned the room, his heart twisted in agony at the thought, when something caught his eye. Among the burnt rubble was a flash of cream parchment. And a dagger. His stomach dipped.

Without a word, he strode to the poisoned note and removed the dagger.

Thomas sniffed. "What does it say?"

The note shook in Jasper's gloved hands as he read aloud.

*"HOWL, howl, howl, howl! O, you **Are** men of stones:*
   Had I your tongues and eyes, I'd use them so
   That heaven's vault should crack. She's gone forever!
   I know when one is dead, and when one lives;
   She's dead as earth."

"OH M-M-M—*CLICK*—MY GOD." Thomas' voice caught on a sob. "Maria's *dead*!"

Jasper's breath quickened, the ache in his heart mounting into a deep, sharp pain.

He shook his head, unwilling to believe it. "Francis wouldn't harm her without first ensuring that I would be there to witness it. His goal is torture of the mind, and *this*"— he shook the parchment—"would ensure just that."

Thomas' eyes glinted with anger and widened with fear. "You mean t—*grunt*—to say that that b-b-b—*click, grunt*—bastard has *taken* her?"

Perspiration tickled the skin along his spine, and an irksome tingling began at the backs of his knees.

"How could we let this h-h-h-happen? How—*grunt, grunt*—could *you*?" Thomas turned an accusatory glare on Jasper. "Y-y-you brought—*click*—the b-bastard into her life!"

Guilt swelled in Jasper's chest. "You're right, Thomas. But Maria is courageous and intelligent. She'll no doubt have already begun planning her escape."

It was his turn to step into the role of command, to prove his worth as a partner.

"We'll find her," he asserted.

"*How*, when you've—*grunt, click, grunt*—heretofore been unable to—*grunt*—find—"

"Beggin' yer pardon, Mr. M?" A short, slight young man stood hesitantly in the doorway, a wrapped parcel in his hand.

Thomas flicked a sideways glance at Jasper before stepping forward, his hand extended. "Good—*grunt*—afternoon, Rupert."

"I'm right sorry 'bout yer 'ome." The man placed the parcel into Thomas' awaiting hands. "That's the last manuscript with the signatures, and the first printed copy."

Thomas nodded tightly, his shoulder muscles stiff and spine erect. "Thank you."

"Boss says it's a pleasure doin' business." The man doffed his hat and made his way from the building.

Curiosity seared through Jasper, but the mysterious package was of little importance when it came to the current threat to Maria's life.

"We must recruit help," Jasper said into the brief moment of silence.

Thomas turned. "What would—*grunt, click*—you suggest?"

CHAPTER 23

The longer Maria remained in one spot, the stiffer her muscles became. Her hips and shoulders were all but entirely numb from the painful position. She ached to stretch out, to rise up off the hard surface on which she lay. She was, however, supremely grateful that the fog had lifted from her mind, despite Francis' attempts to dose her with the bitter liquid twice more.

"I believe that we shall leave the note out of this parcel," Francis mused from his place across the small room, his voice chillingly gleeful. "Our message will come across nicely this way."

Maria remained immobile, her breathing rhythmic and eyes closed. He could not know that she was conscious, for he would certainly bind her wrists and ankles.

"I wonder if he has seen the fire yet," Francis continued in his joyful tone. "Do you think he's heartbroken?" His laughter echoed menacingly in the room, and Maria fought the need to shiver.

Devastated. Merely the thought of all that she had lost made her eyes burn with tears. Now, however, was not the time to dwell on her feelings. She could scarcely feign sleep while weeping.

Instead, she focused her attention on memorizing the precise way in which she lay, the fold of her skirts, her hair, and the exact position of her limbs. When she carried out her plan, it must be flawless, or she would not retain the element of surprise.

She'd listened to Francis' movements, knew when he put his pistols down and when he carried them close.

"There," he said reverently, the sound creeping along her skin. "Now, don't move until I get back!" His harsh laughter grated along her nerves.

There was a shift of fabric and the scrape of wood against wood, and the room fell silent.

Maria hesitated, then cracked one eye open. She was in a dimly lit attic that was shockingly furnished for only *one* servant—the space was designed for at least two—with a writing table and chair placed in a far corner. As much as she might like to learn more about the room in which she was held, she hadn't much time.

Careful to observe where, precisely, she lay, she rose unsteadily to her feet, pin prickles tingling over her aching body. Her head spun in a wave of dizziness, and she quickly steadied herself.

With wobbly steps, she reached the writing table and retrieved her dagger and the loaded pistol he'd left behind. Her breath came fast, and her pulse raced, her stomach swirling with the fear of being caught.

Francis had his weapon, and she did not know from which direction he would return. If she wished to take him by surprise, she hadn't a choice but to lure the man in, and she could not do that by standing foolishly by when he entered.

Before she carried out her plan, however, she *must* know...

Steadier now, she crept silently to the small, murky dormer

window and peered out into the cloudy day. Carriages trundled along the cobblestoned street, finely dressed people strolled along the walk, and governesses guided children toward the green. It was, indeed, a familiar street, bustling with activity, and yet so very far from her reach. Grosvenor Square.

Maria's chest tightened and her blood ran cold as realization dawned. She was in the house directly beside Jasper's! *This* was how Francis was getting inside—through the attic. And Lady Cartwright must indeed have aided him in keeping silent while the servants were abed on the other side of the wall.

She must have paid her servants a substantial sum for them to keep her *guest*'s presence secret while she was alive. No doubt Harris and his men would glean that information from their interrogations, but by then it might be too late.

Francis was frighteningly adept at hiding himself and his movements; if Maria's plan failed, there was a possibility that she would never be found.

With that troubling thought, she carefully positioned herself on the floor once more, adjusting her limbs, hair, and skirts just so. She hid her weapons among the folds of her skirts, closest to the hand that lay curled on the floor.

Her abdomen tightened with anxiety even as hope attempted to show itself. She was grateful for the dim light and cloud cover out of doors, for it lowered the chance of Francis noticing any part of her that mightn't be in the correct place.

Every part of her body protested with pain and tingling numbness as she settled into position. Deepening her breaths, she focused on returning her body to a state of feigned sleep.

"Thank you all again for joining me," Jasper said thickly. Christ, but his body was afire with worry.

He stood in his parlour, facing his sister, her family, Maria's friends, and a select few of Maria's paid staff who had offered their services—in addition to those among Harris' staff currently on shift. Each of them sat or stood around the parlour's seating area, leaning against the wall or a piece of furniture, waiting expectantly for more information.

The room was pregnant with fear and sorrow, and filled with the soft sounds of Thomas' occasional grunts and clicks.

Jasper cleared his throat. "I realize that I am not in charge of this case, nor is it my place to insert myself in the Bow Street women's business. And for that I apologize. Once Maria is found safely, I shall most happily return command to the exceptionally talented Miss Huntsbury." He clasped his hands in front of himself to hide their tremble. "For the moment, however, we must devise a new plan of action."

"Have you not had the Home Office searching this whole time?" Juliana asked, her dark brows puckered in a puzzled frown.

"As a matter of fact," Jasper groused, "we've come to learn that the local magistrate—Sir Ludlow Vaughan—is the man who aided Francis in his escape from the noose. They've been planning a coup not only to gain Francis the dukedom, but also to be rid of our prime minister."

"But that's outrageous!" Juliana exclaimed.

"Holy hell," Mr. Percy Baxter muttered.

"Indeed." Jasper nodded. "Miss Huntsbury has assured me she will deal with the man.

A knock sounded at the parlour door, drawing the attention of everyone in the room. The tall footman bowed deeply and swallowed convulsively, his neck and cheeks growing a deep crimson.

"I beg your pardon, Your Grace, but an urgent parcel just arrived for you."

A muscle twitched beneath Jasper's eye, but he reached a hand out and flicked his wrist. The footman rushed forward and deposited the small parcel in his hand, then hurriedly left with another mumbled apology.

Jasper's attention narrowed to the writing on the parcel. *Francis.*

His skin grew cold, his hands damp with nervous perspiration, and...*hell*, but his eyes began to blur. He was a sodding mess.

Absently, he raised the parcel to his nose and sniffed. It seemed to be simple parchment; no lingering scent of laurel water. With shaking fingers, he untied the twine and opened the wrapping to reveal—

"*Fucking hell*," he cursed low, his voice hallow and hopeless even to his own ears.

He was distantly aware of the others, of their gasps, their cries of horror, and their vows to find Francis as they took in the parcel's contents. Through it all, Jasper's gaze never wavered.

In the parcel was a large clump of brown, curling hair, covered in soot and appearing singed along the edges.

MARIA'S LIMBS had once more moved from pain and discomfort into a state of aching numbness. She wished so badly that she could move, but that was, of course, impossible.

Francis stomped across the room to presumably sit at his writing desk. His movements were stilted, agitated, and that made Maria's stomach turn over with nerves. The man was entirely unpredictable, and when he was angry, even more so.

He'd seemed rather pleased with himself earlier; what could have gone awry?

"The dukedom is *mine*," he muttered, his voice dripping with vitriol. "My father was the eldest. He cannot deny that."

Parchment and fabric shifted, before the sound of a pen scratching against parchment reached her ears.

"He'll not see my siblings dead and live to boast about it. Which is why my next gift must be more meaningful to the bastard." His voice turned pensive and optimistic once more. "Mayhap a finger or two. Or her tongue—he seemed to enjoy it so much, might as well have it as a gift."

Low, menacingly gleeful laughter filled the small room, sending gooseflesh over Maria's skin.

He shifted once more, his steps softer now as he approached her.

"Open up for another dose, now, lovely lightskirt. We mustn't have you awakening."

The gentle *clink* of spoon against a glass vial told her how very close he was. *Come closer*, she silently urged. *This* was her moment, her one opportunity to rid herself—and London— of this madman. This went far beyond her assignment, or her desire to see Jasper and Juliana happy; this was a matter of her life, her dismemberment, her death.

The heat of his breath brushed her cheek as he leaned closer, and she stretched her fingers just far enough beneath the folds of her skirts to pull the hilt of her dagger tightly into her palm.

Now.

His spoon touched her lips, and in one upward arch, Maria sliced through his arm and chest.

Francis roared, scrambling backward and withdrawing his pistol, just as she aimed hers.

"Die, bitc—"

Bang! Bang!

"IT'S HER SODDING HAIR," Jasper breathed, his body buzzing with horror and the burning desire to find his bastard of a cousin and bring him to justice.

"Are we able to trace the parcel's origin?" Mr. Baxter asked.

Jasper inclined his head, his stomach churning. "I've never attempted it before, but I daresay it is worth the—"

Bang! Bang!

Ice froze Jasper's veins. "That wasn't... That couldn't be..."

Mr. Baxter nodded. "Gunfire."

Jasper ran from the room, down the corridor and up the stairs through the foyer, continuing on until he reached the attic, out of breath and damp with perspiration. But it was as it had been before: rows of beds, tables, and the personal effects of his servants. No one else was in his home, and yet...

He turned to the others that had followed him. "Spread out. Search the grounds, the gardens, the scullery, fucking furniture, I don't care. The man must be somewhere nearby, and I *must* know what he's done to—" He couldn't complete the thought, couldn't even imagine that those shots had been for her.

reath hissed between Maria's teeth as she rose to her knees. Fire blazed through the flesh of her upper left arm, and she knew what she would find even before looking down at the crimson stain blooming on her soot-covered frock.

How in heaven's name would she explain *this* to her mother? The woman would be positively—

Francis groaned from his place on the floor across from her, dragging Maria out of her momentary reverie. She would finish it this time.

Ignoring the agony in her arm and the stiff ache in her other limbs, she rose to stand over Francis. Blood oozed from the cut to his shoulder and chest, and the gunshot to his left knee. She shook her head at him.

"You've been a right pain in the arse," she said, more to herself than to him, for Lord knew it was true.

His face was flushed as he clutched his bleeding knee, his eyes bulging in pain and his lips sneering with fury. With a tap to his shoulder with the tip of her half-boot—to ensure he wouldn't reach for her—she bent and unfastened his cravat.

Blood from her wound slid down her fingertips, staining the off-white fabric a deep red. Her fingers trembled and slipped on the rapidly growing red stain, but she managed to tug it off. Gripping his upper arm, she attempted to roll him onto his side, but he fought.

"You'll not take me," he wheezed, wobbling upon the floor.

"If you don't desist your flopping," she grunted, "I shall be forced to find an object with which to render you unconscious."

His eyes full of fiery hatred and mutinous intent, he fussed and fought as she clasped his shoulder and hip and rolled him to his front. Panting with exertion, she slid up his person, pressed a knee into the arch of his back, and pulled his arms behind him. A roar of pain vibrated through him, and she mercilessly wrapped the cravat around his wrists and secured a tight knot.

"Hush, now," she said sternly, a sweat breaking out on her brow and between her breasts. "I thought you enjoyed pain."

Rising, Maria cursed under her breath and removed her pelisse with a groan of agony, the reddened material heavy with her blood. Lord, but she could taste the coppery tang in the air. She hastily sat on the bastard's thighs and tied his ankles with the bulky fabric.

A glance around the space told her that she hadn't many options on how she might carry the man from the room. She couldn't very well leave him there without supervision, for he'd undoubtedly find a way to free himself and wreak havoc upon their lives once more. She hadn't a choice; she must bring him with her. *But how?*

Her gaze landed on his unkempt bed with its dark bedclothes of undeterminable colour, and her decision was made. She stood, pausing momentarily as a wave of faintness spun her head and blurred her vision, before she reached for the thin counterpane and laid it on the floor beside Francis.

The man sputtered, groaned, and swore at her as she rolled him onto it.

"Where is the entrance to the duke's attic?" she demanded.

He spat on the floor near her booted feet.

She glanced about, and said aloud, "The door is on that side of the room, so the attic must adjoin to Jasper's on this side." She strode to the wall and pressed firmly on the wood panelling.

Walking along the wall, she continued to press, blinking through the occasional blurriness. A smooth divot caught her eye, and she placed her fingertips inside and gave a push. The panel moved, just as fabric rustled behind her. She spun and cursed soundly as another wave of faintness whirled through her head.

Blinking rapidly, she focused on the man squirming on the floor. "You'll not be released that way."

He spat again, and she shook her head. Returning to her task, she pushed the panel wider, until there was enough space for her to go through. On the other side of the passage, she slid a similar panel aside, but was blocked by a stack of paintings that entirely obscured the opening.

Frustration bubbled up through her chest as she realized how Francis had evaded their searches.

Careful to keep the blood smears at a minimum, Maria clasped the paintings and slid them along the floor, giving herself enough space through which to move. Then, she returned for her bounty.

Her arm seared hot while the rest of her felt cold, but she gripped one end of the counterpane in both hands and dragged Francis through the short connecting passage and into the storage space in Jasper's attic. Heaving a breath, she pulled him across the space and toward the doorway.

Her back and thighs burned with use, but she welcomed the pain; with every step she was closer to having Francis back on trial and hung for his beastly crimes.

They reached the stairs, and for the briefest of moments, she felt guilty for what she was about to do. But then Francis spat at her, and the guilt faded. With careful backwards steps, she made her way to down the stairs, the man bouncing and cursing with each step. Her head spun, and she fought to keep a tight hold on the counterpane through the stickiness of her blood, but she continued to drag the bastard through Jasper's home.

WITH EVERY HIDDEN nook Jasper searched that came up empty, the knots in his body drew tighter. They'd heard the gunfire, but mayhap it hadn't been Francis. Or perhaps it was, but he was simply attempting—and succeeding—to cause more emotional pain. Whatever it was, Jasper's heart could scarcely handle another moment of this.

The longer they searched, the worse his heart ached. He'd known that his feelings for Maria had grown, but he'd not realized how very *much*. What if he couldn't tell her—

"*Jasper*," a faint, weak voice called from the floor above.

His pulse sped and he darted from the room, racing up the stairs to the third floor.

Thump, thump, thump... A rhythmic thumping accompanied by shuffling, rustling, and grunting echoed down the hall, and Jasper followed the sound to the fourth-floor stairs.

"*Maria*!" His chest swelled for a startled moment before he truly took in her state. "Sodding hell!" He turned to shout over his shoulder, "*Fetch a doctor*!"

She wavered on her feet, and he rushed forward. A crimson stain spanned nearly the entire length of her left arm, which was dragging—

"*Francis*," he spat.

He carefully disengaged Maria's bloody hands from the counterpane and took her into his arms. She leaned against him with a sigh, her eyes rolling backward then sliding closed.

"*Christ*. Maria?"

Knees giving way beneath her, she slid down his person before he lifted her bodily in his arms.

"*Livingston*! *Baxter*! *Thomas*! Anyone within earshot!" he hollered over his shoulder.

Mr. Baxter darted from the third-floor staircase, his eyes widening. "You've found them!"

"Have someone summon a physician. I need another to watch Francis, and send the women to my bedchamber to help Maria out of her clothes. We haven't the time to bring her home; she must be seen to here."

"Right away." Baxter disappeared down the stairs, and Jasper turned toward the ducal bedchamber.

He was dimly aware of others approaching and offering help, but Jasper's thoughts were all but entirely occupied. Nerves wrapped themselves around his every muscle. There was far too much blood. Too much for an injury to her arm, damn it! She was too pale. Her skin was ashen and bore a sheen of perspiration from her efforts.

"Stay alive, my love," he whispered into her hair. "Keep breathing. Stay *alive*."

His entire body taut with tension, Jasper entered the parlour. The low hum of conversation stopped, and the eyes of every occupant turned on him expectantly.

"How is she?" Miss Morgan asked, standing from her position on the settee.

"The doctor is seeing to her wound now. He requested that I give them privacy. But she is still unconscious." His gaze slid sideways to where his cousin sat, bound to a chair and moaning over his own wound. "I came to question Francis, however."

Juliana nodded from her position near the bastard. "I refrained from speaking to him without you present."

Unable to utter a word in response, Jasper dragged an armchair toward the man and sat, facing him. Fury raged beneath his skin, curdling his blood. This loathsome parasite had dogged him and his for far too damned long.

"*Why*, damn you?" he burst out.

A slow, cruel smile spread over Francis' lips. "You know why."

He did, but he wanted the villain to say it, wanted to hear the delusions. "The title? Jean? Hell, Francis, you know very well that—"

"I do *not* know!" he hissed, his features mottling, despite his loss of blood. "When the truth comes to be known about your father's theft of the title and the barbarous murder of my dearest Jean, everyone will revile you. The title is rightfully mine, and I *shall* have it."

"My father did not murder Jean. We—"

"*Yes he did*! We saw her body; we know what he did!"

His emotions in turmoil, Jasper stood and strode from the room.

Shouts of anger and hatred followed him through the corridor and into his study, but while his chest ached, he ignored it. He hastily retrieved the letter from Jean and the informational handbill for Marie Tussaud's exhibit, then returned to the parlour.

"This," Jasper resumed his seat and held the old, wrinkled

piece of parchment out for Francis to view, "is the handbill for an exhibit of death masks from the Reign of Terror, commissioned by Marie Tussaud. As you see, it opened in May, 1802. My father, Juliana, and I were invited as special guests to view the exhibit at our leisure for the entirety of the month, during which time we stayed in London."

"*Lies*," Francis hissed, his mottled face growing increasingly red. "You were in Derby when Jean was murdered."

Jasper switched the handbill out for a creased letter. "I'm certain that you recognize this handwriting. This was sent to our estate while we were in London; it was forwarded to my father here, but by then, it was too late."

Eyes reddening, Francis reared back in disbelief. "Impossible."

"There were only three people who had the motivation to stop Jean from speaking with my father that day."

The colour slowly drained from Francis' cheeks. "How *dare* you? We would *never!*"

"You and Miles mightn't," Jasper capitulated, "but would your father?"

His skin all but entirely ashen, the man lapsed into silence as he considered the answer. The desire to outright refuse must have been hot on his tongue, but the truth will out.

Jasper cleared his throat. "Now that we've established my father's innocence, there are questions that I would like to ask."

CHAPTER 25

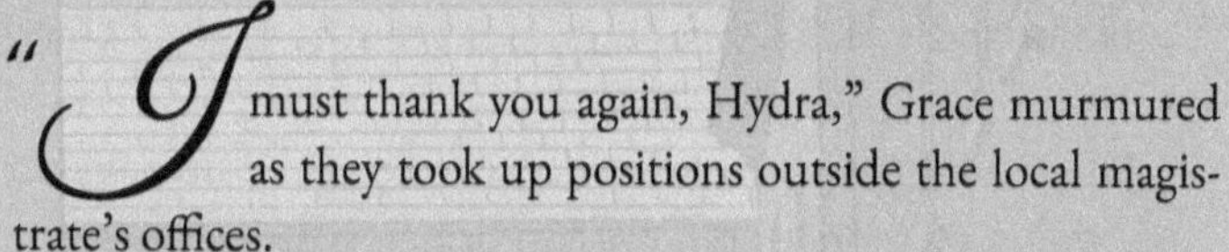

"I must thank you again, Hydra," Grace murmured as they took up positions outside the local magistrate's offices.

Her long-time superior and mentor in His Majesty's Secret Service, Hydra—Sir Charles Bradley—quirked a grin at her. "You were an exemplary spy and great friend; I shall always be happy to help you."

Her chest warmed at his praise, but she shook the feeling aside. Now was not the time.

The outer rooms of the offices had been secured by Hydra's men, leaving only Sir Ludlow Vaughan's office unsecured. Grace pressed her back against the wall outside his door, with Hydra matching her stance on the other side.

Adjusting her grip on the flintlock in one hand and tightening her hold on the handcuffs in the other, Grace nodded her readiness to Hydra. Her pulse was steady and calm, but her abdomen was abubble with anticipation. She'd missed this.

He nodded in return and, as one, they moved, spinning on

their heels as Hydra leaned back to kick down the door with one booted foot.

A GREAT CLOUD of bergamot and lemons surrounded Maria, even as her arm smarted and every muscle throbbed. Her chest rumbled with a low groan, and fabric rustled at her side.

"Maria?" Jasper whispered, his voice pained.

She blinked slowly, taking in Jasper's beloved features, creased with worry, and the firelit bedchamber beyond.

"Good morning," she croaked.

He huffed a laugh, his warm eyes growing glassy. "Good morning."

She moved to sit up and he hastened to help, bracing her back with a plethora of pillows and bringing the counterpane to her thighs.

Someone had evidently found her a previously owned frock, for she wore an overlarge day dress with short-capped sleeves. It was an old style, made with well-worn fustian, and she was very grateful for something to wear that was neither smoky nor bloodstained.

"Juliana found it in a wardrobe in one of the rooms," Jasper explained, following her gaze.

She gave him a half-smile. "It's a far sight better than what I was wearing."

Thomas crashed through the opened doorway, bumping a tray of covered dishes against the door's frame. "Blimey. I've brought us food, Jasper. And the doctor has—*grunt, click*—seen Francis, and says—*holy Christ*, Maria!" He set the tray on a nearby table and stood next to Jasper at her bedside. "How are—*grunt*—you feeling?"

"My arm hurts, and my body aches, but I feel rather well."

"You lost a fair amount of blood," Jasper said thickly.

The vague recollection of her red, sticky fingers gripping Francis' counterpane flooded her mind's eye, and she nodded.

"Thanks to you, we found my cousin's lair, and I've had the opportunity to speak with him."

Maria's stomach swooped. "What did you learn?"

"He's remained frustratingly silent, I'm afraid."

Maria hummed.

Thomas leaned against the side of the bed, his brown gaze curious. "How did you escape, d-d-d—*click*—dearest? From what we found, it—*grunt, grunt*—appeared as though he had —*click*—dosed you with a mixture of laudanum and laurel—*grunt*—water."

Rubbing the soft material of Jasper's counterpane between her fingers in a restless movement, she took a breath and recounted the events of that morning, from the moment she left her home until she dragged Francis through Jasper's attic.

Jasper leaned forward to rest his elbows upon his knees, his scent of bergamot and lemon wafting closer. "That was remarkably shrewd of you."

"Thank you." She smiled, then asked the question that had begun to nag at her. "How did Francis garner Lady Cartwright's trust?"

"I haven't the faintest." Jasper shook his head in apparent self-reproach. "I can genuinely say that I'd not considered the possibility that Francis had taken a lover in town."

"Mayhap she simply found him handsome."

"Whatever the reason, the baron has reached town and is furious at not only being the cuckold, but also at the publication in the paper." Jasper huffed a breath.

She looked beyond the men at the empty doorframe. "Has everyone else gone home?"

Thomas shook his head. "Miss Huntsbury is—*click*—

apprehending the magistrate—*grunt-grunt*—and everyone else is below—*grunt*—stairs guarding our prisoner."

"The magistrate!" Maria's brows rose, and shock rippled through her.

"Indeed," Jasper began. "After receiving another quote from Francis, I went directly to Bow Street..." He swiftly detailed the letter from her acquaintance in the magistrate's office, and the resulting actions taken.

"*'Struth*," she breathed. "How long was I unconscious?"

"The doctor left only moments before you awoke. It has been but an hour, no more."

She nodded, the muscles in her back straining at the movement. Lord, but she must find a way to explain this to her parents. And her apartments! Her heart squeezed and her breath caught on a sob. That loss was devastating.

"Thomas," she rasped, "I'm afraid that our home—"

He clasped her hand in his, his eyes growing glossy and the tip of his nose pinkening. "I know. That was where—*click, grunt*—Jasper and I found Francis' last n-n—*click*—note. Oh!" He rose and strode to the other side of the room and retrieved a parcel from atop a chest of drawers. "This arrived for you while we were there." He handed it to her. "I brought it with me and knew you would wish to see it upon awakening."

His gaze slid sideways toward Jasper as she accepted it. Nerves buzzed through her abdomen. The first copy of her newest novel; it was a moment to be celebrated but, at the moment, she didn't feel quite like celebrating.

Their curious and sympathetic gazes notwithstanding, she hugged the parcel to her chest and closed her eyes. It was all that she had left of *any* of her writing. Her other first copies, manuscripts, contracts, and her current works had all burned in the fire that Francis had set. This parcel was pain. It was hope. It was the end of something, and yet the possible beginning of another.

Her stories would never leave, however; they could never be burned, for they were all in her head. Every story, every idea, every edit and rewrite were all a part of her.

THE COLOUR WAS high on her cheeks, her eyes glittering with unshed tears as she traced the parcel with her fingertips. Suspicion whispered at the back of Jasper's mind, but it wasn't the time for him to inquire about the parcel meant for "Mr. M" and what it meant to Maria. Clearly it meant *something*.

Three sets of footsteps sounded belowstairs, growing nearer as the people ascended the staircase. Maria blinked rapidly, then set the parcel aside with a wince, just in time to admit a footman.

"Your Grace, Mr. and Mrs.—"

Jasper stood.

"Let us *through*, you fool! We're her parents!" The stringent voice of Mrs. Roberts filled the room.

All at once, Maria's eyes flared wide, Thomas' skin grew ashen, and the ostentatious couple burst into Jasper's master bedchamber, colour high and hands flapping.

"Oh Maria, what *have* they done to you?" Mrs. Roberts fluttered to Maria's bedside and put a palm to her forehead, though her gaze was fixed on Jasper. "Aren't you fortunate to have the duke here to dote on you. I daresay his staff will provide anything you desire, if it should make you comfortable. I... What in the bloody hell is *he* doing here?"

The woman turned to eye Thomas with hateful scrutiny, as the man's face contorted with spasms.

Damn. Jasper marvelled at the woman's ability to sound

achingly sweet in one moment, and in the next, spit such vitriol.

Mr. Roberts blustered, his chest puffing up and his face reddening as he caught sight of Thomas. "Wh-wh-*what*? How dare you deign to sully the duke's home with your presence! You belong in Bethlem Roy—"

"He most certainly does not," Maria protested, her mien impassive, though determined. "Thomas is brilliant"—Maria listed the items on her fingers, ignoring her mother's protests —"talented, wickedly amusing, and tender-hearted. He speaks and moves differently than you and I, but he is far more indefatigable in creating a decent life and name for himself."

"That man has a *madness*, you stupid, headstrong girl!" Mrs. Roberts gestured wildly, her eyes bulging with the force of her words. "You've unquestionably lost the duke's favour now! Not to mention ruining any chance your sisters have of a decent match!"

His heart drumming a tattoo against his ribs and anger flaring hot along his skin, Jasper opened his mouth to give the woman a set-down. But Maria spoke first.

"How *dare* you?" she seethed at her mother. "Thomas stands just there, and you dishonour him with your pitiful, spiteful lies and ignorance. I am proud to call him family, but I'm afraid that I cannot say the same for you."

Jasper's chest swelled with pride as the Roberts' gasped and spluttered. Maria was utterly glorious. She needed him for nothing, and yet he was desperate to be partnered with her in life...and hoped she felt the same.

"Mayhap we ought to seek privacy for this discussion," Mr. Roberts put in hopefully, casting sidelong glances at Jasper.

"The duke stays," Maria returned, her gaze locking with Jasper's for a brief moment before returning to her parents. "I daresay he wouldn't pay you a shilling if we married—*I* certainly wouldn't."

"Indeed," Jasper agreed, though the word *if* made his stomach wobble.

"*Maria!*" Mrs. Roberts shrieked. Her face was all but tomato-red, and a vein was bulging from her temple. "Well, I never."

"How dare you speak to your mother that way?" Mr. Roberts raged, his hands fisted at his sides. "Apologize this instant!"

"I will not. It is far past time that I told you what I think about your imprisonment of my dear brother." She reached out to Thomas, and he rounded the bed to clasp her hand in both of his.

MARIA'S HEART clattered around in her chest, her pulse racing with indignation and protectiveness. How could her parents be so...*vile*? It baffled her entirely.

Her mother turned from red to green. "How long has this been going on?"

"You—*grunt*—say that a-a-a-a—*click*—as though—*grunt, click, grunt*—she-she—"

Maria rubbed the back of Thomas' hand with the pad of her thumb. The poor man was so nervous that he could scarcely get a word out. "Shh, shh, brother," she whispered. "It will be well."

He gave her a returning squeeze, his shoulders twitching upward and his face scrunching in a grimace.

Their parents cringed in disgust, and Maria's heart ached even more deeply for the man beside her.

Thomas stiffened his spine and cleared his throat. "I do not need your—*grunt*—approval. I h-h—*click*—have a wealth of love and friendship, as well as—*grunt, click*—funds enough to give me a happy life. I—"

"You'll have none of *my* funds, boy," their father said, his face reddened with rage.

Notching his chin higher, Thomas gave him a mocking smirk. "I have no n-n-n—*click*—need of your funds. I'm fully capable of—*grunt*—providing for myself."

"How could you do this to us?" Their mother spun on Maria with an accusatory glare. "How could you have released him? And where have you been hiding him, for pity's sake? The hospital will receive a shocking letter from me, I daresay. *Shocking*! They owe me my sodding money back, by God!"

How could I? Maria mused. Pain prickled in her chest, but she felt a new sense of detachment from her parents. She'd known that they were monstrous for locking Thomas away without giving him even an opportunity to fit in with society, and for not thinking twice about their decision. But now, faced with evidence of his success, they remained unmoved and unchanged in their opinion.

"I have done nothing to you. I have merely provided someone whom I love with a chance at a life greater than you deigned to offer. And I will not stop for anyone, most particularly two people as cruel and ungracious as you. Please leave."

Her mother's face was blotched red, and her father's had very nearly become purple.

"You'll regret this!" her mother spat. "When the news of the duke jilting you has reached the *ton*, we shan't take you in! You'll see that we were right. Your sisters will not suffer for your sins."

With one last glare at her and Thomas, her parents huffed out of the room.

Maria's pulse thudded in her ears, and her empty stomach threatened to heave. She'd done it, then. She had severed whatever affable ties there had been with her parents.

A weight that had settled around her heart for years began to lift, and hope began to replace it.

Her hand reflexively squeezed Thomas', and he returned it with one of his own. The loss of her parents wouldn't prove difficult when she was on the side of love.

Fists and jaw clenched, Jasper resumed his seat at her bedside. "Are you both well?"

"No," Maria whispered, turning to smile up at Thomas. "But I daresay we will be."

"I can't believe you did that, Maria," Thomas breathed, his eyes welling. "You've just d-d—*click*—defied them for me —*again*."

"And I would do so again." In fact, it didn't hurt as much as she thought it would.

He nodded, sitting on the bed's edge and adjusting his grip on her hand. "If you—*grunt*—require it, I should be glad to remake—*click, grunt*—your wardrobe. The payment from the latest batch of c-c-c—*click*—costumes is due to come in, and with your new—*grunt*—book set to print, I'm certain we shall have enough—*grunt, grunt*—funds for a strong beginning." He shuffled closer, his eyes hopeful. "Perhaps I could pick up your assignments—*grunt*—from *The Morning Herald* and you could write them at home."

"That's very thoughtful, Thomas. I—"

"*I* will pay for the fabric," Jasper offered. "According to my steward, soon the dukedom will no longer be in arrears. I would be pleased to provide you with whatever you desire."

A delightful fluttering filled her chest and abdomen, but fear quashed it.

She cleared her throat. "Thomas, would you please give us a moment?"

"I daresay you've—*click, click*—had more than enough moments alone. But very well." He bussed Maria on the forehead, gave Jasper a long glance, and hastily left the room.

This moment was inevitable, Maria knew; it had been planned from the beginning. Though, now that it was here, she detested it far more than she'd thought possible. The happy nerves that had, just moments ago, thrilled her insides, turned to stones that plummeted in her abdomen.

"We have Francis and his accomplice, at last," she began. "Our task is complete. And...my parents' hold on me appears to have been severed." Her hands twisted in the counterpane of their own accord. "I no longer require an engagement to satisfy my parents' demands or to allow me the freedom to continue my work."

"I BEG YOUR PARDON?" Jasper asked, tingles of unease racing up the backs of his legs.

Maria's eyes watered, and she took a quavering breath that gave Jasper the slightest bit of hope.

"I am not an ordinary woman," she whispered. "And while, in the throes of passion, you've stated that you enjoy the more masculine part of me, I am fearful that you would come to regret that."

His chest squeezed. "*No*, Maria. You—"

"I have no wish to bore you, Jasper."

"Bore me! I can safely guarantee that with you I shall never be bored." Shifting closer, he clasped her hand in his and took a deep breath. Now was his moment to put voice to what was in his heart. "I confess, when I proposed marriage, we both were taken by surprise." He rubbed the pad of his thumb over the smooth skin on the back of her hand. Even after her ordeal, she still smelled like parchment, ink, and soap. "And yet, the moment I uttered the words, I knew in my heart—my very soul—just how greatly I desired it."

As he spoke, Maria's grey eyes grew wider, and Jasper's stomach began a tumbling act.

"I've no desire for a fashionable marriage," she blurted. "If we marry, I would require faithfulness."

"That, I can provide." His heart leapt and he moved to sit next to her on the bed, careful not to jostle or bump her arm. "While I cannot say that I have *enjoyed* Francis' machinations, I must admit that it has taught me more about you, *Mr. Mystery*." He let his assumption hang there between them, waiting for her to refute it. She remained silent, so he continued. "And the more I've come to learn, the more I cannot deny my feelings. I love you, Maria."

Tears spilled over the edge of her eyelids and, with a sniff, she wiped them away with her free hand. "I love you, too, Jasper."

The tightness in his chest abruptly released, and his heart soared. Christ, but those words on her tongue! He beamed, and swept forward to press his lips hard against hers. She gasped into his mouth and touched her tongue to his, and his cock twitched. He was utterly enraptured by this woman, but now was certainly not the time to show her *just* how much.

"Will you marry me, Mr. Mystery, Mr. Duncan Robertson, née Miss Maria Roberts?"

She huffed a laugh. "Yes, I will marry you, Jasper."

EPILOGUE

One month later

A sea of brightly coloured gowns and dark male finery swirled around Maria, the air heavy with clean sweat, harsh perfume, and melting beeswax. It was rather like all other extravagant balls to which she had been invited, with two very large differences.

Her gaze slid across the ballroom to meet the stunning two-toned gaze of the man she'd married. To avoid the possibility of her parents refusing the marriage, they had travelled to Gretna Green and eloped. The *haut ton* found it all deliciously diverting.

No fewer than seven women and men surrounded Maria, each attempting to regale her with a bit of gossip or something amusing that they might have witnessed at Covent Garden, Astley's Amphitheatre, or another such place. Their favoured topics of discussion, however, were the perfidious magistrate Ludlow Vaughan, Mr. Francis Sinclair, and their infamous trials and hangings—most notably because Francis had not been permitted to wear a hood to hide his face, in the event that he made another attempt at escape. Now they knew that he was well and truly deceased.

A servant stopped at her side, offering a flute of champagne on a tray. "Have you seen her?" she mumbled.

Maria gave a half-smile to her friend Cordelia—who had been amusingly shocked to learn that Mr. Duncan Robertson was, in fact, Miss Maria Roberts. "No," she whispered back. "Heather says that we'll know the signal when it comes."

She accepted some champagne, and Cordelia silently strode away. This was the conclusion of Heather's assignment and Cordelia's first foray into work as a runner. So, naturally, Maria had offered her aid.

Upon their return from Gretna, Jasper had split his study in half and allowed her to redecorate her side as she wished. She'd since resumed her writing—having to begin anew with her collection of descriptions from abroad—and restarted the manuscript that had thwarted her for so many months. She rather thought that the second attempt was superior to the first.

Fingertips brushed hers just as the strains of a waltz started from the orchestra on the balcony. The touch turned to a clasp as Jasper lifted her gloved hand and pressed a kiss to the back of it.

"My duchess," he murmured deeply. "Might I claim your hand for this waltz?"

Several of the woman around them sighed or flicked their fans faster.

Maria's fingertips tingled. "I would be delighted."

Miss Heather Morgan had planned her timing perfectly. She'd taken up a spot in a servant's corridor with her squirming sack, waiting for the ideal moment. Her task was to orchestrate a distraction, and that was precisely what she would do.

Once the quadrille was under way, she opened the door leading into the ballroom and poured out the contents of the sack.

A shrill scream rent the air, followed closely by others. "*Rats!*"

People moved like a wave along the ballroom floor, shouting or screeching in horror as a plethora of rats bounded heedlessly through the space.

While everyone fled in one direction, Heather went in the other, slipping through an open doorway and into a rear corridor. Maria appeared at the end of the hall, a devilish smirk on her lips.

"Do you think they're sufficiently distracted?" she asked breathlessly.

Maria rolled her eyes heavenward as they drew nearer to each other. "We merely required a few minutes' time in order to search the earl's study for the letters."

"We will have plenty of time, then."

Following the direction that the client had given them, they made their way to the study and began a search. They each took one side of the room, testing each drawer and shelf for any hidden compartments. Cordelia would, even now, be searching the earl's bedchamber for the same letters. Lord knew if they would get another chance.

Parchment rustled behind her, and Maria exclaimed, "Here! I have them. Do you think that this is all of them?"

"I'll make certain," Heather said, taking the letters and waving a hand at her. "Go on now! Return to the ballroom and keep everyone busy. I will count the letters and destroy them."

With a nod, Maria swept from the room and returned to the chaos in the ballroom.

"Six, seven...eight," Heather whispered as she counted. The abhorrent letters were all there.

She turned toward the hearth and, for a moment, her heart all but stopped. *Fire.* The orange flames rippled and lapped at the coals, and her heart thudded in her ears. It was so close. The heat surrounded her, and the faint screams—

The study door slammed open with a *bang* that reverberated through her chest. Pulse jumping, Heather stared wide-eyed into the furious, dark gaze of the Earl of Hanley.

"You *bitch*," he snarled, his lips curling back over yellowing, aged teeth. "I'll tell your aunt about this, Miss Morgan."

This was it, then. The bastard knew her name, knew her family, and had the ability to ruin her life, just as he was threatening to do to their client. *Well,* she mused, *he'll only ruin life for one of us.*

In one swift movement, she tossed the letters into the fire, the parchment instantly catching ablaze, and curling at the ends until they were shrivelled, blackened dust. The tightness in her chest eased a fraction; at least one woman was saved from the man. Now, she merely needed to sort out how to save herself.

The earl's gaze narrowed on her. "I'll see to it that you regret that."